The Marked One

and other stories

The Marked

and twelve other

by

translated from

Philadelphia 5716—1956

One

stories

Jacob Picard

the German, with an introduction

by **Ludwig Lewisohn**

The Jewish Publication Society of America

Library of Congress Catalog Card No.: 56-7784
PRINTED IN THE UNITED STATES OF AMERICA

CONTENTS

Introduction
by Ludwig Lewisohn

INTRODUCTION

by Ludwig Lewisohn

Almost immediately upon the National-Socialist sei-
zure of power in 1933, German publishers, under
threats all the more brutal because they had not yet
been legalized, were forced to discontinue their printing and selling of books by Jewish writers and to
break their contracts with the Jewish authors on their
lists. Publishing houses in Jewish hands were taken
over and Nazi managers installed. It is only fair to
record that not a few Gentile publishing houses with
long and honorable business records took these en-
forced measures with reluctance and with shame. But
defiance of a police state means not only ruin but
physical liquidation. Hence the Jewish writers of Germany found themselves silenced and Jewish readers
unable to buy books by even the most equivocally or
remotely Jewish authors.

To measure the significance of these circumstances

one must remember that German-speaking and German-reading Jewry was probably the most literate group of people in history. The Juedischer Verlag (Jewish Publishing House) of Berlin was a prosperous business and its prosperity was due not least to a series of massive scholarly enterprises which were easily absorbed by Jewish subscribers. Among these were the magnificent German version of the Babylonian Talmud by Lazarus Goldschmidt, the five-volume *Juedisches Lexicon* and the ten-volume set of Dubnow's *Weltgeschichte des juedischen Volkes* (World History of the Jewish People).

The Juedischer Verlag continued, of course, to function until the final destruction of the Jewish community of Germany in November 1938. Meanwhile new Jewish publishing enterprises arose. Two of these are and will remain historically memorable: the distinguished house founded by Salman Schocken and a Jewish Book Club under the name of Juedische Buchvereinigung (Association for the Jewish Book). The Schocken records are, of course, safe, while the history of the Jewish Book Club remains to be written. This club sought to give its circle of readers works less scholarly and less stringent in their demands than either the Juedischer Verlag or Schocken. Yet sound enough scholarly works, such as Arthur Eloesser's *Vom Ghetto nach Europa*, a literary history of Jews during the liberalistic era, were written for the Club, as well as some far from ephemeral works of the creative imagination. It is one of the latter, perhaps the most distinguished of all, which is herewith presented to readers of English.

Jacob Picard, born in a South German village, may be said to be—as a story-teller, as a writer of fiction—a product of the National-Socialist catastrophe, although some of these stories were written as early as the 1920's. A singularly sensitive and delicate spirit, he had been in more normal times primarily a lyrical poet. He had written some criticism; he had practised law. But for his special village origin and past, he might well, like the majority of Jewish writers in Germany, have been totally absorbed by the surrounding culture; he might well, like Georg Hermann of Berlin, or like Schnitzler in *Professor Bernhardi* and *Der Weg ins Freie,* have written of the sophisticated Jews of the great cities who were, almost by definition, disappearing *as* Jews. But tenacious memories and profound loyalties, memories and loyalties sharpened almost unendurably by the catastrophe of 1933, caused him to seek by imaginative recreation to save, to preserve, to commemorate a phase of Jewish life in Western Europe that might, but for him, have fallen into oblivion.

It was doubtless his brooding, poetic temper, his *Jewish* attachment to the South German earth, that caused him to linger where he had so many more roots than the urbanized Jews. He did not seek to escape until 1940 when, fleeing by way of the East he finally made his way to America, under what incredible anguish of spirit can be well imagined. But in—of all historic times and seasons—November 1938, that accursed month of final terror and destruction, he sent me his volume of novelettes and short stories published two years earlier by the Jewish Book Club and called originally *Der Gezeichnete,* the "marked" man, marked and destined to a peculiar fate (included in this volume as "The Marked One") and other Jewish stories of a century.

I saw at once, a thing not difficult to see, that here was both a work and a document of singular preciousness and significance. As examples of the art of fiction these novelettes and stories represent an authentic narrative mood and rhythm. They may be said to belong to the kind of narrative practiced by the great Swiss story-teller, Gottfried Keller. This type of narrative is meditative rather than dramatic; it is freighted with deep historic and spiritual implications; it creates the patina of beauty and historicity without effort. For a parallel in English one has to go to the best stories of Hawthorne and to the more memory-laden stories of Henry James.

But what at once excited me more than the beautiful art of these stories was the circumstance that here, in this small volume, there was saved an almost unknown section of Jewish life, unknown, almost unsuspected, the life and history of the village Jews of Southern and South-Western Germany. Who were these Jews? Who were the members of that German Jewish community who were left for Hitler to destroy or drive forth? They were the descendants of the remnants left by the massacres of the crusades, left by the even fiercer massacres of the fourteenth century, when the Black Death, the bubonic plague, swept over Europe and decimated its peoples and when we, the Jews, were accused of causing the pestilence by poisoning the wells and were burnt at the stake—

the whole community of Strassburg, for instance, to the number of two thousand souls, on their cemetery, their *kever avos*—and when, by the same token, all debts owed to Jews by the gentry and nobility of the Holy Roman Empire were wiped out. Casimir of Poland, called the Great, invited the remnants of the German Jews to his realm. They trekked East and took their Middle High German of Franconian tinge with them, whence arose the Yiddish language and Yiddish literature.

Those who did not flee, tiny communities, fragments of fragments, remained in the towns and villages of the German-speaking lands and from these descended both the illustrious modern communities of Berlin and Frankfurt-am-Main and those villagers in the South and West whom Picard describes. From the time of the Protestant Revolt on through several centuries, persecution diminished; the relations between the village Jews and the peasantry became more and more humane; almost from the days of the French Revolution on, Jews, too, owned and cultivated fields and farms, dealt in the produce of the land and, especially, in cattle and attained a security in fact and in feeling which was not broken until the Hitler era. It is from the point of view of this new persecution that Picard writes. His stories are all retrospective and told under the aspect of this new, unheard of, unexpected *gezerah*. It is this that gives the tales, quietly as they are written, their immense poignancy, their touch of tragic grandeur.

What is now to be emphasized is the character of the community which Picard delineates. All the world, even beyond the confines of Jewry, knows of the historic development of those German Jews who fled to the East of Europe and became so great, so populous and so expressive a community. Everyone knows, if only from the tales and novels of Perez and Sholem Aleichem, or from the Hasidic evangels according to Martin Buber, or from such prose elegies as Abraham J. Heschel's *The Earth Is the Lord's,* what that community of Eastern Jews was like. In the tentative rebirth of Jewish knowledge and of Jewish commitment which is taking place; everyone knows Sholem Aleichem's Kasrielevke and its people; everyone knows that in Berdichev dwelt the Rabbi Levi Yitzchak. No one thought upon these German communities, which were the parent communities of those great and famous Eastern ones. German Jews were identified with either the assimilationists alone or with the eminent, equivocally Jewish scientists and poets of universal repute. No one remembered and few knew that in Germany, too, there had been and had survived a *shtetl* and an integrated holy community, that in Germany, too, until, as it were, the other day, there existed that strange Jewish community—different from all the other communities of men—a community which, despite its rogues, its misers, its oppressors of the poor, was a redeemed community in that it acknowledged its obligation to live by God's Law and feared, as Picard's people were wont to say, the *averah* of any breach of that Law.

The coloration of landscape, custom (*minhag*), speech, was, of course different from that of the Eastern Jews. Picard's villagers speak the local dialects

of Baden, Würtenberg, the Black Forest, Alsace. Or
else, they speak normal modern High German learnt
at school. What will strike contemporary readers as
strangest is their pronunciation of Hebrew, of which
they use a good deal. They did not share, of course,
the East European phonetic changes of, let us say,
Hebrew *mora* (fear) into Polish *moire* or Lithuanian
meire, but said *mauro* and, by the same token, *Tauroh*
—the diphthong *au* being equivalent of the English *ow*
in *now* or *brow.* And I have carefully preserved this
evidently very ancient pronunciation in my English
text in order to guard the savor and tonality of Picard's
narratives.

This savor and this tonality are very distinctive. A
legendary air belongs to these stories, even when they
are of the earth earthy, even when they are broadly
humorous, as "The Wooer" and "The Fish." Nor does
this legendary air rob the characters of either edge or
passion. It is achieved by the employment of historic
memory exercised at a given moment of time. These
Jews, once more exposed at this late age to the fires
of persecution, remember what they are and what
their fathers were and how they came through the
centuries to be what they are in this hour of the renewal of a tragic fate. Thus it is clear that, in this
handful of stories, Jacob Picard has strongly, tenderly,
beautifully rescued from a probable oblivion an entire
world of our people and has added this community both to the realm of history and of the human
imagination. Of how many books in all literature can
as much be said?

The Marked One

and other stories

THE MARKED ONE

Had a man deeply aware of the trend of things and happenings been asked at the birth of our good Sender Frank concerning the child's future, he would have foretold that its life would not take a customary or a tranquil course. Yet he would not have been able to foresee what, in fact, happened in the end. For Sender encountered obstacles far more unusual than those which are our general portion to meet and to overcome within the days that are granted us.

Strange and uncommon was the very moment in which he was born in the small house of his parents, built of the gray basalt blocks of the Rhone region, in the little village of the sterile mountains, half of whose inhabitants were Jews. It came to pass that his own mother detested the notion of bringing him into the world on what seemed to be the appointed day; for it was the secular New Year's Day, nor was it a random one, but the first day of the new century. But nature took its course and so his eyes first opened to this cold

3

world on the first of January of the year 1800. This
circumstance alone set him apart from others. He de-
veloped with the century, as people were wont to say
and tease him with that observation. It is understand-
able that his fellow villagers did not forget the day of
his birth, for there was none other among them who
had been born on that day; in fact there were very few
born in that entire first year of the century, which was
to be followed by the ninety nine others and the occur-
rences which they were to bring forth.

It was, to be sure, not this circumstance alone which
marked him from the beginning, but it was this one
which produced all the others.

Do you of today remember what was meant for a
long time by the appelation of "familiars" in certain
territories of German speech, to which the Austrian
lands belonged too? Few will remember today. Yet
generations of our forefathers suffered under these
regulations which oppressed them during the whole
course of their lives; indeed, they hindered the fulfillment of life in its entirety.

For the issue of these regulations was a matter of life
and love and death, because no human being can
attain perfection or fulfillment without the love between man and woman and the begetting of children
to prolong one's mortality, to please God and to attain
blessing both for oneself and one's family. Those, who
at that time were permitted to found families, were
given the appelation of "familiars," and precisely what
that meant in that dark period must be made clear to
those who are alive today.

What could this have been? Was not everyone permitted to marry, to follow the native impulse of the heart and of the instincts, to unite with another in holy unity in order to be sheltered and to have a refuge in face of the mysterious powers and uncertainties of the struggle for life? No, not all were permitted to do so. Only those might marry who received permission from the government, and the number of these was always definite and small. And how did all this come about? You must be told that in order to realize what kind of a human being this Sender was in his time.

It came about as follows: the great distrust of the world, which grew out of ignorance of our fathers and of their true character, had inspired in the mighty Empress of Austria a groundless fear of supposedly secret actions by the Jews against her ancient realm. She was deluded into thinking that, by diminishing increase among this small part of the many peoples over whom she ruled, she was protecting the others and guarding them against harm. Hence she issued the decree, renewing it from time to time, that in every Jewish family, wherever Jews lived, whether in city or country, only the oldest son in each family would be permitted to marry. Only one, then, of the often numerous sons of a house, could establish a family in his turn. This law prevailed, as it had done before in older periods, for a century and more. It extended almost to the days of our grandfathers and included the lifetime of this poor Sender Frank, of whom we are speaking.

We need hardly try to prove what everyone can easily imagine, that this harsh edict of the government

caused the fates of many men to be difficult and in-
tricate. What strange things could not happen if two
young people loved each other and knew that they
could never be united; how many other possibilities
of strange alliances and separations did not necessarily
arise under the harshness of this unnatural law?

Senderle, or Little Sender, as he was sometimes
called, although he was by no means small of stature,
was the third born of a small family, following a sister
and a brother, a child almost of his father's old age. He
had been born when the oldest son was mature
enough to marry and did, indeed, do so soon after the
little boy had been born.

And this too was a consequence of the unusual day
of his birth, which really caused all that came over
him and pursued him, as we shall see. For no one can
avoid the law of the Eternal, blessed be He, nor withdraw from that mighty plan, for whose fulfillment He
employs inscrutable means.

Sender had, as it were, slipped in between the ages
and their involvements as they were manifest in that
poverty stricken village. For soon it grew clear that
his fellows, seeing that he was rather homely, thought
they could deal with him according to their pleasure.
Not long after his birth, he being still a very small
boy, his mother and father died after the briefest
interval. He came under the care of his almost adoles-
cent sister, Rivke, in the straw-thatched little house
near the river, on the roof of which moss grew in
furry tufts because it was always in the shadow. His
sister had to bring him up and take care of him, because between herself and the elder brother there

had arisen an enmity on account of money matters, for the man's wife was greedy after possessions, as well as of an unveracious and vicious tongue. She refused to let her husband perform his sacred duty by his young brother. And so the latter was all alone and without protection. And since the other members of the *kehilla* had an instinctive notion of this fact; and since, to mention it once more, he was totally unprepossessing as well as penniless, it happened that he could offer no resistance to them and also that they imposed on him every duty and obligation which they disliked.

Burdens were imposed on him in his narrow life—since he had no knowledge of anything except the village and its compulsions—from the observances of the Law, which none sought to escape; and it was long before he knew that flight was possible for one who suffers from his fellow men on account of his peculiar character.

We must now explain something for those among us whom the Eternal, blessed be His name, has brought back to us through the sufferings of these latter years, but who are ignorant of His Holy Law and of the old customs, in order that they too might understand the involvements which overwhelmed Sender because he was alone and there was none to take his part.

It is a great honor for the men in Israel to be called up in the House of God in order to pronounce the blessing over the Law before the congregation. The order in which men are called up is dependent on the esteem which is granted a man in the *kehilla*. But

there is one *Shabbos* and one *parsha,* or Scriptural
portion, which a man is not required to bless. He may
refuse to be called up, *mi she-yirtze,* on account of the
consequences, which were generally feared and which,
even to this day, are here and there attributed to the
reading of that passage among the faithful.

The section of the *Tauro* which is read on that
Shabbos, which is called the *Shabbos Bechukkausai—*
it occurs during the period of the *Omer—*is the passage
which contains the words of the *Tauchocho,* wherein
are written the curses which the Eternal, blessed be
His name, threatens to execute in case we do not obey
Him and the law He has given us, in order that we
set an example of faith among the nations.

All the evils which He may send us from His hands
to punish and correct us, are written in that passage of
that day and he, who is called to the *Tauro* and stands
on the *almemor* to pronounce the blessing, affirms the
passage as he proclaims it before the congregation.

Hence from of old and also in this period there was
a hesitancy among the men to pronounce the *berocho,*
the blessing, over these words. They feared the effect
that these curses might have upon them and their
families, great as was the honor on all other occasions
to be called up to the reading of the *Tauro.*

You may call this the superstition of a dark age. But
it arose out of reverent fear of the Eternal and His
boundless might. At all events, the custom had arisen
in all the congregations to call up for this passage
someone, whether he wanted to be called up or not,
who was alone in the world, who had neither wife nor

children to whom these imprecations might bring hurt, illness, humiliation and even death. And none who was so chosen dared to refuse; he believed that he must undergo this as a part of his fate and to make this sacrifice for the others. It happened inevitably that someone was selected for this duty whom the harsh law of the secular power kept from marrying, as we have set the matter forth. Rebellion was impossible, seeing that the individual is always weak and helpless against the majority of the congregation. This custom had obtained for centuries.

This portion, as we have explained, is read at the time of the *Omer,* when daily the faithful, at *Maariv,* at dusk between *Pesach* and *Shevuaus,* say the memorial prayers in memory of the bloody and cruel period, a thousand years ago, which our ancestors suffered in the German lands for the sake of their holy faith and which left only those few in life who begot us.

Thus it was almost inevitable that shortly after he had become a *Bar-Mitzvo* and was received as a man among the men of Israel, Sender—especially since Shlaume, his predecessor, a feeble little old man, could no longer perform the duty—was burdened with this heavy and supposedly humiliating burden and duty and was obliged to submit himself to this supposed sacrifice for his fellow men.

He consented, firstly because he had no way of resisting and, also, because in the early years he did not know that he had the right to resist according to the correct interpretation of the Law.

Thus they all became accustomed to having him per-

form this annual service and it seemed inevitable to
him too. This was his job, like the job of the *chazan*
and the *schauchet*, equally necessary for all.

This was the heaviest part of the lot imposed upon
him by the strange day of his birth. It was, in his individual case, too late a day; as well as too early a one
from the point of view of the history of our people to
liberate him from the shameful compulsions of a
previous age. For it is so among men, that evil always
begets more evil if no resistance is offered against the
earlier evils which are dragged on from age to age.

At first Sender hardly noted the fact that he was
less respected by the others and held to be a lesser
creature than they. He grew into the precise situation
which he occupied among them and was satisfied with
it, as we are all apt silently to accept what we behold
as customary among our neighbors, until we are mature
enough to begin thinking for ourselves. To sum it up:
he had no voice among them for himself.

Life was hard enough for him and for his sister who
managed the little household in their straw-thatched
dwelling with the mosses on the roof, which never the
sun shone upon. It is easy enough to imagine that.
From their parents they had inherited a milch-goat,
which had been the cause of the conflict between
themselves and their brother's wife. Every few years
they had to buy a new one, one of those kindly
animals with the pendant udders. This did not take
place too often, for these creatures attained a great
age. Thus brother and sister were barely able to exist
and their house smelled of the goat. They also had a
little garden behind their poor dwelling; there the

sister planted every spring cabbages and a few potatoes
and leeks and also horseradish for the holidays. A little
extra profit arose from a sparse trading in chickens
and in old clothes. Almost without noticing it, Sender
had slipped into these occupations. It is understand-
able that all this did not make him respected among
the people of the *kehilla*. On the other hand, shepherds were glad to listen to him and to chat with him
when he sat with them among their sheep at pasture
on the mountain meadows far from the village; so
were plowmen when they stopped a little behind their
plow or while they were sowing seed and he stood
near them, entirely absorbed in their work and occupation and in the fruitage of their fields.

In this way many years passed and his sister Rivka
showed the signs of age and sorrow. The winters were
full of want and chill; they could hardly find food for
the goat which helped to sustain them. The summers
were hardly less difficult, when Sender wandered out
under the bright sky into the neighboring villages to
bring back a few pennies. And it was really only the
religious festivals which, according to God's will,
brought a little cheer and courage and confidence.

Then, one fine day, Sender awoke and realized the
nature of his fate.

Hitherto he had accepted everything as inevitable
and had resigned himself to passing a life of loneliness,
without wife, without children, without the tranquil
joy of home. And yet each member of the *kehilla* took
an interest in his life, because they knew that he
marked the continuance of the century. This was the
strange thing about him; the very children knew his

age; they cried it out after him. He seemed to age differently than the other people of the community; he seemed also to belong to it more than any other, because he was always needed on that precise day of every year in order to keep the others free of that curse which might threaten them if they pronounced the blessing over the threats of God.

Annually on that day on which it is necessary to read that portion of Scripture in which God's wisdom threatens us with punishment, all the men of the congregation turned around to look at the place in the last row of the *shul* where Sender stood defenseless and alone. He would stride forward hastily, as though to excuse himself for some wrong in the face of the others, and arrive at the *almemor* to perform the bitter duty imposed upon him.

Yes, Sender awakened on a given day and beheld himself as an accursed one; saw himself suddenly as a stranger would have to see him, objectively and from without, himself and his entire existence.

It was on a certain evening, on *Simchas Tauroh*, on a still warm and summery day of October, filled with the fragrance of the last harvest and of the latest flowers, that this thing took place. The young people of the *kehilla* had gathered in the house of Feivel Baum, the largest in the village; they gathered for the sake of the son, Josel Baum, who had the good luck to be able to get married—and was old enough to be— and also on account of the daughter Gela who had been promised in marriage to Eisig Stein from the neighboring village of Laudenbach. This young man was spending the last days of *Succaus* here. This was the chief reason why this gathering of young people was taking place.

They danced to the tune of a fiddle played by a white-blonde vagrant with a wild beard, such as could be seen wandering about the land in those days after the wars of the mighty French Emperor. And they danced the new dance which was called waltz. The French soldiers who had been in occupation here, or had kept marching through for nearly twenty years, had left the waltz behind them. It was only now that people hereabouts dared again to be gay and festive; several years had now passed since one needed any longer to fear the foreign soldiery. The peasants, too, had calmed themselves in that region between the Spessart and the Rhone, where the war had been followed by sundry years of famine which had driven people to despair and to violent deeds against the Jews, although the latter, as everywhere and always, had been pursued by the same misfortunes and had suffered the same want as their neighbors. But now several abundant harvests had been granted and people began to feel some confidence in a better future.

They had, in fact, not been so cheerful for a long time; the very young did not remember the bitter experiences of their elders, having been born during the years of the war. Eisig Stein, of whom they knew that he had lived for half a year in the great city of Frankfurt and had learned the delicate ways of it, danced every dance. He also wore a short, black coat of the latest fashion. We need hardly say that he and Gela were the center of the celebration.

Others danced with the girl too. But how could

Sender have undertaken to ask Feivel Baum's Gela to
dance with him? At first he just stood near the door;
later he sat down at a table near the exit; no, not even
really at the table but just half leaning upon a free
edge at the end of the bench. They hardly spoke to
him. He smiled to himself between his *paiyes* under
his black somewhat greasy and tilted visored cap. It
was a somewhat bashful smile with which he sur-
veyed the scene.

Of a sudden it came over him that Gela was
blonde, like the wayfaring fiddler who lured them all
with his exciting outlandish tunes and, as it were,
symbolized everything strange. He saw that she was
different from all the others, the black-haired girls of
the *kehilla*. And so he loved her from that moment on,
because she had never before revealed herself to his
eyes. It never occurred to him to show how he felt or
to admit it to her. What deterred him was not the fact
that he knew her to be promised in marriage to Eisig
Stein of Laudenbach. No, it wasn't that. But how
could he, the son of a poor man, who had himself remained so poor, have dared to think of marriage with
the daughter of the rich Feivel Baum, the chief man
of the *kehilla*? Yet when she walked through the
village, which didn't happen too often on weekdays
and only in the pursuit of definite errands, Sender
often met her. He just passed and saluted her; rarely
did he speak. Once, however, he said: "Gelele, you
look like a little canary bird."

The girl perceived something of what went on
within him and started to run, after she had cried out
to him: "Are you *meshuggah*?"

He continued to harbor the love in his heart. And from this arose another attitude. One fine day, as he was wandering from one village to another between the ash trees from which the red tufts hung, he met Josel, Gela's brother: "Well," Josel asked him, "are you doing a big business?"

It did, truly, sound a little arrogant and as though he wanted to show Sender his place.

And so Sender snapped back: "As big as yours or that of your *ovaus avauseinu!*"

Now that was, to put it mildly, an exaggeration. And how did the humble Sender come to say a thing like that concerning the *mishpoche* of Josel Baum, whose preeminent position in the community was universally acknowledged? They were not only rich and prominent, but on the mother's side related to the *Bal Shem,* the great sage of Michelstadt in the forest of Oden, who hadn't been dead so very long. But Sender had determined that this belittling of him should come to an end. He was going to show them.

One day he declared to Rivke, his sister, that he was going on a long journey into foreign parts. He was fed up. He didn't explain what he meant. The elderly spinster, quite overwhelmed, thought her brother had gone out of his mind and in her helplessness ran for advice to the *Parnes.* The *Parnes* with his long white beard came to their poor house. It was too late. Sender had gone. He had packed an old valise with a few necessaries and had disappeared. They ran after him; they peered along the eastern and the western village streets. He was no longer to be seen. For, suspecting that he might be pursued, he had gone across the fields and soon found refuge in a forest of spruces. When, after several hours, he emerged upon the nearest highway, he was already in the neighborhood of a distant village where the peasants regarded him distrustfully.

It was late autumn. The fields were bare. Across the hills the shepherds in their ample cloaks wandered with their slow and patient herds through the wind beside the low juniper bushes.

In his home village the excitement lasted for weeks. A thing like that had never happened before. No one could imagine why Sender had left. His sister Rivke wept when the matter was mentioned to her and pitied herself mightily. And yet one couldn't talk to her about anything else; in fact, she expected the matter to be discussed and consolation to be offered her. Only the blonde girl Gela had a dark monition that perhaps she was the cause of this flight. And the men of the *kehilla* were already worried as to who would pronounce the *berocho* when the *Tauchocho*, the imprecations of God, would have to be read. For, alas, man is so made that each one contemplates another's misfortune in the hope that he be not made to share it.

When Sender had set out from home, he had only a very obscure notion of what he would undertake out in the world. On the first day he passed through a region with which he was still somewhat familiar, even though he knew only the name of the village, in which he decided to spend the first night. A peasant let him sleep in the hay of his barn and also gave him two eggs, which he drank raw and ate with them a morsel of dry bread which he had taken with him from home. The people paid little attention to him; it was quite customary in those days to give wanderers casual refuge, for the various sections of the country were united only by roads and rivers and the fare in vehicles or ships was high. Next day the country grew stranger and stranger to him. Descending from a hill he saw the sparkle of a river. Its silvery band between the red and yellow forests of autumn soon disappeared from sight, but not before it had given the wanderer a moment's feeling of breadth and freedom. Thus several days passed. He always found tolerable shelter and needed not to pass a single night in the open or surreptitiously among the haystacks.

One evening, when he saw from afar two towers and the walls of a little city, he was at first afraid. How would it be among so many people? As he drew nearer and turned the corner of a forest, along which the road now led, he observed ahead of him a little man whom he at once recognized as a fellow Jew, for the latter wore a black visored cap and a long coat and in his left hand held a sack which kept moving and stirring so that it was clear that it contained a living creature. Chickens, probably, Sender reflected. How often had he himself returned home thus with the sparse result of a day's wandering?

When he had come near enough to the other to be sure that he was not mistaken, he said: "*Sholaum alechem.*"

The little man turned around. A blonde curly beard surrounded his friendly face.

"Alechem sholaum!" he replied and added: "Where are you going so late?"

"Into the town. Do you live there?"

"Surely! Are you a *Ben-Yisroel?*" asked the little man although he had seen with whom he had to do. "Have you business among us?"

"I just want to stay overnight."

"Just overnight? You are *mochel* with me. If you don't know anybody else, stay with me. I consider it a *koved*. I am Boruch, the *schauchet* here."

"I thank you kindly; I am glad to accept."

The little city was beyond the boundary. It had recently been incorporated in the Duchy of Baden. Here, from of old, Jews had lived among the guild craftsmen and the peasants. When Sender accompanied his host into the house and in the low-ceiled room had been greeted by the skinny Frau Breindel, whose forehead was almost entirely hidden by her smooth, parted wig, Boruch said to him once again: "Be you *mochel* here."

They sat down and partook of a simple meal of fried potatoes and pot roast. By this time, of course, Boruch could no longer repress his curiosity as to the whence and wherefore, the aim and goal of his guest. The answers which Sender gave him were not very clear. From the yard one could hear the cackling of the chickens and the bleating of the goats from their stable. Frau Breindel had already taken the day's booty into the chicken house. All this reminded Sender of the little house at home. It was Thursday evening and so it was fitting that Boruch invite him to stay over *Shabbos*. How happily he consented to stay. He felt so united to these people by blood and by the old holy law and the good customs. And they, for their part, were proud to show the *kehilla* that they had a guest over *Shabbos*.

Next afternoon, after *Minchah*, they stood in front of the house on the irregular flagstones with their neighbors, their hands in their trousers' pockets and their long coats spread out so that their gaily embroidered waistcoats of velvet and of silk could be seen. They discussed various matters and naturally again questioned Sender as to whence he came and whither he would go. But how could he have given them a clear notion of his plans? He had escaped the narrowness and the humiliation which his consciousness had suddenly realized. When he thought of it, it came all over him again. He replied:

"I want to learn something, like a trade, and then go back home."

This had come suddenly into his head; he hadn't thought about it before. And when he had said it, the others looked at each other and shook their heads and lifted their eyebrows, and they didn't pronounce the word which was in their minds, namely, the word *meshuggah*.

Only one of them, a man named Itzig Kallmann, gave it as his opinion that the idea was not so unreasonable nowadays, when Jews had all civic rights and could do what they liked, according to the new laws. The Grand Duke of Baden, their new sovereign, to whom the land now belonged, had, carrying out the will of Napoleon, expressed a benevolent attitude to the Jews. Hence it would not be a bad business if someone started to learn a trade or craft. It happened that at that moment the textile dyer Thomas Walz, Kallman's neighbor, passed by, slowly and with dignity, as was his wont, his hands in his trousers' pockets under his leather apron. He had just come from working at the great trough next door where he rinsed his textiles in the indigo solution. Kallman stopped him and asked, half jocularly and yet firmly:

"Could you make use of an apprentice? The fellow is a little mature, but maybe he would understand things more easily."

"Indeed, I could," the dyer replied. "You know very well that I'm looking for one. Who is it?"

All the others laughed. But Itzig Kallmann, a man of character who carried out his intentions, took Sender by the arm and, followed by the master dyer, stepped to one side.

A long consultation took place. The others watched and gradually fell silent.

Walz was a clever and a liberal man. In his youth, moreover, he had worked as a wandering journeyman in the French Republic and had witnessed the Revolution against oppression and exploitation. There he had heard about the rights of all men to live on an equal basis. And so he said:

"Why shouldn't I take a Jew as apprentice or journeyman? If he is a good worker, he is just as useful to me as a Christian. Done! You can come to work on Monday."

And so Sender became an apprentice in the indigo dye works and print works, although at first he really had no notion of what it was all about and to what

he had consented and what he would later do with
whatever he would learn. For his chief conscious aim
was to give his absence from home and his life here
some meaning and purpose.

He learned quickly; he was willing and satisfied
his master as well as anyone. Soon he learned how to
split up the precious cakes of indigo, so that nothing
was lost of this rare substance from far away. He
learned cleverly how to dilute the substance to a handsome blue color and, above all, how to treat the
textiles, whether wool or linen, in such a fashion that
their color was homogeneous and that the purchasers
were satisfied.

The people of the *kehilla* boarded him among themselves. He ate each day with a different family. And
although most of them, not unprosperous cattle dealers,
did not quite consider him their equal, yet they were
not displeased at the fact that he showed the non-Jews
how one of their own could exercise a skilled craft.
He soon became known among the burghers of the
town as the "Jew apprentice"; for so they called him.

Nevertheless he felt lonely and often thought of his
native village. Yet he sent no message home. For it
made him melancholy to remember how he had always
been rejected by the others there and despised without cause. Here he was a free man, even though these
people knew little about him. No one jeered at him on
account of the day of his birth. They did not know
his age nor, above all, did they force him, on the day
on which the *Tauchocho* had to be read in *shul,* to
take that curse upon himself. Here this sacrifice was
exacted by the others of an old man, who was not

anymore wholly master of his senses, as had happened
at home before his time.

One day, however, before Sender had worked for
quite a year, it came to pass that a strange journeyman
entered the employ of the other master dyer of the
town. He came from the far north and spoke German
in a fashion which no one hereabouts had ever heard
and also immediately acted with great self-importance.
People listened to him, because he was very clever at
his trade; his master, too, was proud of him because he
introduced an important new method of imprinting
colors and patterns handsomely on the textiles, and,
finally, because the strangeness of his being made an
impression on the people of the town. Now this chap
gave it as his opinion that it was not proper for a Jew
to be received into a guild and learn a trade. For this
tended to limit the opportunity of Christians and also
went counter to all tradition and belief, not to mention the circumstance that, according to the wont of
the guilds, this fellow was far too old to be an
apprentice.

And so the journeyman and apprentices of the other
workshops put their heads together, the tanners and
the weavers, the wheelwrights and the smiths; they
all yielded to his persuasion and demanded that
Master Walz discharge his Jewish apprentice. Although Walz at first refused, he could not in the
long run withstand the talk and tumult which arose
against him. So one fine day he gave Sender notice,
although with kind and consoling words. He also gave
him a regular recommendation as one skillful in the
craft they practiced.

But what good did that do him? Even the Jewish people who had given him food and lodging during this period had not been without their own doubts, because they clung to the customary; they had often wondered what he would undertake, poor as he was, when his apprenticeship would end without any certainty of being able some day to work as a journeyman. So they advised him to set out once more and to return home.

Winter was approaching and so wandering through the land would soon have to cease. The fruit trees were already almost leafless and only the ash trees on the edges of the river still formed a sere reddish roof, and mornings found fogs on the river. So, on one such morning, he set out on his way, not through the mountains but along the course of the river in the direction from which he had come; and he was both excited and confident. For the oppressive circumstances that had driven him away had faded a little from his mind and his predominant feeling now was that which each human being cherishes for his original home.

In this particular year the cold of winter set in early. One night while the migratory birds were still on their way south, a frost occurred and in the morning, overtaken by the cold, the delicate swallows, frozen to death, lay by hundreds on the road and on the river bank. Many still stirred their little wings in their last breath. Sender, a lonely wanderer, with dust-covered shoes, beheld these little bodies and their misery seemed to him his very own. Again and again he bent over, wherever he perceived a flicker of pitiful

life, and carefully took into his hand, in order to give
a little warmth to it, one or the other of the birds. But
as though this last movement had been harmful to the
last manifestation of life under these little feathers,
each one died in his hand while from its little beak
there came a last drop of blood. Then he placed the
dead bird on the grass beside the road. They're dying
in alien places on their way home, he reflected, and
perhaps it is better so. Only one of the birds remained
alive; trembling it nestled between his hollow hands
as in a nest. Carefully he held it thus for hours; he
even tried to feed it; he took a little caterpillar from
the bushes and brown grasses or else a little spider out
of its dewy web. Without a definite intention, there
was a vague hope in him that he could take the bird
home to mitigate his own loneliness. But toward noon
when suddenly the sun was warm, the bird slipped
out of his hands and in a great circular flight swung
itself toward the south.

Sender looked after it and murmured to himself:
"Now it's going home." And then he added: "If only
it survives one more night," since he felt that, in
order to reach a goal, it always needs a last exertion
of power and a last help. His heart was downcast,
thinking of his own fate; he didn't know how they
would receive him in his home village which he had
secretly left and to which he was now returning. He
was suddenly frightened of the narrowness there and
of the false words of those who had always been about
him and knew his life from its beginnings; and he
had a premonition that flight from one's original and
permanent destiny is given to no man.

He intended, however, to tell them what he had learned and could do now and beg them to help him open a shop, so that he might show them what he could do and bring profit to them and himself by the work of his hands. He hardly considered the possibility of the thing and whether, in that barren region with its sparse population, it might at all profit to exercise his skill. He thought of plan after plan; at times hope awakened in him of a new life and of the possibility of being as well esteemed as the others. Perhaps he would manage to distinguish himself by his work, by showing that special ability which people required in order to regard another as their equal. All this was half-consciously within him.

On the noon of a certain day he was almost amazed to find the landscape becoming familiar. The fields were no longer strange to him nor the hills covered with juniper bushes; he saw patches of forest that he recognized and soon, standing on a hill, he saw from afar the village of his birth. He was excited and full of dread at the same time and shy at the thought of suddenly appearing in the sight of his fellow villagers. Thus he waited until dusk and then went slowly and slipped, seen by no one, into the sombre old house where he had left his sister. When he suddenly entered by the kitchen door, she cried out: "Sender!" She rushed toward him and embraced him in that exaggerated manner which people use whose feeling for another is mostly a matter of self-pity. Well, she was glad after a fashion to see him back, although she couldn't help wondering what they would say in the

kehilla, all those who had pitied her during the long
period of his absence. That very same evening she ran
quickly over to her neighbor, Perle Schwarz, a widow
woman, who lived alone not far away.

So on the next morning the whole village knew that
Sender Frank was back—Sender, who had run away,
bankrupt and poor. For this appellation—that of the
runaway—now clung to him among the other unfor-
gotten ones. They asked him where he had been. He
was taciturn and in the end merely showed those of
whom he hoped to gain the means for the realization
of his plan to erect a textile dye shop the certificate of
the master dyer Walz in which it said that Sender
Frank had been an apprentice in his dye shop and imprinting shop for such and such a period and had
shown himself to be faithful, industrious, and quick
in learning and had comported himself in the proper
fashion of an honest Christian apprentice, so that he,
the master dyer, was able to express his satisfaction
with this apprentice's skill and behavior and had
therefore been unwilling to withhold from him this
evidence of his good behavior and of his skill, even
though according to the principles of their honorable
craft and guild, he had not completed his apprenticeship, though his interruption of it was due to no fault
of his own.

They laughed because he was called an apprentice
—he, whom they had known so long as an adult; and
they treated him to evil words on account of that expression concerning "honest Christian apprentice" in
the certificate. And it goes without saying that they
did not give him enough to make even the smallest

beginning toward what would have been necessary for the work he wanted to do. Soon the whole village gossiped concerning what he had in mind: this Sender, who marked the century for them, and who pronounced the *berocho* for them over the portion *Tauchocho* of the imprecations—he was going to found an important business without a penny! What was it that had gotten into his head, and what a *chuzpe* it was! They laughed at him, sometimes openly and sometimes behind his back. There was none who even tried to understand him. And now that they knew that they no longer needed to fear the worst for him, namely, that he might have perished, and so recognized that the compassion they had shown his sister Rivke had been wasted, their mood changed completely. What business had anyone to run away and go his own path and escape the control of the community! And little as Sender had been esteemed before, they now surpassed themselves in making him feel how little he amounted to within the community.

A winter of great severity descended. Cold, storm, ice and snow whirled through the streets and lay on the thatched roofs. The small, deep river which came from the hills was frozen early. You could cross it as though it were a street. The people shivered in their little houses if they didn't hug the ovens, and doors and windows were closed tight. They huddled there, each family alone; their hearts, too, grew rigid and forgot that it had ever been summer. A gray sky hung low above them. They saw each other only at the services in the *shul*, especially on *Shabbos*. The *shul* was not heated and so they stood there, changing from

one foot to another in order to produce a little warmth
and letting their sleeves fall over their hands. And
there Sender stood among them as he had always done,
and as though he had never been away. Swiftly they
ran through their prayers which had become a trouble-
some duty.

And one day the worst came about. No one knew
who had invented it. But the children cried and sang
it after him, when they saw him. It was a derisive
ditty:

> "Sender, whither away?
> Out of the century
> From place to place goes he.
> Through lands by night and day.
> Sender, whither away?"

This is what they cried out after him wherever he
showed himself. There was none to forbid them. He
was lonelier than ever! His co-evals, or those who
were nearly so, addressed him now and then. But he
had grown strange to them and quite alienated from
them by the space of months during which he had
absented himself and also by the manner in which he
had disappeared. We are all so bound to the original
circle of our lives and to the community of our birth
that none can loosen those bonds unpunished.

As soon as the extreme cold receded, Sender once
more took up his skimpy trading in the neighboring
villages and farmsteads. But there was hardly any
profit; the peasants had no young chickens yet and the
old ones were just beginning to lay again. Nor were
there any lambs or calves. But it did him good to chat
with the peasants. He told them what he had experi-

enced, little as it had been, and what he had heard
concerning the unknown world out there. Among
other things he told them how many people from
Baden were now going overseas to America to live an
easier life, since there, as the rumor ran, wealth was
accessible to all and easily gained in the freedom
which obtained there.

Again and again he nurtured plans to go away
once more, farther away, and for a longer time. And
when toward spring he walked through the warm
sunlight over the thawing roads, now brown with
manure and earth, he often forgot the immediate
pressure of the day and the bitter scolding words
which awaited him when he returned with empty
hands to his low hut and to his sister who, after a
fashion, loved him within the community of their
wretchedness. But when a man's destiny is fixed from
the beginning, he must bow down to it. These things
upon which he meditated availed him nothing. For
when he had returned home he had still found Gela
Baum there, since it had come to pass that her *shid-
duch* with Eisig Stein of Laudenbach had been
broken off, because her father, Feivel, had at the last
moment insisted on deducting one hundred thaler
from the originally promised dowry and had been
unwilling to yield to persuasion. What he had told
no one was that he simply didn't have the money.

When Sender heard this story, he had become weak
all over and his blood had suddenly surged toward
his heart, even though in the strange places where
he had been for so long he had thought of the girl
less and less. He had, in fact, been quite tranquil

when he had seen her again for the first time and
had greeted her, without knowing how things were.
But during the whole winter he had carefully avoided
her, remembering that last meeting of theirs before
he went away, when he had so wanted to say tender
words to her. Then came Purim. And although they
still derided him and his vain flight, and although
one night, as was customary, masked figures appeared
at his and his sister's door, too, singing that derisive
song and adding to it other insolent and malicious
words, nevertheless Sender went to the festival which
was arranged annually in the parlor of the old inn.
For a Jew must bear derision and malice and even
laugh at them, when it is Purim, when it is that
festival when everything that touches the individual
must seem of little account compared to the reflection
and the joy over the grace through which the Eternal,
blessed be His name, once upon a time saved our
fathers from slander and persecution.

At first they were all a little shy, embarrassed by
the rare fact of being all together and forced to adopt
certain conventions. It was always thus. The girls sat
together and dared hardly to speak, certainly not to
laugh or to peek over at the men; until Leopold, the
professional jester, walked up to one of the girls with
his amusing gait and, dancing up and down before
her, inaugurated the general festivity. Soon they were
all dancing. Only Sender sat alone again, although
so much had changed within him.

Suddenly Gela caught sight of him and, though
she was probably not conscious of it, had compassion

on his loneliness. She went up to him, pretending it
was a Purim jest, and danced with him. Everyone
observed it. She smiled a little, as though she were
not taking the thing seriously; nevertheless she nestled
against him, as to any other partner. But he was
awkward and the others laughed at him. He felt her
breath upon his cheek and felt the delicate softness of
her womanly body. And this did not so much stir
his senses as give him an inkling of that being sheltered by love for which he had always yearned. And
this kindliness which Gela had shown him without
reflecting upon it, quite finally sealed his fate. Now
he knew that he would never get away from the
village. She had danced with him; she had singled
him out, him, who lived in that dark alley and
traded in chickens and goats and could never marry
and bore the permanent shame of having to say the
berocho to the portion *Tauchocho* every year in token
of his being a victim and a marked man and whose
years increased with the years of the century, as
though it, too, would have to cease, were he to die,
and who would never be able to escape this coil of
circumstance.

After that dance life came into all his gestures; his
eyes were radiant as they had never been; his arms
and hands quivered. Now he drank some of the
brandy with them which they offered here after they
had previously drank the yellow wine from Wuerzburg
of which they had caused a whole keg to be brought
and which had cheered them all. He laughed and was
as merry as anyone. They suspected the reason and

began to make fun of him and suddenly one of them, half drunk, began to sing the derisive song which the children had made up:

> "Out of the century
> From place to place goes he.
> Through lands by night and day.
> Sender, whither away?"

Everybody laughed. But Sender seemed by no means angry. Quietly he arose and very slowly approached the man who had sung the song and, when they had all fallen silent, expecting tumult and violence, Sender stood still before the fellow and said:

"*Shem yisborach* (the Holy one, blessed be He) has made your *lev* (heart) hard and will repudiate you—you stuffy stay-at-homes!"

They did not understand his meaning and talked at random to each other. But he turned around and left the room, not bowed but upright and almost proud.

And Gela, as though driven by an invisible force, followed him. In reality it was still the compassion which she had suddenly felt for his loneliness; in addition, a dim feeling impelled her toward him, the strange one, who went his own way. And perhaps she felt a common element in their fate, because her engagement to Eisig Stein of Laudenbach had been broken off and because people gossiped about her, too.

"Come back in, Sender. Let them talk!"

But he would not go back; he said: "No, not any

more. You can go with me, Gelele, if you really want to."

At that Gela realized that she had gone too far and that her action could easily be misinterpreted. For even if she had found it in herself to love Sender, it would have been senseless, since he was not privileged to marry; and so she went back into the parlor of the inn.

"Oi, oi,"—it came to her from the lips of those who had looked through the window and observed the momentary intimacy between her and Sender. And one cried out: "May one say *massel tov?*"

Her brother, Josel, came up to her and said loud enough for all to hear: "What do you mean by running after that pauper? I'll tell Father!"

"He is as good as the rest of you," she replied, not so much in order to protect him, but rather in defiance of the others who were in opposition to her too.

When Sender came home to his sister, who had long given up attending such festivities, she immediately perceived from his bearing that something had happened. Silently he sat down at the kitchen table and stared at its scrubbed and furrowed top.

Rivke asked: "What's the matter with you again?"

He did not answer. She put before him an earthenware plate filled with an enormous pancake fried in fat to a dark brown color and said, as though she knew all about it:

"Let them talk, Senderle, and eat. It's a fine Purim cake!"

He smiled quietly and put his hand on hers, by which she was supporting herself against the table, and ate.

"Why do you go and bother with them?"

"I want to show them. They are to see——!"

No, now he had to stay; now he couldn't leave the village. How could he abandon Gela who, as she had plainly shown, clung to him. Something would have to happen to make it possible for him to marry her. Wasn't it conceivable that his brother might soon die? He kept on coughing and coughing and had remained childless as a punishment for his not doing his duty by his close kin. But Sender tried at once to repel this thought as a wicked and blasphemous one. Wasn't there, however, the faint hope that new laws would be made, seeing that all these years there had been so much talk of civic rights and equality and that, therefore, the marriage laws would be altered? He would have a talk with Gela.

Purim came to an end and they looked forward to spring, even though in this mountainous country it came late enough. But at last they started their preparations for Pesach, and the women of every household were busy scrubbing and making everything ready for the holiday.

And so it was difficult for Sender to meet Gela and have a talk with her. In addition, he was in doubt concerning her answer, deeply as he yearned for a favorable one. He knew well enough what reply she was almost bound to make; but was there no possibility of being liberated from the heavy yoke of that old law? He tried to persuade himself of that again and again. And couldn't Gela, in that case, live with him and his sister in their little house? There would be room enough. He would have it renovated inside and out. Surely the shepherd, Karl, who was a skilled bricklayer whenever his sheep were in their winter folds, would do this work for him for little or nothing. He nursed these dreams for weeks.

Meanwhile the whole village gossiped about him and the girl, as was to be foreseen after that incident on Purim. He, himself, had at first no notion of this, for it all went on behind his back.

It was Gela who suffered under it. At home her parents and her brother reproached her; her girl friends made fun of her; she, herself, became ever more indignant because she had never dreamed of any real relationship between herself and Sender and had, on that occasion, showed him only an apparent feeling out of pity, out of *rachmones,* as she insisted. So now she avoided him.

And so it came to pass that, on the second day of Pesach, Sender, returning from the *Maariv* service in his *Yontef* suit, stood leaning against the basin of the village fountain at the corner of the upper village street, and waited for her because he knew that she would have to pass by there on her return from the house of her friend Channa Loeb. She did come and so out of the depth of his innocent confidence he spoke to her there in the dusk.

"Gelele," he said, "may I go with you? I have so much to say to you."

Recognizing him, she strode on rapidly without a further glance and said:

"Let me have *menuche* (peace)." Stricken to the heart he remained behind when she added: "Am I to share your curse?"

That left him standing. Silently he pondered: Curse? Is everything that happens to me accursed? Dully and almost paralyzed he walked along the houses on the downward street and felt, as never before, that he was a stranger here at home. That was it; that was his guilt. Never would he be able to get rid of it; always would it cling to him, if he did not help himself. And when on the next day, as he was taking a walk in order to forget his misery, he accidentally met Gela in the village street and she looked past him, as though she had never seen him before, it hurt him to the very quick, but he accepted it as necessary until he himself would somehow have conquered his fate. There was a rebellion within him, but he did not know where to turn or whence help would come.

The days of *Yontef* were past. Now the land was green, both the oak forest near the village and the stingy fields of oats; the yellow rape climbed the hills in broad bands; the wild plum bushes looked like islands of blossom and soon the crabapple trees displayed their reddish white loveliness. Sender beheld it all. But already there also shot up the useless nettles near the walls of his house and stood in tall clumps.

And every evening toward sunset the Jewish men hurried to the *shul* for the ceremony of *Omer;* from all the alleys they came hastily and it seemed to them, as it did every year on the occasion of these special hours of prayer, as though they were in flight from dark surrounding forces which threatened them, as they had threatened their ancestors a thousand years ago. Sender joined them on each occasion, oppressed in his soul in a double sense. Rarely did any one of the others address him, for they now considered that he had become arrogant in addition to everything else.

And now there approached that *Shabbos Bechuk-kausai,* when the Scriptural portion concerning the blessings and the curses would have to be read, as has been related. And they were all glad enough that Sender was here again on this day, for to them it seemed to go without saying that he would again dedicate himself to the service of the community, especially since in late summer old Schlaume had died, he who, during Sender's absence, although he could hardly speak any more, had necessarily been called up to say the blessing over the section of the *Tau-chocho.* They had been very conscious of the fact, however, that this could not have been pleasing to God, since Schlaume had no longer been in his right mind. And Sender was now lower in their esteem than ever, on account of all that had taken place since his return.

It was a brilliant day of early summer. The garden edges were magnificent with all the flowers of the season, with roses large and small and with late lilac on the bushes. A *Shabbos* in all appropriate beauty and tranquility had arisen. But its festive light seemed inappropriate to the difficult *sedra* which they, as Jews everywhere, were destined to read according to their Holy Law. Meanwhile they were looking for-

ward to *Shevuaus,* the happy festival of the Revelation
of the Law. . . .

The *chazan* prayed and sang and the *kehilla* prayed
and sang with him. Upstairs, invisible, stood the
women, the old and the young, in their black and
gleaming wigs under their veils, softly praying, each
following the lead of her husband's voice which was
recognizable to her from below.

The Torah scroll was lifted out of the Holy Ark
and the men were called up one by one: *Rishaun,* the
first; *Sheini,* the second; *Shelishi,* the third; *Revii,*
the fourth; and finally they came to the point at which
the blessing over the section of the *Tauchocho* would
have to be pronounced and it was fully expected that
Sender would arise and go up to the Holy Ark.

Suddenly the women raised their heads. Why was
there such a long silence? On the instant the silence
was broken. The women in the front row could see
how all the men turned around, first only a few, then
all of them. And they stared at a place in the last row
of seats near the door where Sender stood, his *tallis*
over his shoulders, and looked at the floor and did
not move.

Then one of the men cried: "Sender!"

But he did not stir. And another cried out:
"Sender!" And next several at the same time, and
finally there was a great crying and calling in the
shul: "Go on, Sender, go on!" And again and again
they cried out.

But he remained calm and silent and unmoved
by their loud demand to sacrifice himself for them,

although they despised him and though they were
now by their cries desecrating the sacred place. They
had all turned around now and gazed upon him and
were filled with fear. And also the women upstairs
huddled together and pressed forward in order to see
what was taking place.

But Sender did not stir. And no one else summoned the courage to say the *berocho* over that
passage of imprecations in his place.

And so it remained unsaid on that occasion and
they were full of fear that this *avereh* would be a
permanent burden on the whole *kehilla*.

Deeply cast down they left the House of God after
the Torah scroll had been returned to the Ark and
the last prayers had been said. The sun of May
warmed the houses. But it seemed to these men and
women as though a dark veil lay over this day and
over their lives. How could that which had taken
place be made as though it had not?

Sender was the last to leave the *shul*. A few still
stood near the door. They cried out evil words to him;
no one joined him as with slow tread he went toward
his little house that stood in the shadow of a lane.
But from a swallow's nest above the door under his
roof, the young birds twittered at him from their
yellow beaks.

When he entered, his sister Rivke, her veil still
over her head, sat weeping and did not reply when
he wished her a good *Shabbos*. She wept as though
someone had died.

"Rivkele," he said, "don't be angry! I had to do that.

Shem yisborach, the Holy One, blessed be He, will
welcome me nevertheless and will forgive me. He sees
everything as it is in truth."

But she would not be quieted and for days did not
address a word to him.

Nor did the others from now on ever speak to
him. They all avoided him because they considered
him guilty of that threat of doom which they felt
hovering above them on account of the *avereh,* the
great sin, which had been committed.

For it is thus among men that the majority will
never admit its own guilt, but seeks to project it upon
one who has separated himself from it, because it
has forgotten the duty of compassion and takes its
empty common words for deed and truth. And it is
also so because men apply only their own inner norms
by which to judge others, so that the good must suffer
through the wicked.

Thus they thrust him further and further into
utter loneliness; and, while they had formerly jeered
at him or been angry at him, he had now become a
mere burden and stumbling block, whether they met
him or not. And one day he became aware of the
fact that he no longer heard the song of jeering
which the children had made up. The *Parnes* had
forbidden that it be sung; no one was to show a consciousness of his existence. And on another day when
Gela met him on a narrow path outside of the village,
she promptly turned around when she caught sight of
him and hastened back.

He, himself, walked only in the lanes and alleys

in order to meet no one. Soon, too, he felt a change
in the attitude of the peasants round about. They,
who were strict in the observances of their own faith,
had been told that he had refused obedience to his.
Only an occasional one would talk to him at all when
he met him on the farm or in the stable or on the
field. Often he sat in the stable with his neighbor,
the cooper, in silence and watched the cattle, the
cows and the young calves as they took their food
of fresh grass and hay out of the mangers and slowly
chewed it. This calmed him. This single friend had
some understanding of his fate because he, himself,
was nearer than others to the truth of life.

The summer faded. The second harvest had been
brought into the barns and on the empty fields the
black ravens gathered the stalks that remained and
intoned their wintry cries. Even the last penurious
crabapples had been garnered. Clouds and perpetual
fog succeeded the first long rains of autumn. If now
and then they lifted from the hilltops which now were
almost constantly swathed, soaking the meadows and
the fields in dampness, then bluish flames were
kindled here and there and spread their flags across
the countryside. Soon there was no more refuge for
the lonely man amid the goings on of earth and
growth. . . .

And so one day the rumor went through the village
that Sender was gone again. He had not returned
home during two whole days. A sense of guilt began
to oppress them all once more, but they could not
make out what it was that weighed them down.

Rivke ceased asking for pity in silence. She scolded
and screamed and ran about with disheveled hair and
accused everyone.

After a week the serving man of Sender's friend,
the cooper, Conrad by name, reported that he had
seen Sender from afar on the top of a hill. It had
certainly been he. And he had walked around and
around a tall nut tree and had caressed the trunk
and the bark as though these were living things
which belonged to him. But so soon as Conrad, evidently seen by him, had offered to approach, he had
turned away and, bare-headed and as though pursued, had taken refuge in a nearby grove.

Never again did they see Sender Frank in that
part of the world. They went looking for him in the
forest round about; they sent inquiries to that town
from which he had returned the year before. They
found no trace. But many years later, when Rivke
had long died and Gela had married a horse trader
in Prussia and the children who had once sung
those jeering verses were grown up and had children
in their turn, there arose a rumor that in America,
whither people now traveled in steamships, there was
a Jew named Alexander Frank, who was a German
by birth and who had earned immeasurable riches
as a manufacturer of precious, many-colored textiles.
But all this was vague and uncertain. For on another
occasion they heard that in a great city of Eastern
Europe, where men still clung faithfully to their an-
cestral faith, there lived an old *Rav* who was wise
above all men and rich in good deeds and who bore
that name which had not been forgotten during an

entire century, because the events of long ago continued to be related from generation to generation.
But this, too, was only a rumor.

And so it seemed to remain true as the elders of the
congregation had decided, namely, that none dare refuse the sacrifice demanded of him by the community
and that therefore Sender had been punished, even as
the section *Tauchocho* threatens the people of the
Holy One, blessed be He, for all time to come.

THE LOTTERY TICKET

Exodus 20.21

For long hours now Hirsch Bernheim had been tramping through the snow. It was cold and from the steely sky fell small frozen flakes, almost like hailstones. He could scarcely find the path which, even if it had not been snow-covered, could hardly be called one; in fact, the wanderer would never have found it, had he not known the region for very many years and had been able to be guided by the dark, snow-covered fir trees which, singly or in groves, were visible both near and far in spite of the whirling snow.

It was the period during which there, in the southern Black Forest, not far from the land of the French, both Christians and Jews were stirred by the report of a frightful rebellion of the French people against the king and the aristocracy, as well as by the premonition of uncertain mishaps in the future. There

45

was famine in the land and, especially in winter, the poor Jewish peddlers of the little towns and villages scarcely knew how to escape the extremes of need and survive the long cold months. Their small peddling trade barely fed them and their numerous children in whom, in their piety, they took delight and who, in truth, gave them the courage to live at all and whom they regarded as the rewards of God's grace for their lives of obedience to His law.

Hirsch was worn out. The wind blew in his face and took his breath away and the weight of his pack pressed sorely against his back, well used to it as he was. He had now been on the road for four hours, seeking an isolated farmstead which had belonged to the peasants named Kromer within the memory of man. His father, of blessed memory, had traded with that family and had exchanged such articles as he carried in his own pack for silver coins, when the peasants had them, or for butter, for dried healing herbs, such as camomile, mint and juniper berries, or for the pelts of foxes and martens, as well as for the dark and fragrant honey of the fir trees; even, at times, for wooden objects, bowls and brooms, products of the peasant labor in the period when there was no work to be done in the fields, as well as for linen of home-grown flax which the peasant women spun on their wheels during the long winter months.

And what merchandise did they receive? Hirsch, as a matter of fact, did not carry with him only the things which his father had carried with him all his life. He reflected on this matter in his loneliness. He was moved at the memory of his father who, now long dead, had worked so hard up into his old age, and he remembered vividly how he had taken him along for the first time on one of his wanderings through the region, proud of the reception which father and son were accorded by the peasantry. Well, there was the fact of mutual need. As things were now, he had brought more than the traditional wares; he had always sought to furnish his clients with new things and had not lagged behind the times.

Precisely today he had merchandise on which he set great hopes: a new kind of iron nails, brightly polished ones for all kinds of carpentry work. They were very cheap, much cheaper than those hammered out on the anvil one by one by the smiths of the neighborhood. Hirsch had gotten these nails from Basle, where he was well known; thither they had been imported from England, where machines in factories were said to produce them by the many thousands according to a new method. They would yield a good profit and yet the people on the farmsteads would buy them much more advantageously than they had hitherto bought nails from the smiths. But it was just these nails that so increased the weight of his peddler's pack. Also he carried with him wax candles, consecrated candles of lovely yellow beeswax, blessed in the monastery of Einsiedeln, as well as reddish-brown sealing wax and leather shoe laces with metal points. These, too, he carried for the first time. And he had added little toys for the children and gaily colored candies; for it was the period of Advent, a few weeks prior to Christmas. Above all, he carried against his body in the lining of his coat a flat leather purse. It had

a little lock of its own and was further secured by a
narrow leather strap which was wound around it
many times. It smelled of leather and sweat; his father
had carried it before him; in it he had secured seven
tickets for the lottery at Zurzach beyond the Rhine.
The drawing would take place at Candlemastide when
there would be the great fair for both cattle and merchandise.

He had brought these for the sake of the modest
commission which he as an agent would earn, and
he was quite sure that he would be able to dispose of
them in the period of several months which would
elapse before the drawing. Even now he had been
able to sell three. These tickets were printed slips
of stiff paper. Figures were printed on them and a
mysterious seal. He could not, of course, read the
words, but he understood the figures. They felt to
the touch like banknotes and looked like them too.
Kromer, the peasant, would surely buy one. Although
he lived on his isolated farm quite alone with his
wife, his children and his servants, he was a bright
and clever man and therefore very tolerant of the
Jews. Never had he permitted his children to use
those abusive terms which Hirsch was quite accustomed to hearing now and then. It was for this reason, too, that Hirsch had set out on the long and
difficult road to this farm, rather than to some other
that was nearer.

For it was Friday. He should have been home by
noon at latest today in order to prepare himself properly for *Shabbos*, so that he might pass the holy day
with his family and in his own *kehilla*. But the snow

had set in yesterday and had fallen uninterruptedly on the old snow of the roads; and when this morning Hirsch had waited for an hour at the crossroads between Bonndorf and Weizen for the post sleigh, he had had to come to the conclusion that the vehicle could not make its way through the great drifts and had also been forced to conclude that he could not get home for *Shabbos*. It was unusual for him to take a public vehicle; one didn't do that; the profits did not permit it. Yet his heart was sore. This thing had never happened yet—not to be home on *Shabbos* with wife and child, not even to be sheltered in a Jewish house, not to speak of not going to *shul*. The whole thing depressed him. What a sin! For he had been on the road since Monday, as was his wont. He determined, if Kromer gave him the reception he expected, to fast and pray the entire day. Thus he would keep the dietary law as well as expiate and beg God for forgiveness on account of the desecration that he had been guilty of by not proceeding homeward early on Thursday. All for the sake of business.

Painfully he tramped through the deep snow, in his long brown coat with the gleaming metal buttons which were too icy to be touched. His ears pained him although he wore a fur cap with earmuffs. He could not even beat his arms crossed upon his breast, as people in the country were accustomed to doing for a little more warmth, because his pack prevented that. Again and again he sank into deep drifts and unseen holes. Under these circumstances his pack was almost unbearable. As a rule, he carried it with ease; for, though not tall, he was a vigorous and stocky man.

If only he had not had those new nails! For a moment
he considered taking them out of his pack and hiding
them under a tree. But how was he to dig through
the snow and then dig a hole in the frozen earth?
Above all, how did he know when he would be here
again. Then there was the danger of his being
observed. No, he had to go on although even his stout
gnarled stick was of no use to him. It slid into the
snow. At least he could shove it under his pack in
order to release his back a little. And it couldn't be
much farther off. He was by now so tired and hungry
that a wave of weakness came over him. All he
wanted was not to move. But just then, beyond a
grove of trees which he knew well, he saw a little
cloud of smoke. That must be it, thank God. And he
uttered a prayer.

At this moment, too, it stopped snowing. Beyond
the fir trees and a little hill, which they half hid,
he saw the great farmstead standing peacefully in the
light of evening. No one was to be seen. The edges
of the straw roof of the high-gabled house almost
reached down to the snow. Only the windows of the
front of the house were visible.

At that moment, too, the watch dog gave voice. It
was the shaggy St. Bernard whom he knew, standing
in the snow up to his belly and barking. Out of the
door came the peasant on to the front steps.

"So it's you, Hirsch, so it's you," said he, recognizing the visitor at once. The latter explained his presence briefly and then continued:

"Give me something to eat, Kromer. Nothing but

two eggs, boiled ones; then leave me all alone. Any moment now *Shabbos* begins!"

On the flagstone in front of the door he stamped the snow from his tall boots. The peasant relieved him of his pack. Firm in his own faith, he went into the house to consult with his wife. Both of them recognized as a matter of feeling, rather than of conscious thought, the common origin of their own faith and that of their guest. They harbored, too, the shy respect of simple souls in face of the others' mysterious way of serving the God whom they, too, served. Thus they took all possible care to make the necessary arrangements for Hirsch to perform his service in peace.

Hastily he ate the two eggs with a little stale bread which he had brought with him and which his wife, Rachel, had baked the week before. He would not even have sat down if his extreme fatigue had not forced him into the broad wooden chair. And he felt the wonderful warmth. Oh, it was warm here! The bright blue tile oven which took up almost one fourth of the wainscoted room, fairly radiated. And now he felt a mood of solemnity and peace, this Jewish man among these people who were strange yet familiar. In the kitchen he washed his hands, pronouncing the blessing and then went back into the big warm room, took up his stand with his face to the East in order to say the Friday evening prayer. His hosts and their serving people were silent. They observed and respected their guest's service of God.

Meanwhile they had lit lights: two tall candles

in cast iron candle holders, for the dusk had fallen.
When Hirsch had finished his prayer, it occurred
to him suddenly that he still had, sinfully enough,
money on his person. It was forbidden to carry anything on *Shabbos,* above all money, the worst of all
things. For surely, by now, the day of rest must have
begun. Hastily he took off his handsome old purse,
studded in front with many colored little stones which
he wore like a girdle, even though it embarrassed
him to have the others see it. He laid it on his pack
which stood beside the oven.

Now, too, suddenly he thought of the lottery tickets.
Were they money? What a question! They were
made of paper, true! But they had a pecuniary value
even now. How much more if one of them were
drawn in the lottery. One could win as much as ten
thousand crowns. To be sure, they were money! How
could he ever have doubted it? He must get rid of
them over *Shabbos;* that was beyond all question. But
where was he to put them and not be seen? So first
of all he took off his coat and hung it on the back of
a chair. That relieved him; that sin at least was
averted.

The peasant and his wife proposed that he should
sleep warmly on the long oven bench. To this he
agreed. He took off his wet boots and Marilie, the
serving maid, put a straw sack on the oven bench.
The peasant's wife, too, looked in once more to see
that all was well and wished him a good night's sleep.
She extinguished the light for him and he stretched
himself out.

He found it hard to sleep. His limbs ached with

weariness on this unaccustomed couch and the day
had been too difficult. All kinds of thoughts beset
him. If only they would not be too frightened about
him at home. How could they know how safe and
comfortable he was? They might well think that he
had met with an accident, that he was in great danger. Perhaps the good Rachel, his wife, would ask
the men to say a *misheberach* (a prayer for his
safety). His keen emotions made sleep impossible.
He lay awake and it did not occur to him that what
principally kept him from sleeping was the great heat
emitted by the tile stove which was fed with long fir
logs from its other side. In addition to all the other
thoughts he was suddenly frightened both on account
of his hard cash and on account of the lottery tickets.
He got up in his stocking feet and quietly lifted his
pack and placed it on the bench at his head. He placed
his money belt beside him. Next he took the leather
purse out of his coat, removed the lottery tickets
from it and placed them under the oilcloth of his
pack among the smaller wares that he had. The recep-
tacle he returned to his coat pocket. Now he was
quite calm.

When a noise awakened him in the morning—it
was the sound of fresh logs being slid into the oven
from without—Kromer stood before him. His brown
round beard quivered with a pleasant laugh. He said:
"Good morning. Did you have a good sleep?" Hirsch
quickly recollected all that happened. In the end he
must have fallen asleep. Now the room was bright
and cheerful and the wainscoting reflected the snowy
light of day. So he too laughed and got up from the

bench and said: "I've slept far too long. But then I was very tired."

But at that moment he saw in a corner of the room, where a round table was standing with a bench, a crucifix high on the wall, a simple image carved of wood. At the sight self-reproach came over him with great force: What an *avereh* to be here and not at home on the *Shabbos* and not to be praying in *shul* with the others! What a sin! But then there came into his mind the words written in the *Tauro* and he repeated them softly to himself: *Bechol ha-makaum asher askir es shemi owau eilecho uweirachticho*—"In every place where I cause My Name to be mentioned, there will I come to thee and bless thee." And he was quieted. Now he would fast and pray.

His kindly hosts understood and respected his desire. They left him alone, seeing that they had to employ themselves and fill the day with their labor in the house itself. The masses of snow were so high that one could not even go into the nearby forest to cut wood. From time to time one of the children, who was still small, peered shyly through the door at the strange man. Thus he passed the long hours of the day in prayer, interrupted by heavy thoughts of his dear ones at home and evermore oppressed by the anxiety that his absence had brought upon them.

But finally the evening came. Hirsch asked for a candle and a small glass of *Kirsch* and performed the *Havdolah* ceremony and softly chanted the prayer, letting the others observe him in their silent tolerance.

"So," he said, "now *Shabbos* is over." He turned

to his hosts: "If only I knew how my family was feeling and who made *Havdolah* for them!"

"I'm sure everything is fine," said Kromer. "Now you sit right down at the table and eat. That's a thing I wouldn't like—eat next to nothing all day long!"

And so Hirsch washed his hands and sat down with the others. He took out of his pack a remnant of dried beef which he had almost forgotten and let his hostess persuade him to take a large round slice of the coarse moist bread of the farmstead, although it troubled him, whether it could be considered kosher. Kromer fetched a tall bottle, flat on its two sides but in the form of a huge drop, into the flat sides of which figures had been artfully engraved: two naked human beings under a simple tree, to represent Adam and Eve in paradise; above them had been carved within a luminous triangle the holy eye of God. The translucent bottle contained clear and pure cherry brandy, home distilled according to an immemorial recipe. The very fragrance did one good. They drank the brandy out of thick low glasses.

Hirsch had many things to tell them. He related to them how the news came from Alsace that the French revolutionary leaders were also giving all the rights of man to the Jews and intended to protect them and that, therefore, a new time was coming. Kromer, the peasant, murmured to himself: "That won't be a bad thing!" And then after a pause he asked in his deep bass voice: "What have you brought along, Hirsch? Let's do a little trading!"

Hirsch arose and went over to his portable shop and threw back the oilcloth: "Good wares I have for you today! You'll be pleased!" he said. First he showed them the toys. That always created a pleasant mood. But the children, two boys and a little girl, were sent out of the room, because these things were to be surprises for Christmas. This trade was soon completed. Then he showed the nails. These were admired at once. Kromer said to his serving man: "If they're as good as the smith's at Bonndorf, it's all over with him!" And he exchanged a bottle of raspberry syrup for a package of nails.

"Have you got candles, too?" Kromer's wife asked.

"Certainly I have, fine and consecrated ones from Einsiedeln."

And he went back to his pack.

But, alas, when he started to take the wax out of a lower compartment of his pack, he saw that the candles were bent and in part had melted under the nocturnal heat of the oven. And when he looked further he saw that the same thing had happened to the sealing wax. The reddish brown sticks had lost their form and had been flattened and some of them had run into blobs and one of them had melted over the lottery tickets which he had hastily hidden near them the night before. Fright overcame him. But most of the tickets were only spotted here and there. Only a single one had been entirely flooded by the sealing wax. Hirsch lamented: "Bad luck has come to me, nothing but bad luck!"

"Let me see what it is," said the peasant. Hirsch explained what had happened.

"That's not so bad. Show me the stuff; I'll take one of those!"

And in fact he acquired one of the tickets, undeterred by his wife's objection as to what he would do with so much money, if he won. He paid for the ticket with a half crown of silver, which he fetched from the bedroom and on which was to be seen the picture of the good Empress Maria Theresia. To be sure, he picked the ticket that was least harmed and had the fewest spots. He looked at the one which had been quite overrun by the sealing wax and so had been more or less obliterated and said:

"That one is probably no good anymore. No one will buy it. You can't even see the number of it!"

This troubled Hirsch little. He was sure that a way could be found. And when he had another good night's sleep and had calmly laid his *tefillin* on Sunday morning, curiously but respectfully observed once again by these kindly people who had sheltered him, he set out, accompanied by Kromer himself, on that road to where the post-sleigh would have to stop. Today it was not hard, for the snow had settled down and there was no storming.

On the evening of that day Hirsch arrived safely at home. There was joyous surprise on all sides, not only among his own family but in the whole congregation, how God had again been gracious to a Jew. And when he told them how he had been sheltered and how he had fasted and prayed, it was clear to the whole congregation that, in view of his piety, none but a happy result could have been expected. True, they had for a moment reflected, whether they had not better perform a *misheberach* for him. But the *chazan* had objected, seeing that no one knew whether Hirsch was really in any danger.

Slowly the recollection of the adventure faded. Weeks passed and months. The snow thawed and so did the rivers and these rose in floods and swamped their banks with the fullness of their waters and as they receded they left fishes lying on the fields, red spotted trout and big whitefish, of which some were not dead and thus furnished welcome food for the people in the little towns. And Hirsch continued to make his rounds in the countryside. Week after week he went from the forest of Hotzen to the monastery of St. Blaize, through the whole valley and again up toward Bonndorf and occasionally across the wooden bridge that leads into Switzerland. Slowly he sold the lottery tickets, first those that had been but slightly injured by the melting wax in the heat of Kromer's oven. Later he sold the others too. Finally he had only one left. In spite of all his persuasiveness he had not been able to get rid of that one, because the distrust of the buyers was greater than his power to convince them. They were sure that a lottery ticket, of which the number could scarcely be deciphered, could have no validity or worth.

So the day of the drawing approached and Hirsch himself was left in possession of the ticket. Sometime before, at the advice of Rachel who was a clever woman, they had tried to remove a little of the hard red mass of sealing wax by warming the paper against the oven. They had wanted to leave nothing untried.

But it had done little good. So the ticket was lying there and, in the end, Hirsch had no longer carried it with him and had almost forgotten it.

The fair at Zurzach came around. Hirsch did not attend it this time. He had commissioned his brother Seligmann to make the necessary purchases for him. It cost too much for both of them to make the journey and it was his brother's turn to go. On his return the brother brought back the list of the chief winning numbers which he had written down in Hebrew letters.

Well, you will have suspected what had come to pass. On that wretched, apparently worthless slip of paper, which had been lying about the house, they were able to decipher a number recorded on the brother's list. It was this number that had won the highest amount. Ten thousand crowns! Ten thousand silver crowns! But first they dared not to believe. They went to the *Parnes* (the president of the congregation) who was a *chochem* (a sage) and asked his advice. He, to be sure, was of the opinion that there was no room for discussion. By right and law Hirsch was entitled to the premium. Nevertheless he proposed that Hirsch was to go himself on the next day to Zurzach and ascertain the facts. He himself would accompany his friend. And so it came to pass. And Hirsch Bernheim was and remained the winner of the premium of ten thousand crowns and thus became the best heeled man in the *kehilla*. No wonder that the Jews and the Christians of the village were long excited by this piece of good fortune which was remembered through the succeeding years.

And that would be the end of the story were we
not obliged to add that Hirsch himself and his excellent wife in the purity of their faith had made it
known and had ever again in the after years emphasized the fact that only through the direct providence
of God had they been deemed worthy of this *massel*
(good fortune), because on that long ago *Shabbos,*
when Hirsch had been obliged to spend the day in
that isolated farmstead in the Black Forest, he had
fasted and prayed and thus chastened himself for
the sake of God; therefore he had been thus re-
warded by the Eternal, blessed be His name. And
all men believed it; and the Kromers too and their
people were equally convinced that God had granted
this favor to one who had faith in Him, because they
had seen with their own eyes how their guest had
turned to his God on that day.

All this is related even to this hour in the old
family of the Bernheim's. Hirsch opened the first
regular shop that the village had ever seen with wares
that came from near and far. Everything he touched
succeeded from that time on and he was soon elected
Parnes of the *kehilla.* His children had many children and their children even unto our own time and
beyond the great war were blessed for a century and
more in well being, good repute, peace and happiness,
in life and love and death. The men were *Parnosim*
of the *kehilla* and the daughters made good marriages
in the land and far into Switzerland, even to Lake
Constance, and into the great cities of Bavaria. And
even today, when heavy trials once more assail the
Jewish people and many of them have had to flee

into foreign lands, they still tell their children that they have become and remained what they are for the reason that a far ancestor of theirs had been a God fearing man and one steadfast in strict belief in the Holy Law.

THE CALL

The life which old Mendele Weil had had for years to lead in the little town of the Black Forest was neither a simple nor an easily bearable one. He had to be supported by the community and one knows what that means: being boarded out among the various families on a daily basis and occupying a little attic room in crooked Shmul's house. Once upon a time he had not been without means and his voice had had some weight in the community. But you know how these things happen: without fault or guilt, fate has a way of attacking a man from all sides; then the end comes. If you can't stop yourself from falling, down you go. . . . Finally, too, all the members of his family and all the friends of his youth died. He was left alone. No one knew rightly what was to be done with him. To be sure, no reproach could be addressed to him; no dishonor attached to him; and so the community took care of him, not even with a sense of irritation, a fact worthy of em-

63

phasis. Nor was it a bad thing for anyone that the
kehilla as such took upon itself the performance of
this *mitzvah*. Moreover, he was not quite useless; he
could be employed for one or another small task and
accomplishment.

As far as he was concerned, it didn't particularly
depress him, even though his mind and his memory
weren't what they had once been. It even had a
slightly childish aspect when he went about smiling
to himself and even murmuring to himself at times.
All the while he felt that he was still a worthy member of the community. He was asked to complete
a *minyan* and thus his station before God and in *shul*
was equal to any other's. And was it not also considered appropriate to set him tasks for one man or
another and, above all, for the *kehilla* itself?

Yet the little man was the object of some compassion when one saw him going about with dragging
footsteps, a little bent and with his spare yellowish
white beard framing his wrinkled face. Sometimes, to
be sure, the boys teased him badly. He took that as
inevitable and let it not wound him too deeply.

But one fine day, as though to recompose him for
all suffering and to show him that Providence was
not forgetful of him, God permitted something to
happen which raised him high above all others and
consecrated him, as it were, for the future, for those
few years which it was still given him to live and
which, in truth, awakened the thought in him that
all his fated suffering and sorrow had come over him
only in order that in the end he could pass into the

World to Come easily and as one consecrated by God
Himself.

It was a gray day of winter which the mild light
of the snow did not brighten and on which the earth
was frozen hard. They had told him to carry a cord
of firewood, which had been prepared for the oven
in the synagogue and which lay in the yard where
a hedge separated it from the garden into the room
meant for it within the building. The old man took
this work very seriously. Busily he went back and
forth, carrying, pressed to his bosom, several but never
too many of the longish thin logs.

He had been busy thus for several hours when,
above him where the road mounts the hill, coming
out of the little town between the gabled, ancient
houses, two boys, whom he did not see, wandered
along, as boys are accustomed to do after school hours.
They were Jewish boys. They saw the little man
below them and, as they had done on other occasions
in a different place, one of them cried out his name:
"Mendele." The cry was faint. The little old man
barely heard it and barely raised his head. He knew
well enough that not to shiver in the cold in his thread-
bare garments he must not stop too long the physical
activity of his work.

But after a period, even though again from very
far and without his being able to see the boys, because
a house stood between them and him, the call came
once more: "Mendele, Mendele!"

Drawing himself half erect, because he still had
a bundle of the logs in his arms, he stood quite still

and remained thus for quite a while and gazed and listened. But for the moment he heard nothing more. So he carried his burden to the appointed place and returned to the yard and approached the pile of wood.

And as he stood there in a moment's meditation, the voice arose again, far, far away and high and clear, and passed through him like a gleam of light: "Mendele, Mendele, where are you?"

A sudden cognition arose in him. He turned about and ran, as fast as his old legs would carry him, into the House of God straight up to the *almemor* and stood with rapt head before the Holy Ark and cried in a loud but trembling voice: *"Hineni!* Here I am, Lord, here I am!"

And he threw himself on his face in fervent prayer, and lay thus for a long time, his forehead in the dust of the floor. And he knew that the Eternal spoke to him as to one of His elect. . . .

And when the little old man stepped out under the wintry sky again, in the coat which someone had given him and which was far too large for him, he was as one transformed and his heart was lighter than it had ever been in all his previous life. Thus did God take the oppressed Mendele Weil, whom his fellows regarded as the most wretched member of the congregation, and made him for the rest of his days the happiest of them all; for he could go about among the people cherishing within him the great and blessed secret that he had been the elect among them all and above them all through Him above and for eternity.

THE FOX

Wherever, a hundred years ago, Jews were found living in the villages of the German countryside, it was not uncommon that ten or more children were born to each family. Thus Jews fulfilled piously the command to be fruitful and multiply. But this obedience to God's law had two aspects. It was a fine thing for a father, praying in *shul*, proudly to survey his sons about him. But when they were grown up, there arose the difficult question of how they were to become independent; how each was to attain a way by which to be supported. This was hard. It was all the harder because in those days in the country there was really no occupation but peddling. From time to time, to be sure, rumors came to them from the cities how here and there one of them had risen in the world and gained what seemed to them inconceivable riches; how, indeed, it had come to pass that there existed great Jewish lawyers and physicians of acknowledged merit. They heard, too, that in certain regions, especially in the southern part of the Fatherland, there were not a few jews who had for long been living on their own earth, owning their own fields and woods, and thus wholly integrated with the homeland.

And thus the day came when Leib Gump, in Werblingen, had to begin to take thought as to what was to become of his four sons, seeing that he was old now and desired to retire from business. Well, what could he do except follow the long, long custom of his kind and time? In the district in which he and his forefathers had long traded and had been well esteemed, he distributed the six villages with their adjoining farmsteads among his four sons. Thus they, industrious as himself, could build themselves a future, undisturbed by the other families of the *kehilla* who, for their part, carefully observed the boundaries of their customary districts. This method assured a peaceful life among the Jews of a given area. They found their happiness in the sacred observances of the Jewish year, about which their whole lives revolved. And it occurred to no one to act differently or to breach the circle of the accustomed.

And so Leib Gump had four sons: Elias, Jikel, Moses and red haired Jonas, the youngest and the most vital. They were mature enough by now, although none of them was married yet. Three sisters had to be brought under the *huppa,* before it was their turn. Two of the girls had been married off with appropriate dowries which the sons, as was right and proper, had helped earn. And that hadn't been easy, in view of the limitation of their trading; for they belonged to those members of the village community who had not fared too well in the matter of the distribution of trading areas. In addition, the land had experienced difficult years of bad crops and dearth. Yet they were industrious fellows. And so the father, who was far beyond sixty, had already "handed over the business," as the saying went. That is to say, the sons needed no longer to work for the total family, nor render him an accounting on Sunday morning concerning their achievement of the past week. They could begin to save and accumulate their own capital. The whole thing had been far from easy. How were the six villages and farmsteads to be distributed among four?

What could be done except assign two of the villages to a pair of sons in common, in addition to the village which each of them had alone? The method involved limitations by streets or by upper village and lower village; for the villages were situated in a hilly country and had no more than two or three streets a piece. At bottom everything proceeded in orderly fashion, for the boys carried moral discipline in their very bones. Once in a while difficulties arose and small disputes, principally because the youngest boy, Red Jonas, was—how shall we put it?—too shrewd and able. His whole aspect betrayed his character whenever one saw him coming along with quick, short steps, his head held sidewise and bent a little forward, as though seeking to spy out an opportunity. Also, he had tell-tale freckles on his hands.

Once upon a time he was walking through Fischach, a village which the oldest, Jikel, shared with him. And although he really had no business there be-

cause the upper village, through which he was saun-
tering, was his brother's special territory, yet he let
his quick looks dart hither and yon and also exchanged a few words with the friendly peasants.

It was earliest springtime and the sowing had
already begun. As he was standing at the gate of the
Salen farm and chatting with its owner, Pankraz,
what was it that he saw? From the brown, tarred gate
of the stable there hung for drying, nailed by its four
feet, a handsome fox, a yellow-reddish fox pelt in
its richest winter thickness with fine bushy tail. There
it hung, the shrewdness still in its aspect, in spite
of the glassy eyes which had not helped the creature
whose greed had led it into the trap.

"Did you shoot it?" asked Jonas and went nearer
and felt the pelt with his freckled, expert hands.

"No, I caught him in the trap. You see, there's no
bullet hole in him. The pelt is whole. I never had
a finer one."

"What will you take for it?"

"It belongs to Jikel, you know. Only I haven't seen
him around lately," said the peasant, thinking of his
trusted business friend and desirous of guarding his
rights.

One is not to suppose that Jikel didn't know that
the pelt was hanging there. He had seen it long ago.
Calmly he had let it hang; that was all right. There
was no need for him to hurry; no one was likely to
interfere with his bit of business. The peasants did
not buy such articles. They were finally sold to the
gentlemen in the cities; and the furrier Boehni in
Dusenhofen beyond the Rhine, into whose hands

it would finally fall, didn't take walks in the country. If the Jewish traders had not existed, the peasants would not have had their small additional income from their hunting and trapping.

Ah yes, Pankraz needed the money. He had been a little short of the purchase price of the seed which he had required in the past few weeks. And so, finally, upon Jonas repeating his question, he answered: "You can have it for four thaler."

That wasn't a great deal of money; but it was just the amount he needed, and it was high time to buy the remaining seed. They shook hands to seal the bargain, as was then customary. "Done!" Jonas had quickly calculated that beyond the frontier, in Switzerland, he could get at least a gold Napoleon for the pelt. . . .

When he came home with the pelt which he had wrapped in a cloth, his father was in the house. He perceived the gamey scent; yet he asked his son: "What have you got there?"

The latter, well aware of his offence, stepped to one side. But the old man had already grasped the cloth and lifted one end of it and had seen the fox.

"Where did you get that?"

Now there was no getting out of it.

"From the Salen farm."

"From the Salen farm? How do you happen to drive a trade with Pankraz and thus rob your brother?" he asked at the top of his voice.

"He didn't go to fetch it; Pankraz himself told me that."

"Didn't fetch it! Didn't fetch it! We may be sure

that Jikel knew well enough why he hadn't done so.
But now Pankraz the peasant will be thinking what
kind of a son I have—a son of mine who will be
cheating his own brother by poaching on his territory. A son of mine!"

Jonas wanted to smooth the matter over and said
at once: "I can turn the pelt over to Jikel. I didn't
pay too much for it."

"And the peasant," the old man demanded, "the
peasant? You don't care what he thinks of us, do you?
You take the fox straight back to him and tell him
that Jikel will come to fetch it."

"He won't want to take it back; he will want to
keep the money," said Jonas.

"Then let him keep the money! The pelt must be
taken back and kept for Jikel. Pankraz is good for
it; he won't take the money twice over!"

And so it came to pass that Red Jonas carried the
pelt back on that very day, although he had to be on
the road until late in the night.

Thus it is clear that the peasant, Pankraz, could
have sold the same pelt twice over, had he been so
minded. And the far too clever Red Jonas with his
freckled hands was put to shame before him and
also suffered some anxiety during several days on
account of his four thaler, because his father insisted that there be peace in the house and that no
enmity arise between his sons just for the sake of
money and, above all, that the honor of the Gump
family be kept intact, not only in the mind of this
peasant, but of those of the whole countryside.
Discipline had to be preserved; unscrupulous shrewdness was not enough.

THE PARNES IS TAUGHT A LESSON

They were both named Moishe, the proud *Parnes,*
Moishe Levy, with his big farm and his six daughters,
of whom he had already married off three with proper
dowries, two of them as far away from home as Baden
—whence you may learn concerning his prosperity—
and also the little man Moishele, who was so poor that
people had forgotten his family name and whose age
no one knew. He might have been forty or even sixty,
or, if you like, more. And it seemed to everyone as
though he had always been around.

You may well ask why the two were called Moishe
and not Maushe, as everywhere in Germany, especially in the South. Well, it is because of the dialect
spoken in Upper Alsace, not too far from Basle,
and the name derives from the French word Moïse,
which is the name of Moses, our great teacher. Yes,
the scene of the story which is to be told here is
in Upper Alsace; it is to be the image of happy and
serene days and also as a sign of the possibility of a
Christian teaching a lesson to Jewish people as a

rare recompense for that which our Holy Command-
ments have given them through the millennia, and
how the Jews involved were grateful for the lesson
and glad of the oneness and community of moral
attitudes.

It was in that part of the country which was the
homeland of that good and true poet Johann Peter
Hebel, the same in which, on the other shore of the
Rhine, there was born several centuries ago that good
man and great helper of our ancestors, Jossele von
Rosheim, and whence he set forth whenever it was
necessary to protect his Jewish brethren anywhere
in the great realm of the Germans. And the time of
the story is that period of French dominance when
the second Napoleon, who called himself the third,
and his vain wife Eugénie, produced turmoil in his
great country, to which Alsace belonged at that time
and brought trade and activity to it but also rest-
lessness and finally the misfortune of war, as his
uncle had done before him. But the Jewish people
of Alsace lived very well. They cultivated the land
just like their fellows and had had time by virtue
of many decades of peace and freedom and equality
to attain prosperity. Nevertheless, though no one was
in want, yet there were some who had no more than
what was barely necessary, no more and also no less;
and it is ever thus among us that there are those who,
despite pains and industry, have no particular luck.
They never truly prospered, and this applies to whole
families who seem to lack luck and the favor of
Heaven. Thus, while most members of the *kehilla*

were able annually to lay aside several hundred golden Napoléons, yet there were a few who managed just to live and not to go hungry. This was the best they could do and ready money was always lacking to them. To the latter group belonged Moishele, as you may have suspected.

Ready cash? He was the village barber, the barber of the Jews. What is that? Well, to put it precisely, he was the hairdresser. But even that does not define it correctly, as must be done if the people of today are not to receive a false impression. If you imagine that he ever used a razor, you are wrong. A pious Jew and a razor—those things don't go together. So what am I telling you? Yet you must know. But if you imagine that in those days and in that village even the most *bekoved* man in the *kehilla* employed the barber on weekdays, on ordinary weekdays, you are mistaken. Not even the *Parnes* indulged in such luxury. It was on *Erev Shabbos* that this thing was done, and then only with a bent, dull pair of scissors which rattled through the thick beards of the men.

They could always see Moishele coming from afar in his wooden boots and his blue linen smock which reached down to his knees and which had two wide-open pockets on his chest from which one could see protruding the scissors and a whitish yellow comb of bone. First he went to the house of the *Parnes* Moishe Levy, and this was the little man's most important moment of the week. He seemed to himself indispensable then and was delighted when the mighty president of the congregation asked him:

"Well, what is there new among the people, Moish-
ele?" And he could answer and tell all he had heard.
He always made a point of knowing something, even
if he had to make it up. To come back to the practical matter, you will realize that there wasn't much
ready cash involved in this service which Moishele
rendered. He was, in fact, the poorest man in the
kehilla, if you omit the two feeble-minded sisters
Bloch who, like himself, lived in the Bach alley in
little one-storied huts. So he could barely buy himself garments, although those he had lasted for
decades; far less could he indulge in any luxuries, not
even in tobacco in order to use it, as the others did,
in a clay pipe or to roll cigarettes.

One day, it was the first day of the *Chol Hamoed
Succaus,* Moishele sat early in the morning on the
milestone that stood in the bend of the road which
led from the lower to the upper village on the way
to the synagogue. It was a solid white piece of sandstone from the Champagne country. He sat there in
his blue smock, his hands on his knees and gazed
before him. He wasn't cheerful, to be honest, under
the black pointed cap which they all wore in those
days. His hair fell down a little over his forehead
and his gaze was absentminded. It needn't have been
the good Hans Brohme, the *Maire* of the village, as
they call the burgomaster in that part of the country—who was placed above both Jews and Christians
by the Prefect and who took notice of everything,
even as his office demanded—it needn't, I say, have
been he. Anyone else would have turned to Moishele
and asked him why he looked so miserable and down-

cast. But the *Maire* considered it his official duty to find out what was wrong and approached the little man with mighty tread. "Well, Moishele, what ails you? What's the matter with you? You sit there as though the hail had killed your crops."

To begin with, Moishele was silent. He just sat there and looked up at the *Maire* with melancholy eyes. After a little while he shook his head and struck his knees repeatedly with the palms of his hands.

"Well, come on! Answer me, man!" the *Maire* said impatiently.

Finally the other replied:

"They didn't call me up to the *Tauro* on *Yontef*, not on *Rosh Hashono* and not now again on *Succaus*."

"Why didn't they, Moishele? You're a Jew, the same as the others."

"That's true. But it is because I can't make a contribution for good causes, because I have no *mesumen,* like the other people, the rich ones."

"Because you have no *mesumen!* But that won't do at all! Our dear Lord doesn't care about that; what He cares about is the heart and faith. Aren't you a pious Jew?"

"That I am. But there's nothing you can do about it."

The *Maire* reflected briefly.

"Oh yes, there is something to be done about it. Let me see to it. And don't tell anybody that I know. Are there any more days of *Yontef?*"

And Moishele with a dazed look at the *Maire* told him that on the next Thursday it would be *Shemini*

Atzeret and the following day *Simchas Tauroh*. And
the *Maire,* who was a peasant, had a pretty good idea
of this festival and its meaning, because for nearly a
week now the *Succaus* had been standing in front
of the Jewish houses, covered with foliage and adorned
within by the fruits of the harvest. He patted the
shoulder of Moishele, who had risen, and said:

"Have patience, Moishele, we'll attend to that!"
And he went on his way.

Now came the penultimate day of the festival and
next that happy day on which we rejoice in the Law
and hopefully seek to forget all evil. From all the
streets men and women walked to the *shul* that morning. So, also, came Moishe Levy, the *Parnes.* He
wore a broadbrimmed, gray, top hat, which grew narrower at the peak, the black coat with the high collar
that reached almost to his ears behind, and the
trousers checked in gray and black. It was the Parisian
fashion before the last. The top hat he had recently
bought in Strasbourg when his daughter, who knew
how to manage horses, had driven him there for the
purpose of selling his wheat in the big city. Next to
him strode his wife Henriette, a member of the
Bloch family in Gebweiler, known to everyone in the
land, with her distinguished, broad East Indian shawl
over her shoulders, which was held together by a great
brooch of twisted gold woven like a bird's nest and
from under whose wig hung down the appropriate
earrings of blue enamel on gold like handsome heavy
fruits. And the others were clad, even as these were,
in more or less sumptuous garments. They were all

in a happy mood. And it seemed to the men as though they were still carrying the festive *lulav* with the green willow wands from the edges of their own brooks, as well as the rare *esrogim* in their silver bowls. For there had been a rich harvest this year, which was equally favorable for trade. The grapes had had enough sun as well as rain at the proper time, so that the clusters had become sweet all over the land and as far as Baden; the ears of the wheat had been fuller than for long and the maize and hops had been rich. On the slopes of the nearby hills the foliage was still green and as far as eye could reach were the pines and fir trees on the dark summits of the Vosges mountains. Moishele, the barber, also had donned his *Yontef* garment which wasn't even of the fashion before the last.

In happy mood they stood between the pews of the *shul*. And who can describe their amazement when suddenly—the *chazan,* Shloime Ruef, had just begun to intone the prayer—they saw a strange and yet familiar figure enter the House of God with their own people. Unquestionably, it was Hans Brohme; it was the *Maire.* For a moment they were of two minds, hesitating between the scruple of a Christian in the House of the one and only God—a thing much rarer in those days in the country than in the cities, although Christian and Jews were not ill-informed concerning each other's customs—and, on the other hand, their satisfaction in that the *Maire* considered it important to stand with them before God on an important holiday. In the end their pleasure in the community of

faith overcame their scruples. They smiled and nodded
to him, especially his friend Moishe Levy who was,
next to him, the most important man of the community. And, as they observed, Hans Brohme, too,
was festively attired and, moreover, had about his neck
the silver chain of his office and in the buttonhole of
his black morning coat the gleaming red ribbon of
the Légion d'Honneur.

Had anyone ever heard of such a thing? In no other
village, in no other country was that possible. Only
among them, where all men lived in peace with each
other. And how tactful, how significant it was that
for this sign of good will the *Maire* had chosen precisely the feast of *Simchas Tauroh*. They were not
likely to forget this.

The service proceeded. Brohme stood with a serious
and even solemn expression near the door, while the
Jewish men about him, led by the *chazan,* sang the
old holy prayers with such fervor that he, too, was
moved.

Then the Torah scrolls were lifted from the ark in
their white silk coverings and were carried about the
synagogue with the ringing of bells and with singing
and finally there began the reading of the Scripture
portion of the day. The first one called to the Torah
was naturally Moishe Levy. Slowly and loudly he sang
the *berocho,* as one had not heard it done for a long
time, as though it were a question of showing their
friend and through him the whole of Christendom
how the Jews here in this village, and indeed everywhere, praised the greatness of God. Already the rich

Parnes had named his contributions: five *livres* for the
Chevra Kaddisha and five *livres* for this and five
livres for that, so that they all looked at each other and
nodded at each other because they had so generous a
Parnes. Already the *chazan* was calling: "*Jaamaud
sheini,*" and the latter, the second one called up, was
the fat Jacques Brunshwig with his little black Napo-
leonic beard, who was the second most powerful member of the *kehilla,* needless to say. He was already on
his way to the *almemor,* when a sudden voice arose:

"Why don't you call up Moishele? Moishele must
be called up. I'll contribute for him. He can contribute
today as much as Moishe the *Parnes.*"

It was the *Maire.* No doubt about that. Consterna-
tion seized upon them all. So that was why he had
come. First they hardly knew how to treat this unheard
of and painful situation, that someone interfered in
the accustomed course of their service. They didn't
even at that moment consider whether it was an *avere*
which was being committed here. But they would not
have had the best and best respected *Parnes* in the
whole of Upper Alsace, if he hadn't found a way out.
Swiftly he went up to Jacques Brunshwig who was
about to intone the *berocho,* conferred in whispers
with him and next with the *chazan,* Shloime Ruef,
whereupon the former left the *almemor* with a smile
and returned to his seat while the latter, commissioned
by the *Parnes,* hastened to the good Moishele and
whispered to him.

He had probably been the only one in the synagogue who had been morally uncomfortable during

the incident, at least so soon as he felt that what was taking place here concerned him. Indeed, a feeling of guilt came over him.

But immediately the voice of the *chazan* rose again and cried: *"Jaamaud sheini."*

Nevertheless, after a moment of hesitation, Moishele, finally not without pride, walked up to the consecrated scroll and spoke—no, sang—clearly and without a trembling of the voice, the *berocho* as he had probably not sung it since his own *Bar-Mitzvo*. And the whole congregation perceived the special quality of the moment and were delighted with the experience which had been given them.

Was it because, in the person of Moishele, Hans Brohme had in a sense been called to the Torah, one of the other faith and in him, too, the Prefect of the region and thus the whole government, including the Emperor Napoleon in Paris? Or was it that they received a satisfaction from this particular *Simchas Tauroh* because a Christian friend had taught them a lesson which they were bound to remember, that the value of a man was not to be gauged by his ability to contribute for causes however good, but by the sanctity of his will, by his being a pious and honorable man who did well his day's work, however humble it may be?

We would like to believe that both motivations were active.

What is certain is that, in the succeeding years on *Simchas Tauroh*, it was always the poorest man in the *kehilla* who was called third to the Torah, after a *Kohen* and the *Levi*. The *mitzvah* was bought for him by one of the rich men. But neither the name of the latter nor the amount of his contribution was ever revealed. Such was the fruit of the lesson which the *Parnes*, Moishe Levy, learned for himself and for the others and which was motivated by poor Moishele. For, when at the end of the service, the *Parnes*, with his wife between himself and the *Maire*, had proceeded on his way home and they had shaken hands all around, he had promised himself never to forget the lesson he had received.

THE WOOER

They were among the most comfortably off in the village, which was a good thing for Izzie; for how else would he have been able to satisfy his voracity or, to be perfectly frank, his boundless gluttony? Their house stood tall and high-gabled on the edge of the village, where the road ascends toward the neighboring hamlet. It stood almost isolated, with its stable and barn between the orchards and the fields which belonged to it, and one could see from afar that its inhabitants led a comfortable well-ordered life, so well was it all kept. For so long a period had the Leisers been settled here among the peasants with the other Jewish families that no one remembered any more when they had come. They belonged to the village, just as it was, in its peaceful community of a mixture of inhabitants.

To get back to Izzie. Although he was a young man, scarcely in his middle twenties, there was already a saying in the community which defined him precisely

and assigned to him a place, such as each of the older
people in the village had even to his life's end and
sometimes beyond, one by virtue of this quality and
another by virtue of another. If a man was seen to be
eating a great deal people said, and knew that they
were understood: "He feeds like Leiser's Izzie." The
Jews called him briefly the *Acheler* ("Gorger").

Well, you know how such things are. There was
neither contempt nor malice in the saying. For, since
he had left school ten years ago, he had helped his
father very ably in the cattle trade and was considered
all of a man, not to mention the circumstance that he
had served three years with the Black Dragoons and
had been made a corporal. Even his figure was im-
pressive and by no means laid him open to contempt.
He was a mighty man and freckled and tall and his
gait was a swinging one, such as one sees in seafaring
men, although he himself had never seen the sea. So
he could well afford to be differentiated from others
by this special quality and people laughed in a pleased
way when they thought of his excessive appetite which
meant more to him than anything else in the world.
Many anecdotes were told about him. When they
reminded him of an especially mad escapade he would
smile good-naturedly, almost as though pleased with
himself, as for instance, when he thought of the feast
of goose cracklings that day at Aunt Fradel's, as the
whole village called her, that eating contest at which
he alone had taken into himself the cracklings of two
heavy geese, without taking any hurt, even though he
had not drunk so much as a *Kirsch*, as was customary
in such cases. At most he would say: "You don't

exactly live on air either, you *chamorim!* You donkeys!"
Well, he wasn't exactly a sage.

The story we are going to tell about him was not at
all the most fantastic, but it was the one most preg-
nant with consequences; that is to say, it gave rise to
consequences that were not supposed to ensue. As we
have said, he was in his middle twenties, the period at
which in those days young men thought of getting
married. They were able to do so, too, because they
made good money, quite differently from nowadays.
And so parents considered it their duty to look about
in the neighboring villages, and even beyond, for a
shiddach not only for their daughters but even for
their sons; and though in general they were distrustful
of everything unfamiliar, yet, if a *kalle* came from far
away, the more distinguished did she seem to people
with her strange dialect and her strange ways.

You realize that the first thing that they inquired
about was the prospective bride's *mishpoche* and her
dowry. No bad marriages were those which grew out
of these customs which are, as one knows, followed
among peasants and princes to this day. And sometimes it happened that love, too, awakened in time.

Now old Leiser had a business friend named Meier
Ortlieb, who from time to time sold him the handsome
beige cattle from the low countries, which calve so
well and are so satisfactory to the peasants. At least
once a month these two friends met at the market in
Heiligenzell. For it took Meier several hours by train
to get there, while the Leisers could very well arrive on
foot. It was a five hours' march—five hours, truly, but
no great matter for the pedestrians of that period. On

this long trudge they took along dry bread and boiled eggs, for all the food on the road was *trefe*. It goes without saying that Izzie endured this with heroic piety. Never would it have occurred to him to eat at a goyish inn, aside from the circumstance that in those prudent days he would have considered it an extravagance.

One fine day Meier Ortlieb said to his friend Naphthali Leiser, the father of our Izzie, that it was high time to look around for a *kalle* for the boy; nay, that, he might as well be frank with him, he had already done so and he knew of a wonderful *shiddach*, than which none better was to be found far and wide. As though made for his son was the girl and the *mishpoche* and everything. It was the daughter of Baruch Wolf in Mühlingen, first class family; for years the grandfather had been *Parnes* of the *kehilla*. And the dowry! Oh, something very special! The child was blonde even, and just of the right age.

Naphthali rocked his head to and fro, almost from one shoulder to another. And although he felt flattered by the choice which Meier had made for his son, and although he himself had thought a good deal about the future of this self-same son and had spent long hours of the night discussing with his wife Hindele the necessity of finding a wife for their son Izzie, of whom they were so proud, and of the difficulty—we know exactly why—of doing so, nevertheless he said: "You make yourself *tzores* for other people! You seem to be in more of a hurry than I." Then, after a few minutes' silence, he said indifferently: "It's probably a fine bargain that you're trying to make. A man has to be on his guard with you."

Yet, since Meier would not desist, they continued to discuss the matter. To be sure, it gave old Leiser pause that the girl lived so far away.

Well, things have a way of working out. It happened that the sister-in-law of Leib Gump, a neighbor, whose wife was from Randegg, had married a man from Mühlingen and so lived in the home town of the proposed *kalle*. Through this circumstance exact information was obtained. Then the fathers had had a talk; Meier Ortleib had arranged to have them meet at Heiligenzell. Finally an exchange of letters had ensued, and one fine day the preliminary understandings had been arrived at and the moment had come to go and look at the intended bride; for up to this time Izzie had not seen the girl who, moreover, was called Clementine, a name not used in this part of the country and concerning which Mother Leiser had at once said that it showed the influence of Alsace and was a French name.

It was autumn after *Yontef* and the leaves were beginning to fall in the early storms and the fields were bare. The last apples had just been plucked from the trees, those that don't get mellow till *Pesach*. And since the cattle trade was slack too and St. Martin's day, when rents had to be paid, was still several weeks away, one could well leave home for a few days.

So at the peep of dawn on a Friday morning father and son fared forth; for it was necessary to arrive well before *Shabbos*, not only on account of the *avera*, but

also on account of the bad impression which would
have been created. They were to be the house-guests
of the parents of the prospective bride, although
naturally the sister-in-law of Leib Gump and her husband had declared that they would insist on putting
them up. But finally and after mature reflection, in
which Frau Hindele shared, Father Leiser had accepted the invitation of the Wolfs to stay with them
and not rob them of the *koved,* as they said in their
letters.

Before they left, father and son had to eat. For all
day long on their journey they would have nothing
warm. Of course, Hindele had wrapped up in a brown
paper package three fine portions of goose and had put
these, together with slices of bread spread with goose
fat, and four hard boiled eggs for each of the men,
into a handbag, not to mention a bottle of dry red
wine. The boiled garlic sausages, which usually were
destined for the eve of *Shabbos,* the mother had prepared for early morning, even though an hour before,
namely at five o'clock, the men had already had coffee,
without milk to be sure, in order that this second
breakfast an hour later would not, God forbid, cause
the *avera* of a mixing of the meaty and milky.

And now, while the father ate two sausages, Izzie
consumed four with the delicate stinging horseradish
and the potatoes fried in goose fat. The mother, seeing
him eating thus in his accustomed manner, besought
her son once more, as she had done for days on end:

"Do me a favor, Izzie, please do it for my sake"—
she emphasized *my*—"and be careful! The few days
won't kill you. Don't eat so much; take only one help-

ing of each course; behave yourself nicely. Those are
bekoved people; they're not used to it. How will they
think you've been brought up?"

"Don't worry, mama; I know what's fit and proper
and what I must do. How often have I told you? I'm
not a child any more," the son answered.

"Well, I know you, you know. You can't blame me
for warning you."

The father was silent. But when Izzie was out on
the dark street with the black handbag, which was
flat on top and broad at the bottom, Hindele still delayed her husband at the door and said:

"Make him promise you once more, with his hand
in yours, that he'll be careful. Make him do it before
you leave the train."

"I will. I will," he replied with his foot already on
the stair.

It was an hour's walk to the railroad station. Shortly
after they had left the village, the mayor of the village,
Kaspar Lohle, joined them; he was on his way to the
city for a meeting of the county council. He and
Naphthali had known each other from their youth on,
and he, like the rest of the village, knew what was in
the wind. After they had conversed for a while about
the height of last year's wheat and the calving of the
cow which Naphthali had obtained for the mayor the
spring before, the latter suddenly said:

"The girl that wants to be Izzie's wife will have to
be a mighty good cook!" He laughed and gave the
young man a smack on the shoulder with the palm of
his hand. Naphthali answered: "She is! You may be
sure that we inquired."

When they took leave of each other, Kaspar called out to them from afar: "Good luck to you!"

Shortly before their arrival in Mühlingen, Naphthali remembered the advice of his wife and said to his son: "Now remember to be careful, as Mother told you. Put your hand in mine and promise that you will not take more than one helping of each course and that only when you are asked."

Izzie hesitated and assumed a stuborn expression and looked out of the window. "Hurry up now!" the father admonished him. The son gave him his hand and drew it back quickly and said: "If it makes you feel better." It did, indeed, make the father feel better.

At the small railroad station, which was some distance from the little town, Baruch Wolf was waiting for them. He had on his *Shabbos* clothes, the long black coat and the stiff hat and, his hands behind his back, was nervously pacing up and down. His anxiety had two reasons. First, there was the embarrassment of the unaccustomed and singular position of being the father of a prospective bride, and furthermore there was just one hour left till *Shabbos,* and there was so much that had still to be done within that hour.

But everything went on quite according to program and very well. They saw at once that both families had the same good manners and, above all, Baruch was quite pleased with the young man. Today there would be no talk about the reason for the visit, nor would there be on the next day; the matter was to be adjusted, as was fit and proper, on Sunday morning. By that time everyone would be better acquainted. It was a delay which was to bridge the gulf of embarrassment created by a delicate situation.

They went down the main street of the little town with its antique houses between the two lines of well cultivated hills and saw the people standing there and watching them, clad like themselves in their Sabbath garments. It went without saying that Naphthali and Izzie Leiser had put on their *Yontef* clothes for the journey. And here, too, everyone knew of the nature of the visit and scrutinized father and son shrewdly.

At the house they had just time for introductions and formal salutations. The daughter Clementine stood modestly aside. Izzie at once observed her slightly red hair and could not help thinking that Meier Ortlieb had promised blonde hair. Well, blonde or a little reddish, that was almost the same thing. On the table the Sabbath candles were already lit in two tall silver candlesticks. Yes, Naphthali reflected quickly, these were certainly *bekoved* people.

The mother observed that the gentlemen were probably hungry; it was a pity that they had to go to *Shul* at once; but afterwards their appetite would be all the better. Izzie thought to himself: I smell fish, all right. It was Friday evening; he would be able to stand it. He remembered, moreover, that on the journey his father had let him have two of the cold roast goose drumsticks and that, in any event, the services would not take long.

At the synagogue everything seemed particularly solemn, as it always did when strangers came to worship there. Thereafter they went to the house and

wished each other *Good Shabbos* and the fathers
blessed the children and everybody sat down to table.

The first course was noodle soup. What other soup
would it be on Friday evening except noodle soup?
The noodles were as delicate as threads and flavored
with fresh green herbs. The aroma was excellent.
Comfortably Izzie sucked up his soup. In those days it
was good form to suck up one's soup nice and loud in
order to show one's appreciation and enjoyment. But
he took only one helping, although Frau Wolf tried
to empty the great filled silver soup ladle into his plate
a second time. No, thank you. Although at home he
would have taken at least two helpings, if only for
the sake of the flavor, this temptation was easy to
resist. Soup is only soup.

Then came fish. Fish, of course. But what kind of
fish was this? He had never seen a fish like this, with
a broad head and a mustache. Aha, carp, his father
said knowingly. There was a brown sauce with raisins.
At home you got delicate blue trout or else pike out
of the lake with a wonderful golden mayonnaise,
which his mother prepared better than anyone in the
village. This fish was full of small bones; you had to
be exceedingly careful; it was really no pleasure, even
though the thick sauce was excellent. Consequently he
took no second helping this time either and found
his renunciation not too difficult.

Thereupon the soup meat was served, fine succulent
beef, just as at home, with grated horseradish and
young beets and tiny new potatoes. That was good.

They conversed, seeking to discover common
acquaintances, able to start of course with the kins-

people of Leib Gump at home, who had been the first
intermediaries. They were coming to call after dinner.
Clementine and Izzie said very little, as was seemly.

Yet the soup meat almost led to a catastrophe. It
must be remembered that after the long exertion of
the trip Izzie's hunger was very great. Frau Wolf
offered him a second helping and he was on the point
of pushing his plate forward a little for the handsome,
oblong rib portion, when his father, who sat next to
him, gave him a gentle, apparently accidental thrust
with his elbow. Izzie drew his plate back and said in a
feeble voice: "No, thank you. Really no."

Frau Wolf said at this: "But listen, I don't understand how a young man like you lives on so little. I
almost believe you don't like my cooking."

And now it was the father, Naphthali Leiser, who
made the right remark and said: "Yes, you are right,
Frau Wolf. We have the same trouble with the boy
at home. His mama is sometimes so worried over him
because he eats so little. All persuasion is in vain."

To be sure, Naphthali must have doubted the
wisdom of this remark. He bent over the table and
looked deep into his plate.

And so Izzie overcame this danger, too.

But now when the dessert came in, the *lokshen*
shalet, his father had pity on him. It was a shalet with
special ingredients, which were not familiar to them at
all—an Alsatian recipe, the old man thought—very
lightly baked and full of almonds and of fruits and
very rich and so, when Izzie's plate was empty and
Frau Wolf asked, he said: "I have aplenty, thank you."

But the father came to his aid: "Now I am fed up with you myself. Take some more."

And so Izzie took some more and thanked his father with a grateful look. But, of course, his hunger was far from appeased.

The evening passed comfortably and well. The brother-in-law of Leib Gump and his wife came and they talked about their home town and the men talked about business and about the opportunities here and there and about the hardness of the times.

The young people sat next to each other. They had very little to say. What could they have talked about? There was as yet no cinema nor tennis nor the habit of travel nor new books, which it was necessary to have read. At least Izzie didn't know of any such. They all pretended, in addition, as though no one knew what the purpose of the party was. Only once a chap who sat next to Izzie winked at him and said: "Well, what do you think of her?"

That was a bit heavy and tactless. And when Izzie did not answer and just smiled shyly the other one added: "She can cook like nobody else. Eh, what, Clementine?"

Next morning, with his coffee, Izzie could at least have two big pieces of the huge coffee cake, which was just as good, it seemed to him, as his mother's at home, with almonds on top and many raisins inside.

Then they went to the synagogue for morning services. When they returned at the end of two hours and he entered the house, Izzie smelled the soup, which had been warming over night in the oven, the bean soup, to be precise, and the highest thing on earth to him. And now he became fully aware of the fact that he was hungry and that he had not had anything proper to eat for a very long time.

On the way from synagogue the two fathers had agreed that the young people should be left alone together for a little and that the mother should see to it that they were. Well, she arranged the matter expertly and tactfully. "Clementine," she said, "show Herr Leiser the scenery around here. Take him a little ways toward the forest and let him see how beautiful it is."

We can afford to pass lightly over this excursion; it has no great bearing on the outcome of this story. Only so much need be said that Izzie was filled with a kind of dread, because Clementine kept telling him about her experiences in the French boarding school and her French—fancy that: French friends, and sometimes she even used an outlandish expression. The whole thing was uncanny and uncomfortable, even aside from the fact that he was preoccupied by the violence of his hunger.

But at last, at last, the hour of noon arrived and when those two came home the others were already waiting for them in order to sit down to eat.

Old Leiser thought: soon the worst will be over. He greeted his son cheerfully. The parents of the girl had expressed a very kindly opinion of the young man. The first course was the bean soup. Frau Wolf herself said that no one had better take a second helping of it, because it was so filling that no one would have the proper appetite for the principal course. Next came a delicate veal ragout, spiced with cloves and served

with cauliflower. If this is the principal course, Izzie
thought to himself, it's too light to satisfy a man's
hunger even if he could have all of it that he wanted.
He had become irritated and impatient and said to
himself: I won't eat any more of this stuff, even if
they were to urge me.

In addition we must not forget to observe that this
course was accompanied by a white wine, which
seemed too sweet to Izzie. The bottle bore a label in
a foreign tongue and Herr Wolf had pointed to this
wine as a special treat.

Then, at last, arrived the chief course, stuffed roast
goose, and everything came to pass as was inevitable
according to our knowledge of the situation. It was a
gigantic goose, golden brown and looking very distinguished with white paper frills slipped over the
ends of the erect drumsticks. And what drumsticks
those were! Izzie made a rapid estimate of them. And
the animal had not been flayed, but retained its thick
fat skin. And this was not all. Next to the goose stood
a dish of exquisite purée of chestnuts; if his memory
served him correctly, they had had that at home only
one single time, on the occasion of his parents' silver
anniversary.

The goose was carved on the table; Herr Wolf had
to give his aid. His wife, who believed now that she
knew what Izzie required, after she had served his
father, served Izzie a portion which she considered
plentiful; to him, of course, it seemed wholly in-
adequate. He ate. And when he had finished and his
hostess asked him a little shyly if he wanted more he
simply helped himself to the huge drumstick which re-

mained. Yet that would not have been so bad, had he
not, without ceremony, grabbed the two ends in his
two hands and, recking of nothing, as it seemed, in
broad based satisfaction, begun to tear off with his
teeth the huge fragments of meat, silent and utterly
absorbed, not to speak of the huge mouthfuls of purée
which, with his fork, he stuffed in at intervals. He
had been taciturn before; he was utterly silent now.

Gently his father poked him with his knee in order
to remind him of his promise. When Izzie continued
blindly he gave him a violent poke and at last
whispered to him:

"Stop! Is that the way you keep your word, *chamer?*"

To that the son replied half defiantly and half
desperately and a little too loud:

"Oh, let me eat; I don't want the girl anyhow . . . !"

And he ate and he ate. And what thereupon ensued
you can easily imagine.

The question has never been clarified, whether
Izzie really did not marry the girl because she actually
displeased him, or whether things came to pass as they
did because he succumbed to the great passion of his
insatiable hunger. We would not and need not go
farther into that question. What, at all events, resulted
from the affair was a lasting distrust, if not an actual
enmity, between the people of Mühlingen and our
own people, which made it impossible ever again for a
shiddach to be arranged between the two *kehillas,* and
on account of which, it was right and profitable that
this tale be told.

THE FOREST

The situation in Werblingen was never such that the Jews had to repel the reproach of being cowardly among their gentile fellow townsmen. For, aside from the fact that they had Muchel in their *kehilla*, the strongest and the most intrepid man in the whole region, a fact which none ever denied, they were too well known from of old for such notions to have occurred to anyone or, above all, have been expressed.

For that very reason it could not but be observed if there were one among the men who made the impression that he would not immediately react positively—that is, in brief, not be brave—when faced by a decision which required the conquest of certain inner inhibitions. To be sure, nowadays that we have experienced and seen so many things in the great war, we know much better the curious circumstances that may surround the quality of courage. Not a few who at home or in the barracks yard seemed small and insignificant among the others and were even laughed at, because they made no soldierly impression, so confirmed themselves on the field of battle by their spiritual force and will power that they were respected ever afterwards. And such people were usual among us Jews, because for well known reasons we had done little to exercise our bodies. Well, this circumstance applied less to us Jews in the country; we of Werblingen did not require the test of battle not to be maligned among the others. The stories of Muchel, whom we have mentioned, must be kept for a future occasion. It will suffice to recall the incident of that autumnal storm on the lake when he set forth in his small skiff across the raging waves in order to save Black Naphtali, whose boat with broken rudder had shipped water and was tossed helplessly about. Yet he and Naphtali were deadly enemies on account of a matter known to all the village.

In those days, long before the war, it was tests of this kind which made it clear as to who would act the man in an emergency. Now the brothers Shmul, Eisig and Fromel, were never considered heroes; in fact, one knew all about them in this respect. Many small characteristics of their lives had served to give a picture of them which, though they were esteemed for their astuteness and honesty in business, made them a little ridiculous. For among natural people in the country you cannot expect anyone to be regarded wholly as an equal who has not some measure of physical sturdiness. These two were considered, to put it mildly, a little fearful. It was known, for instance, that neither of them was fond of wandering alone in the countryside, that is to say, on their way to trade with the peasants on their farmsteads or to go to the monthly cattle market in Heiligenzell, where everyone knew them.

Rarely had one seen either of them alone on the roads between the bordering fruit trees or on the narrow field paths at the edge of the wheat fields or in autumn among the stubbles. Almost always they were together out on the roads. Now this would have been, it must be admitted, a very handsome thing as between two brothers, had they been united in a spirit of comradeship and mutual affection, each ready to help the other. But closely looked upon, this was hardly the situation of those two.

For their characters were very different indeed. Eisig was thoughtful and fond of deliberating, shaking his head in doubt when someone else asserted something or desired something. His brother Fromel was hot-headed and self-willed and something of a braggart. Thus it came about that they were in a continuous state of quarrelsomeness with each other; there were probably not two weeks out of the whole year in which they lived in peace with each other, in spite of the impression they created. Often, for months, they would not be speaking to each other. Nor did they ever trade together or have a common piece of business, as would have been appropriate for brothers. And it was not without reason that, on *Yaum Kippur* when all who had in any way been at enmity in the course of the year in the *kehilla,* became reconciled to each other, these brothers, too, deeply moved, took each other's hands and begged each other for forgiveness.

Only in one thing were they wholly united, in the circumstance which we have mentioned, namely, that they always accompanied each other, even when they did not speak. When, among the paths through the fields, this was no longer possible, because each had business in a different village, they yet stuck together at least until they had the great forest behind them. Only then did each venture forward alone over the frozen ways in winter fog and through the desolation of the leafless trees, or else through the summer air, fragrant with the growth of plants or of approaching thunder. This was their custom from Monday on, when they went forth for the week, until they returned on Thursday, happy in the goodness and tranquility of *Shabbos*. No one knew whether they had made this explicit agreement with each other or whether old Shmul, their father, had made them promise this to him before he died, or whether it was a tacit agreement between them, because each was glad to have it so.

This was known about them as a certainty. Not far from the village, perhaps half an hour's walk, after one had left it in the direction of Weilhofen, there stretched for another hour's journey the well known forest. It was not especially dense, yet it was a real forest with all the trees mingled that grew among us, oaks and firs and spruces and very thick undergrowth, composed of a variety of bushes. It was a real forest and a forest can be dangerous. Nor was it as well taken care of as it is today. The underbrush was very thick, and when you walked through you could often hear the rustling and rattling and hissing and dragging of

small animals. Well, it had been a long time since
dangerous animals had been encountered in our part
of the country. There were hardly any wildcats left,
not to speak of larger beasts of prey. All that was in
the past. Small animals rushed across the paths, such
as foxes or occasionally a weasel or a marten; now and
then you beheld in a clearing the noble figure of a
deer munching leaves, while hawks and herons floated
high in air.

Nevertheless it was a forest. Think of all that might
happen in its secret places. And it was true enough
that, years ago—not in their lifetimes, but their father,
of blessed memory, had told them the tale—a man
from not far away had been slain in the forest near
Holzlingen. It may be that they were subconsciously
aware of this incident. So, if it was rare to see either
alone crossing the fields, never were they unaccom-
panied when they ventured to pass through the forest.
And the curious thing was that they went with no one
else from the *kehilla,* only with each other.

And everybody knew, in addition, that the brothers
did not travel silently through the forest. Many a one
had heard what took place. Hardly had they arrived
at that bend of the road where the sandy path leads
from the fields to the first fir trees and the forest odor
of decay and of new growth received them, when they
both began to whistle. They whistled and whistled.
They whistled marching songs and military tunes, as
they had heard them from the soldiers and recruits
coming from the cities. Their favorite was the Federal
Swiss March of Berne. They knew best its solid con-

fident rhythms, which came from across the frontier.
Nor was this all. While they indulged themselves in
the rhythmic swing of these songs, of the words and
meanings of which they were mostly ignorant, they
marched, bravely and with military bearing, deeper
and deeper into the inevitable forest. Thus these
heroes produced the necessary courage and strength
within them to traverse the threatening way between
the old trees and high bushes. Uninterruptedly they
whistled and the sound and the echo of their whistling
filled the forest and broke its uncanny and inhuman
silence. If, at times, the breath of one of them failed
and he had to interrupt himself on account of the dry-
ness of his mouth out of which he had been expelling
the whistling air through his teeth, he poked the other
in the ribs in order that he, at least, might not cease
from emitting the shrill tones.

Nor could it be said that the forest of dark autumnal
days, when the moisture dripped from the leaves, was
more oppressive to them than the summer stillness
with its shadows and its unmoving leaves in the
silence of the trees. No, precisely the latter seemed
more uncanny to them, with the great vault of the
heaven above and the coolness of the trees which hid
the sun as with a wall. At that time it would happen
that Eisig, who was tall and vigorous, cried out to the
shorter, quick stepping Fromel: "Louder, louder!" The
latter would then put into his mouth four of his
fingers, the index and middle finger of each hand and
produce a whistling, such as nowadays we are accustomed to hear from locomotive engines. For Eisig did
not have the talent of turning himself into a signal

whistle, superior as he was to his brother in all other physical matters. It is clear that this special outburst filled them with uncommon courage; they felt that they had frightened the very forest; also, that they had impressed any possibly threatening creatures upon this difficult way and had frightened them through their own intrepid behavior.

Once, to be sure, even these devices failed them; they had to try other means, a last help, as it were, in greatest need. It was a late afternoon in August, shortly before *Tisho b'Av* and they were coming home together. As usual, the melancholy mood of this period was upon them. They had come from Riedlingen and had agreed to meet at a definite time under a tall willow tree hard by the bridge over a certain brook in order to traverse the forest together. Each had slowly arrived with dusty shoes from another direction. Hardly had they greeted each other, when silently they set out. The harvest was over; wheat stacks were visible here and there; from afar one could see now and then a peasant returning to his village. They faced the forest and were about to enter into the shadow of its silent trees, when suddenly behind them a man with yellow face and drooping, black mustache arose from the moat. Never had they seen him before. He wore long English trousers, narrow at the ankle. He had no coat and his shirt was soiled. In one hand he carried a gleaming, longish object which they did not recognize but which they took for a weapon.

"Shemah beni!" cried Fromel and was about to whistle. But whether it was their conviction that their well tried whistling would be of no avail in view of

this event, or whether it was that fright had suddenly dried the mouths of both, the fact remained that they were utterly unable to produce a sound. And swiftly they went on without looking behind them, although the man now cried something out to them, which they did not understand and so considered to be in a foreign language.

Thus the stranger remained behind them. But now and then they heard his footsteps when his shoes struck against the stones on that furrowed path. They had not gone far when in a sudden clearing deeper in the forest, which made the sunshine seem sharper, they became aware of several other men and of a woman who, as they approached, arose and called out to them too.

As with one breath they uttered a cry of terror and conjuration: *Baavaunes!* They redoubled their speed, especially since at this moment they heard the first man cry out to the others and being answered by them. The protective whistling now died entirely in their throats. At the sight of this strange man and in view of the strangeness of the whole experience, the paralyzing fright went through all their limbs. What they had feared in anticipation, without ever having expressed it, had come to pass. A band of robbers, of *gaslonim* and *ganovim*, had been lying in wait for them. There was no doubt. If, on previous occasions, they had met someone, a thing which, of course, happened now and then, they had had but to look more closely to recognize someone from their own neighborhood, a peasant, a wood cutter, or a fellow Jew. Today it was different. Whistling would do no

good. How would that frighten such questionable
characters or fill them with respect? This time they
would not come forth unharmed from the forest. That
much was certain. Panic came over them. There was
no help. The unescapable was here.

At that moment, as though suddenly inspired, the
big brother began to sing. He sang in that thin, high
voice which didn't at all suit his figure and had always
tended to reduce his natural dignity. He sang:

"Yigdal! Yigdal elauhim chai vejishtabach . . ."
With all his might and with deep feeling he sang the
lofty prayer as it was wont to be sung in the synagogue. And without being bidden to do so, his
brother sang it too. And they did not cease singing
until the song was over. But since they had still an
hour to go, which is a long time, especially in such a
situation as theirs, and since there are few songs which
last long enough to fill so much time, they repeated
it. But since it is a sin to misuse that which is holy
and consecrated, Fromel, after they had repeated the
Yigdal, intoned at the top of his voice another song,
in spite of the fact that it was summer and that the
sweat of their exertion ran from their foreheads,
namely, the song that consecrates Chanuka:

"Moaus zur jeshuosie lecho noe leshabeijach . . ."
And with a sense of liberation his brother joined him
in the singing. Now this song was somewhat longer
than the other; also its rhythm lent itself better to
marching than that of Yigdal. It almost lasted them
until they came to the milestone which marks the
boundary between Werblingen and Weilhofen and
whence it is not far to the end of the forest. And this

very song, although it is meant to be sung in winter only, obviously helped them. They had gained confidence and courage and were sure that no evil could overtake them, nor any ambush or pursuit frighten them any more. And so they found that they could whistle again and trumpeted, as it were, the March of Berne as though it had an inner relationship to the *Chanuka* hymn. When soon thereupon the trees grew sparse, Eisig had the courage to look behind them. He saw no one, and it was quite quiet among the big bushes by the way. As they emerged from the forest and the meadows of the village lay, friendly and familiar, at their feet, Fromel took a deep breath and said: "I wouldn't pass through that again, God forbid!"

And his brother replied: "A good thing we thought of *Shem yisborach* (the Holy One, blessed be His Name). One must have trust in Him."

And so they set out homeward, trust in their hearts and bound in affection to each other as never before. Within their hearts they made resolutions, as after the performance of a good deed and Eisig said: "We have survived a great danger, because we were true to each other; let us never quarrel with each other any more." And he began to pray under his breath, the prayer prescribed for those who had survived a great danger.

The people who had caused this commotion were harmless good natured wanderers, tinkers and scissors-grinders from Slovakia, such as sometimes in those days passed through our countryside.

RAPHAEL AND RECHA

It might well have been that Raphael Baer, now in his fiftieth year, could have carried on his life with his wife Recha, who was ten years his junior, and the daughter of a very poor *shames* in a neighboring village, as he had now been accustomed to do for more than a dozen years, until old age overtook him. What made that impossible was, in the end, the matter that came to pass concerning his tenant Debele and the consequences that arose therefrom. Other, similar things had arisen before, all due to the greed and de-graded avarice of his wife, which in this instance over-came him with a fateful force.

For, though usually trivial causes give rise to harm-less enough consequences, so that a habit of patient endurance is gradually formed, so it can happen on the contrary that, through the sudden addition of definite actions and unforeseen circumstances—even as poisons can arise from the blending of apparently innocuous chemical substances—decisive and evil

effects can fall upon people who hitherto have lived
their prosaic lives as though nothing could ever change
them.

From the point of view of our generation the cause
of the whole matter was, as will be seen, an apparently
trivial one; to the people of that period it was so uncommon that it was talked about for many years.

In the dusk of an evening of late autumn Frau
Recha was standing idly, in her rather shabby black
cotton dress with the violet flower pattern, under the
kerosene lamp of her living room. The lamp had a
broad globe and the curtains were starched and
gathered. She was reckoning out what she owed to
Lizzie, the woman who went out among Christians
and Jews for day's work; that is to say, she was a
seamstress who made the clothes, the skirts and blouses
as well as the underwear for the women and children
in their homes and also, naturally, did the mending.
She received her food and a meagre wage. In addition
she was the only midwife in the little town. For
thirty years this good woman had helped bring into
the world all the children of the community and had
thus had her hands, so to speak, in many destinies. By
the same token she was a competent witness to the
circumstance that had necessarily made Recha what
she was, namely, that she had been unable to have
children. Perhaps it should be mentioned that Lizzie
was primarily employed by Jewish families in both of
her callings, of which the second may be likened to a
true vocation. . . . She sat at the sewing machine surrounded by fabrics and patches, as Frau Recha was

making up their account. Well, Lizzie was her match. She was accustomed to Recha and knew, as every one did, that the woman was an ill customer to deal with where money was involved. The scenes that took place in this house were nothing new to her. Lizzie was paid by the hour. She had worked ten hours a day for two days with needle and scissors and yardstick and at the sewing machine, the innovation of very recent years. She had worked very industriously and had accomplished a great deal for her wage of thirty *pfennige* per hour. The mark, at one hundred *pfennige*, had just then been introduced into the country and it is easy enough to reckon out what Recha owed her without any chaffering. But Raphael's wife chaffered and bargained, as the saying goes, and tried to reduce payments always and wherever it was possible, even though hard and tight agreements had been made. So much everyone knew. And if she succeeded in squeezing out only a single farthing through the toughness of her arguments or through her total insensibility to the feelings of others who were less tough-minded than herself, then she was really contented and considered herself ever again as the ablest manager in the little town. This gives you an insight into what kind of a woman she was. Well, Lizzie was an able opponent who knew what she was doing. No spate of words helped Recha. And although she almost shed tears, describing the evil times which had now overtaken all those who had no shops to keep and although she grew insulting over what she called the greed of the seamstress, the latter was not to be moved and did not permit the deduction of fifteen *pfennige* for her alleged slacking during half an hour around noon of the first day. She remained firm and Recha had to pay her the six *mark,* cash down, consisting of two silver *taler.* When Lizzie had finally gone, Recha sat down at the kitchen table and pored over a little, shabby black account book with a wax cloth cover which was filled with figures. She had taken it out of a drawer and now reckoned and counted and considered where and how she could squeeze out another *pfennig* to compensate her for what, according to her opinion, she had just lost. To herself she abused the seamstress, called her evil names and determined to employ her no more, although she knew perfectly well that she had no choice in the matter: there was no one to take Lizzie's place. She tried to reckon out too the amount she would have had to pay Lizzie in the old fashioned currency, before the *mark* was introduced. And if the actual figure in the old currency was a higher one, that comforted her mightily. And maybe it would be possible to reduce by a little the wages of Jachet, the serving girl, who took care of the two cows in the stable and milked them. If only the girl's mother would not raise a howl in the *kehilla!* That she wouldn't like. So she sat there with her ill sharpened pencil and, as usual, a strand of hair had gotten loose and hung almost down to her shoulder. No, it can't be said that Recha was very neat. But to that, too, Raphael had long become accustomed, he, whose mother had been an admirable housewife as is appropriate to a pious, Jewish home in whose interior everything had always shone with cleanliness.

As Recha was sitting there she heard quick, furtive

footsteps, as though someone wanted to pass by both hastily and unobserved. And as though she had been lying in wait for just that, she arose swiftly and poked her head out of the door and said:

"Debele, where is my rent?"

The man stopped as though he had been caught and turned to her. He had been about to climb the stairs to the attic room where he had lived as a tenant for several years. For a moment he was silent; he didn't know what to say. What was there to say, if he were to stick to the truth? It was that he couldn't pay; he simply, in God's name, didn't have the two months' rent for which he was in arrears. But he dared not say that, since he did not want to evoke the wild and abusive screams which he had experienced once before. He couldn't bear that. He had to act humble and seek to calm her by promising her that he would soon get hold of some money. Leib Kahn, as she ought to know, had been able to drive a good bargain in the matter of a *beheme,* a head of cattle, through his inter-mediacy and would pay him his commission within the next few days when he himself got his money from the business. That was the situation. All he wanted to do was to silence her and to calm her until her husband, who had gone on a buying expedition of a couple of days, would come back. He was a man one could talk to. In fact, Raphael didn't care whether the few *mark*—fifteen and not easy to earn for poor Debele—came in earlier or later. As a matter of fact, as Debele knew, he would gladly have forgiven him the indebtedness, if only for the sake of *Gemilus Chesed,* that is, for the sake of a charitable deed, if it had not been for

Rechele, his avaricious wife. To be sure, Raphael himself had recently threatened to throw him out. But he
had said it with a smile; he was only jesting. And he
probably said it only out of fear of Recha who had
probably talked him deaf in order to have her will.
Everybody knew how she forced him to yield to her
determination. And Raphael was a pious man, although he was so well to do; even as in that period
all those members of our community who lived in the
villages and little towns sought to fulfill their duty
toward the Eternal, blessed be He, even though they
were well off and had no cares of their own.

"What do you mean you're going to pay soon?"
Recha said irritatedly. "Is that any way to do, to live
in a place and keep owing the rent?"

In those days it was most uncommon, in fact it had
never happened among Jews, that, if a man could not
pay his rent, his neighbors even considered robbing
him of the roof over his head, merely on account of
money. This thing which is common today in the cities
and even in the villages that the stronger thrusts aside
the weaker—this is a thing one would not have considered possible among the Jews of former times.

"Now look," Debele ventured to say. "You act as
though I had never paid my rent; I have lived with
you going on five years and it's only in the last year
that I have sometimes been slow in paying." He
shouldn't have said that. It irritated the woman who
could ill bear contradiction at any time.

"How? You want to resist me, too! That's a little
strong. You just wait. We have nothing to give away.
You'll see. Just wait till my husband comes home!"

"What do you want me to do? I just can't pay right away, and it's bad enough for me. You should have a little *rachmones* too. It isn't my fault." Thus he humiliated himself asking her to pity him.

And so the wretched man moved slowly along with his drooping shoulders and climbed up the stair to the attic room, of which the walls lay between the beams of the roof and which was a part of a larger attic room which had been filled for decades with the cast-off objects and the trash of the house. In all corners and especially between the beams and around the chimney the spiders' webs and the dust were thick.

Recha could not restrain herself from screaming after him: "Not your fault! Maybe it's our fault! If a man works and isn't a *shlemihl*, he can pay his rent."

He couldn't even reply to the great sin of which the woman was guilty, the sin against one of our most stringent commands, namely, not to be *mevayesh*, not to put a fellow man to shame.

After some time he heard the well-known steps of the master of the house on the stairs. Raphael was coming home. Shortly thereafter, he heard without being able to make out the words, the loud and pertinacious and never wearied voice of Recha. She permitted no answer; at least, her husband's voice was not to be heard. Debele sat on the single chair in his room, of which the seat was an old board. He sat there like one accused in a court of law, whose fate was being discussed. He did not stir and stared at the floor. That it should have come to this with him! As into the shaft of a mine he peered into the depth of his past and of

his fate and wondered what had brought him to this
pass.

Downstairs a door was suddenly opened and then
slammed shut; in the meantime he heard the voice of
Raphael:

"Aren't you ashamed? Don't you ever feel any
shame—ever?"

It sounded like a cry of despair. Ah, thought
Debele, that one has no easy time; everybody in the
little town knew that. But how did that avail him
who had no notion where he was to get hold of the
money quickly? And that he owed the rent was known
to everyone in town, too. Recha had seen to that; her
greed impelled her to gossip about it. And although
everyone knew that she was the most avaricious person in the whole *kehilla* and grudged everyone whatever he had, yet they gossiped too and he was ashamed
to show his face. Yet he had to associate with other
people. He made up his mind to talk to Raphael once
more.

They lived in the prosperous old town on the slope
of the mountains, at the confluence of two small
streams which, a little beyond, flowed into the great
green river. The appearance of the little town had not
changed for centuries. There were only a few narrow
but cozy streets, paved with smooth stones. And it had
been but a few years ago that the railroad had connected the town with the great world.

Early on the morning of the next day Raphael and
his tenant came from the *shul* together, as every day
from the *Shacharis* service, through the moist and

foggy air. Each carried in his hand his red velvet
tefillin bag with the holy letters embroidered on them
with threads of gold. For, although Debele was only a
poor *bocher* and not too highly esteemed among the
others where business was concerned—he was, to be
frank, just a little agent and commission man—yet
Raphael, because he was pious, treated him with the
respect which is due to every Jewish man who recites
the prayers in *shul* and can be called to the *Tauro,* that
is to say, he regarded him as an equal and treated
him accordingly. The two were not unlike in character; only that Raphael was a man of means because
his father, who had been industrious and had a happy
touch, had left him a house and broad fields and cattle
and a considerable capital. Raphael, himself, was no
man of business, properly considered. If it hadn't been
for Recha! Well, it is useless to end the sentence. We
know her a little by now. And yet he was highly
esteemed among his fellows, which is clear even from
the circumstance that they had given him no nick-
name nor even called him by a diminutive of his own.
As they were walking home from *shul,* then, he said,
as though they had already discussed the matter and
as though this but continued a former conversation:

"Look, don't take what my wife says to heart. She
is the way she is. Don't worry. As far as I'm concerned,
you can stay as long as you like. I'll see to it that you
do."

And after a while, although all that Debele had
said was: "May it be reckoned as a merit to you,"
Raphael added with a great sigh:

"It's hard to get along with her—hard."

But Recha gave him no peace. For that bit of business with Leib Kahn had finally failed entirely. Because the head of cattle which was to be sold through the mediation of Debele was found to have a fault which rendered it *treif*, so that the seller had to take it back and thereby Debele's little commission was lost. And Recha scolded and insisted because a couple of additional months had passed. In his utter despair Debele decided to talk to Michel Bloch. If anyone could help him, it was he. The poor chap went over and over this in his mind.

Bloch was considered the wisest man in the *kehilla*, as well as the most popular. With this opinion he himself agreed. No one was his enemy, because he told everyone what that one wanted to hear. Also he was a great teller of anecdotes. He knew many and, of course, the latest ones. Wherever anyone was sick, he went to visit that one and of course he was present at every funeral, not only in this little town and among the Jews but also whenever a respected Christian had died, and not only in his own community but equally in the neighboring ones. In brief, he was considered an *ish yosher*. Oh yes, he always had the appropriate words for everyone. In addition, he was quite prosperous. He had a draper and notion shop and he sent out two traveling salesmen who called upon the peasants to a great distance round about.

So Debele accosted him as he was on his daily walk for his afternoon coffee in the Crown Inn, where they were accustomed to playing at cards. He was very modest, as the occasion required, and explained the whole situation to him. He besought him to act as a mediator between his landlord and himself, or—and here he paused for a minute—to help him in other ways, because their fathers had been friends before them. But Bloch was in a hurry, as such people always are, and he said: "What do you think I can do? Leave me out of it. I don't like to mix into what doesn't concern me; one has nothing but annoyance in the end. Do you expect me to start a quarrel with Raphael and his wife? I have no time anyhow; I'm being expected."

That's all that good Debele got out of him. But over his cards Michel Bloch made what he just heard a subject of conversation, adding that the matter was really one for the *Chevra Kadisha,* and one man there who belonged to the governing council of this charitable organization declared that he would bring the matter to the attention of the *Parnes* who was the presiding officer. And so it came to pass. Several days thereafter, when *Shabbos* was over and when, in any event, they had planned to meet at the house of the *Parnes,* Menke Guggenheim, the matter of Debele or David Levy, was on the agenda. In order that the group might be comfortable, Bela, Menke's wife, had placed before them her well known anise cakes and nut liqueur in the rough little glasses with the blue edges which her husband had brought home from a trip some years ago.

On this occasion Michel Bloch asked for the floor first. He thought he had a right to do so, since the matter was being discussed at his suggestion, as he did not fail to point out. And, as in his interview with Debele, so now too that the time had come to do something, to accomplish something more than the mere

saying of words, he found the right excuses and the
best reasons for avoiding the supposed obligation; he
spoke, as people of that kind always do, when they
want cheaply to withdraw from an action which might
entail some sacrifice. It wouldn't do, he pleaded, to
create a precedent of this kind, which would always be
appealed to in the future and instigate claims of the
same kind which would finally quite exceed the possibilities of the *Chevra*. It had never happened before
that someone's rent should be paid, not to mention the
fact that bad business conditions were being expected,
as they all knew. He added, as though accidentally,
that just in the past few years many non-Jews had
emigrated on account of the bad economic conditions
at home, in order to seek their fortune, to make it clear
and definite, in the new world.

The others had no effective replies. Old Avrohom
Meyer agreed with him, after he had offered all round
a pinch of snuff out of his carved beechwood snuff-
box and then had partaken of one himself through his
white beard which was brown with tobacco stains. But
he had one suggestion to make that might be helpful:
they should persuade Raphael to let Debele stay on for
a while, until some better opportunity offered itself;
this, he declared, was a *mitzva*, quite in the spirit of
the *Tauro*, pleasing to God and man.

"I wouldn't like to persuade his wife," Elias Gump
said with a laugh. He was a forthright man and not
on the best terms with Michel Bloch. He was the only
one in the *kehilla* who sometimes spoke the blunt
truth to Bloch. Therefore he added now too: "I am of

the opinion that Michel should take up the matter
and talk to her, since he brought it before us."

Bloch resisted this suggestion violently until finally
old Meyer, tapping his snuff box with his fingers,
undertook the task, after he had made the motion and
caused it to be recorded in the minutes with this
reservation, that it would suffice to speak with Raphael
Baer alone, that it was, indeed, contrary to wont and
custom to deal with a woman. This was a cheap way
out; that's why it was chosen.

On the very next day Avrohom Meyer met Raphael
and talked to him very impressively. He spoke of
Gemilus Chasodim, of the command to love one's
neighbor in general and the duty of brotherly kindness in particular and, above all, he said none of them
doubted that Raphael would be charitable, seeing that
they all knew him as a benevolent and generous man
who, in case of need, would give away more than
the commanded tithe. He added that one really should
have *rachmones* with poor Debele who had certainly
not deserved so hard a fate.

From all that has been related here it is clear that it
was not difficult to persuade Raphael. He was not the
man ever to dispute with someone who was insistent
in a given matter, of which he himself recognized the
fairness. And in this case it was a religious duty which
he was asked to perform, the chief duty which is imposed upon the Jew by his Holy Law, namely, *Zedaka,*
and its carrying out in *Gemilus Chesed.* Finally,
Raphael had already promised Debele precisely what

he was requested to do. Voluntarily he had given a
pious Jew his word to spare him.

He had never cared greatly to acquire money, since
the happy situation of his ancestors had made him independent and beyond all need. He paid little attention to it and had never considered it an end in
itself. He was far removed from those who have risen
from narrow circumstances, even though not actually
poverty, and who, by whatever happenings, accidents
or persistent industry of their own have gathered
fortunes for the mere sake of gain and who are far
more inclined to overvalue money and to regulate
their lives and their attitude to their fellow men by it.
They are easily recognizable. And such not being
Raphael's situation or character, he immediately replied to Meyer:

"You don't have to try to impress me. I've already
promised Debele that he may stay. That is certain! It
doesn't matter about the few marks. And I'm perfectly willing to promise the *Chevra* that I will not go
back on this agreement, God forbid!" Such were his
words and it is clear what meaning they had coming
from a truly pious man.

When he came home that same evening and tried
after supper very carefully to make it clear to Recha
that he had given his solemn word in this matter and
that she must be tolerant of their poor tenant, this
resistance against her definitely uttered wish, against
her arrogance and her greed, so enraged her, that she
passed all bounds. She screamed and raged; she ran up
and down the room so that the set of glasses on the
whatnot tinkled and complained loudly over her mis-

fortune of having to live with a husband who was a wretched *shlemasel*, a luckless fool. She was impelled —quite differently from her husband—to overestimate the value of money and of gear and could therefore never attain tranquility; for she had been brought up in the narrowest circumstances and trained by her mother to value everything, especially human beings, exclusively according to cash and not according to any real or inner worth. Thus she was really unable to understand the character of her own husband, which was utterly different from her own, which was the reason, too, why he had steadily declined to assume any office in the community and to be talked about in it, as she had demanded of him. Yet she did love him and was profoundly allied to him through the many years of their common life, as well as through the feeling of possessiveness and exclusive possession. This was *her* husband. And, precisely because he was as he was, he had married her to the astonishment of his *kehilla* and of hers too, without any dowry, only because she pleased him with her gleaming black curls and the lovely vitality of her youth. He did not consider, nay, he did not know, that man and woman should be permanently united only when they belonged to the same human strata and have had the same customs and habits for generations. For as it is easy for one to sink from his position, if fate is hostile, so it is equally difficult for the individual or even for a whole family to rise and to be comfortable according to new ways and to take these ways for granted. In her vulgar pertinacity which, after all, usually led to little or nothing, Recha now determined to nullify her husband's will. She knew that in the long run he couldn't withstand her and usually gave in when she insisted and gave him no peace, whether she used words or actions. What she did not suspect was that he had been spiritually so worn down that he finally could not endure to listen again and again to her loud and violent reproaches. And this condition of inner exhaustion had arisen in just this period of the conflict about their tenant.

And she left him no peace, whether by day or night. When they lay side by side in bed and she perceived that he was awake, she murmured lamentably to herself and yet so that he could not but hear: "I have to have a husband who is a *shlemihl,* and such a *shlemihl! Shlemihl, shlemihl."* Stealthily or directly she injected the matter between the words of every conversation, so that at last he didn't know what to do except to seek some way out, to escape a decision in the dilemma between his desire to have some peace at last from the perpetual pressure exerted by his wife, which had torn him to pieces in the course of the years, and the solemn assurance which he had given to fulfill a religious duty.

Well, in those years the thought of divorce occurred to no one, as it is practiced so lightheartedly nowadays. It never even entered Raphael's head. In his old fashioned piety he considered himself indissolubly bound by the Eternal to his wife, be she what she may be, during her life time. And so he tried to find a way out. He had long ago given her power of attorney to act legally for him in all business matters, as was customary in other prosperous families, so as to be prepared "for any eventuality" as the saying went. Only Recha had not waited for him to give her this customary sign of trust and unitedness, but had insisted on it with many violent words soon after their marriage. And while none of the other women dreamed of making any use of this privilege which had been given them and tactfully considered it only as a custom among the better families, satisfied and proud to be of use to their husbands and families in their households, so, on the contrary, Recha took satisfaction in injecting herself into affairs and into practical business matters which, in those days, were the exclusive preoccupation of the men. And she acted as though this were her clear right, though the assignment of power of attorney was regarded merely as a form, as a symbol.

Raphael had, therefore, been put to shame on many occasions through her forwardness. She had thrust herself into matters with which the women of her time were supposed to have nothing to do. She always injected an evil word or a demand that gave rise to disputes and quarrels. In addition she had no lack of effrontery in her arrogance and was not reluctant contentiously to appear before a court of law. And it must be remembered that in those days it was considered humiliating among self-respecting Jews to have anything to do with the secular courts of law, even though the cases were purely civil in their character and had nothing to do with the possible imposition of punishment. There are people to this day who are reluctant to push a difference to the point at which it has to be adjudicated before a

judge. But Recha had had to appear twice before
the court in Heiligenzell because she had opened
her big mouth and uttered libelous words against
others. She had been quite undisturbed by these matters. She ought to have been the wife of some poor
grocer or draper who had next to nothing and who
was trying to get on in the world. She could well
have stood in a small shop and chaffered over minute
sums and put the money, which she loved for its
own sake, into a cash drawer. That would have given
her an almost sensual satisfaction. As it was, she tried
to satisfy her lust for gain by little additional profits,
of which her husband was usually quite ignorant,
however small these profits were. So in winter she
would stuff geese with imported grain until they were
morbidly fat and had hugely enlarged livers. These
she would sell to the city physician or to the pastor
of the church.

Raphael, for his part, pursued, as we have seen,
his quiet way in the consciousness of his inherited
security which permitted him and his wife to pass
their lives without too much exertion. He was in-
different to her constant haste and business, even
though he might himself buy a head of cattle in order
to re-sell it at a modest profit to a friendly peasant
or to a neighbor whose fields adjoined his own beyond
the limits of the town. In autumn, too, he might sell
the fruit of his orchards gathered in sacks and willow
baskets, insofar as he did not store them in for his
own winter use or tread his grapes for wine. They
had so many advantages over many others. They
needed never, for instance, to buy wood for their

winter's need. For all, whether Christians or Jews,
who, like Raphael and his family, had long been
native here, had had for many years the right to cut
as much wood as they needed in the communal forests which surrounded the little town on its hills.
Indeed, many a one could have sold a surplus of
wood. So favorable was the situation of Raphael and
his wife. And, indeed, the people of that period in our
part of the country were nearly all in a position where
they could pass their lives tranquilly and without
interruption in the regular change of the seasons and
the years and could grow old and blessed before the
Eternal in their piety, if now and then wicked im-
pulses had not prevailed within them, as is frequent
among men, also according to His will.

Like the other men, then, Raphael passed the
greater portion of his days in the exact practice of
the holy commands and the prescribed customs. Early
in the morning he laid his *tefillin*; he went to *shul*
for the *Shacharis* service; he washed his hands before
every meal; he was present at every memorial service;
he paid in his tithe as a matter of course. The divi-
sions and the course of the year he marked exclusively by our holy festivals which were the center
of his existence. He conducted his *seder* service
with deep emotion; he was merry at *Shevuaus*; long
before dawn he went to *shul* on the days of *Selichaus*,
deeply aware of their meaning; on *Succaus* he proudly
carried through the ill paved streets of the town his
lulav and his *esrog*. Never had an unrighteous deed
of his set the tongues of men wagging. In him, as in
his father and grandfather before him, they saw a

true ornament of the congregation. Without any real awareness of it, he felt himself to be, as it were, a measuring rod for others, altogether honorable and feeling his *yichus* in his very blood like an ever living element. Yet there was no arrogance and no pride in him.

It must be admitted that he had periods of apparently uncaused depression, since all was well with him. At such times he would speak to no one for days on end; he would scarcely say a word to his wife who, however, scarcely felt the deprivation. Long ago the brother of his mother had taken his own life in an attack of melancholy. Without any observable reason the man had simply walked into the river near their native village. It had been in the middle of winter when the ice floes were in the stream. The case had been a matter of much talk in the whole region. His mother had told Raphael the story as something which had not ceased to oppress her. So the family was prone to melancholy spells.

It was at this period that the more prosperous people even in the little towns and villages began to acquire certain complaints because gay watering places had been established. So they would make trips there, in order, as they thought, to recuperate, but assuredly also tempted by the notion of meeting other Jews there from far-away places and to converse with them concerning the common holy destiny, concerning the state of business and also concerning the general situation of the Jewish people, taking pride in the circumstance that these strangers were yet so closely akin to them and felt like them and recognized their common bonds. And how delighted were they, these simple people, when they were privileged to converse with some eminent metropolitan rabbi or with some old and pious *rav* from Poland who still wore *paiyes* and velvet hat and *caftan*. Then they had a great deal to relate when they returned home.

And so it came to pass that precisely in that year and in early summer old Avrohom Meyer decided to go to pass four weeks in Badenweiler, where he had been several times before, and that he communicated this plan of his to Raphael in an accidental conversation. To Raphael this seemed like a sign from heaven. He recognized his opportunity and quite unexpectedly asked Avrohom whether he might not join him. The latter was more than willing. Not only was he glad of Raphael's companionship; he also considered that the attention and gossip in the *kehilla* caused by this trip, would be distributed between two people.

We need hardly say that, when her husband explained his plan, Recha's first reaction was a storm of angry words. How could one throw away good money in this fashion on a barren and unproductive adventure, especially at a time of misfortune when one was suffering losses through this wretched tenant, as well as through one's own fault! And how did it occur to a man as young as Raphael to want to go for a cure? She forgot entirely, of course, that for years and years she had been nagging him to take her to Baden-Baden for the September races which, at that time, had become the chief social event in the whole of Europe, to which fashionable people came from everywhere, especially from France. She clamored that

the wife of the *Parnes* Rothschild in her native village, with whom she had gone to school, had already
been there twice. He took advantage of this notion. He
promised her voluntarily to permit her to take this
trip the following autumn; she could take it alone;
there would be no dearth of company for her; perhaps
Frau Rothschild would join her. This calmed her at
last. The following week, then, Raphael and Avrohom
set out, both in their black morning coats and their
high round hats; for in those days that was the cos-
tume in which people were wont to go upon extended
and rare journeys.

There is not much to tell of Raphael's experiences
at Badenweiler, because they are irrelevant to what
in the meantime took place at home during his absence. It goes without saying that the two *balabatim*
lived in a kosher hotel in which the three daily services were piously conducted. Beyond that, they took
walks in the forenoon and in the afternoon. They
sat on the benches of the great promenade, especially
in the shade of a rare palm tree which had been
brought there from some southern land, perhaps even
—how could one know?—from Eretz Yisroel itself.
They had never seen anything like it before. They
also made the acquaintance of other men from nearer
and farther places, as we have said before. All this
time Raphael was very taciturn.

One day Avrohom Meyer, offering him a pinch of
snuff, asked him, as it were, by the way, how that
matter of Debele had been settled. He replied:

"How do you suppose it was settled? He's going
to stay just as he has been doing. I'm not going to

throw that poor *bocher* on the street and make myself guilty of such *avereh!*"

Avrohom made no reply, although he was thinking of Recha and her ways and although it was on the tip of his tongue to ask whether she agreed to this plan.

The days passed and the weeks and the two men prepared to return home. Raphael had received several letters from his wife; these letters had dealt with no concrete matters; he had the feeling, on the other hand, that she kept something from him. But their tenor deceived him. She expressed herself in general terms, such as were customary at that period between married people. She said nothing but handsome things and in some of these he seemed to feel a genuine warmth; once, indeed, she expressed her loneliness and affection. Nor need we suppose that this was hypocritical on Recha's part. She had, in fact, loved her husband from the beginning, although her unworthy instincts had often intended to estrange them. It must be added that Raphael wrote her only a few lines now and then because he hesitated to speak insincerely, nor did he want to reveal the moral oppression which he had taken with him from home.

In the meantime Recha had not been idle. She could not bring herself to consent to shelter Debele for the rest of time without pay. It robbed her of sleep; it did not leave her through the occupations of the day, nor had she anyone, since Raphael was absent, on whom to wreak her rage. The thing left no rest. She exchanged no word with that pauper, that beggar, that good-for-nothing, as she kept mur-

muring to herself. She pretended that he did not
exist. And although Debele was hardly at ease because he suspected evil, yet he paid no attention.
At least there was peace and no humiliating words
were flung at him. However, it was not entirely two
weeks when she had come to a decision.

Early one morning she marched on foot to the neighboring town, which was a little bigger than her own
country town and was the nearest seat of a court.
She made her way to the secretary of the court and
asked him to institute a suit of dispossession against
David Levy, to be effective within twenty four hours,
on account of the non-payment of rent for such and
such a period. She signed the affidavit with her short,
stumpy fingers, such as you will find the avaricious
to have.

At that time the law had not yet any provisions for
the protection of poor tenants; hence Recha's scheme
had quick results. On the day on which Debele was
summoned to appear at court, he tried to explain to
the judge that Raphael Baer had given him unlimited
time and had assured him that he could stay in spite
of the fact that he was in arrears with his rent; he
affirmed, furthermore, that Baer, being a pious Jew,
would not be in agreement with what his wife had
undertaken to do during his own absence on a journey. He tried to make all this clear. But since he had
no concrete proof of his assertions and because he
was inexperienced in the ways of the secular law
and unskillful in speech, and since Recha showed
the document which made it clear that her husband
had given her power of attorney to act for him in

the management of his fortune, Debele was condemned at once, even as the action of the wicked, greedy and arrogant woman demanded it. The procedure at court had not, however, been without witnesses from the community. Michael Bloch of their own *kehilla* stood in the back of the courtroom among the other spectators. He had come in the matter of a cattle deal which was brought before the court. Even before the court was in session he asked Frau Recha why she was here. Unwillingly she explained her presence. And when he tried to persuade her, even though not too emphatically, to wait at least until Raphael's return, she replied:

"Mind your own business!"

That's what he got for his interference.

With her little hat, set with black pearls, a little askew on her head and a strand of hair hanging down, Recha left the court house. She found that her satisfaction was brief. And now, too, that poor homeless David was faced by the undeniable fact and had nothing more to lose, and the shyness which had prevented him from an adequate explanation to the judge had vanished too, he went up to Frau Recha and said to her: "May an evil fate overtake you, you and your whole *mishpoche!*" Thus he cursed her and her evil deed which contravened the sacred prescriptions of our faith.

It is not to be denied that this imprecation went through and through her. She knew just what it meant: this calling down upon another of the wrath of Heaven. She got no good of what had happened. A bad conscience throbbed within her. Suddenly she

wished her husband were back and an anxiety for
him came over her. For although her instincts had
always bidden her to concentrate on earthly possessions, yet from her youth up she had been acquainted with our Holy Law, which forbids us to
oppress the poor, which demands of us helpfulness;
and she knew, too, that her husband took these duties
very seriously as, indeed, the majority of the community did too. Ah, yes, she missed him now. She
felt terribly alone with the burden of what had happened, now that her will had been satisfied according to the rigid ways of the secular law. To this may
be added the circumstance that they had never before
been separated for so long. All the hateful annoyance
which she had caused him in the weeks before his
departure was forgotten; indeed, all the disputes of
recent years which had arisen from trivial circumstances and had usually been caused by herself—
these were forgotten too. She hoped for better things
now that that stranger would have to leave her house,
although she was irritated too by the fact that she
would have to renounce any rental for that attic,
since it would be quite impossible to find another
tenant in the little town. Yet it never occurred to
her to reverse the entire situation and so to eliminate
the chief reason of their quarrels by giving in and
telling Debele that he could stay, whether he paid
rent or not. She had defended her rights; the secular
court had confirmed them. She would not give in.
Yet she rejoiced in Raphael's approaching return; she
wrote him one of those letters, which we have de-

scribed, in which she used tender words but did not
indicate what had come to pass.

These words surprised him and awakened in him,
too, a desire to return home, seeing that we are all
inclined to forget evil and renew our hope in the
goodness of man. Sitting on a bench on the promenade under the light gray parasol, which the men
of that period used, he had read the letter and smiled
over it, so that Avrohom Meyer was impelled to ask
him what good news it contained. Raphael answered:
"No special news. But why does a man gad about
when he has a wife at home?"

Recha, for her part, prepared to receive her home-
coming husband as it was customary to do among
people who rarely traveled far or long and usually
within a narrow region and only for purposes of
business.

As she had seen other women do under such circumstances, she had all the hangings taken down in
both the living room and the bedroom and had them
washed and spread out on the lawn beside their house
to dry, a most uncommon thing at this time of the
year, commonly done only at Pesach time or at *Rosh
Hashono,* so that the other women of the *kehilla*
were surprised and gossiped about it. Fanny Rothschild, for instance, who was a bit frank and, as some
thought, even malicious, said to the wife of Elias
Gump that Recha would do better to determine to
refrain from her eternal quarrelsomeness and screaming upon her husband's return, and omit these un-
seasonable goings-on which were not meant to please

him but were only undertaken to show others what
a careful and able housekeeper she was. As if they
weren't on to her! This time, nevertheless, they were
not wholly in the right. Recha cooked and baked;
that is to say, she had her servant Jachet do these
things which she had never learned properly and
in which she had no skill, although she bragged
to the other women of the hard work that she was
putting in. She fetched a smoked tongue from the
butcher Guggenheim, because Raphael was very fond
of it. Nevertheless it had been a rare dish in their
house, for Recha always reckoned that ordinary meats
were cheaper. Jachet had derived her skill in the
preparation of many dishes and, above all, of pastries,
from Raphael's mother, in whose service she had been
and from whom Recha had taken her over. She was
indispensable and a necessary adjunct to the house.

Jachet had already talked to Debele who had complained to her of what had taken place; she had tried
to console him with the prospect of the return of the
master of the house. But the poor tenant was through,
as he said. He had his notion of *koved* too. This
thing would revenge itself upon Recha who was nobody in particular either, that she had acted so harshly
and heartlessly and greedily toward a *Ben Yisroel*,
especially toward one of her own *kehilla*.

In the meanwhile the day of Raphael's return approached. Everything was in order and the whole dwelling smelled of cleanliness and paint. The floors were
freshly varnished; the curtains hung stiff and starched
at the windows; even fresh flowers stood on the table
and the bureau. It was before the time when artificial

palms were placed among the pompous furnishings, never renewed and always full of dust. Recha was especially proud of one cake. She had taken the recipe from Bela, the wife of Menke Guggenheim. It was a hazelnut cake with icing. She bragged of this cake to every woman in the neighborhood and of the labor it required. She herself came to believe this, although it was the servant who had baked the cake.

On a Sunday afternoon of mid-summer, the train of two or three coaches stopped at the little hut of the station with its garden in which tall sunflowers bent their umbels. The train had begun to whistle from afar. Raphael and Avrohom Meyer were the only passengers who descended the steep steps of the coach. And there stood Recha to welcome her husband. She was bareheaded, that is to say, she wore nothing on her head except her pious wig. She had put on her *Shabbos* frock of black taffeta. Since, however, it was not *Shabbos,* she wore a little apron of gray silk lace. At her throat she had fastened a longish brooch of grayish-green, iridescent stones that were then called cat's eyes.

Raphael saw his wife and went up to her and kissed her on both cheeks and said with a smile:

"God greet you, Rechele."

"You're looking well," she said on their way home, looking up at him sidewise without meeting his eyes. His face was slightly tanned from the many hours which he had passed on the benches of the promenade and the gardens, in spite of the gray parasol, which now hung from his arm. In the other hand he carried the embroidered satchel which he had inherited

from his father. And since we are all prone to let
the agreeable moment cast its veil over the past and
thus also take a cheerful view of the future, so on
this way through the familiar streets Raphael's mood
was a bright one. He was glad that his wife had come
for him, and when the moment came to say goodbye
to Avrohom Meyer, whose wife was waiting for him
at home, he called out after him:

"Give our regards to your wife! It's really good
to be home again, isn't it?"

Recha walked beside him, hoping that she was seen.

The street was strewn with the remnants of dried
hay. Many inhabitants of the little town had meadows and fields and cattle. It was the time of the early
harvest and the hay, dried by the sun and with a
slight burned odor, had been brought in within the
last few days. Here and there, from house or barn,
from door or window, a welcoming word was called
out to the returning traveler.

They entered their own house. Above the second
inner door before one mounted the stairs, Recha had
caused to be nailed a white placard on which was
written in red letters: "Welcome home!" The inscrip-
tion was surrounded by a wreath of oak leaves. It
was cool within these thick old walls which never
quite lost a slightly mouldy smell, of which the cause
was unknown. Raphael felt agreeably the atmosphere
of all the things to which he had been accustomed
from his youth. And as they were mounting the worn
wooden stairway, he heard from the yard which led
to the stable the snorting of the two cows which

furnished the household with milk. As though to greet him one of the two cows let out a broad and good-natured moo.

"Are the cows all right?" he asked, just to be saying something.

"Why shouldn't they be?"

Recha's words were so impatient and querulous that he, suddenly reminded of reality, turned to look back at her on their way up the stairs. Ah, there it was again, all that he had been dreading. Yet this dread disappeared. At the head of the stairs stood Jachet, who had just come out of the kitchen, wiping her hands on her apron.

"How are you?" she said in a slightly embarrassed fashion, "Did you enjoy yourself?"

Upon his saying that he had she disappeared hastily in the kitchen which was in the rear, calling back from the door: "I still have a lot to do!" She acted as though she fled from being questioned.

Before he entered the living room Raphael lifted his right hand to the doorpost and let his fingers touch the *mezzuzo* lingeringly, while he softly repeated the blessing.

Slowly he then went through the living room, rubbing his hands together. There stood the sofa with its crocheted white antimacassars; above it hung the familiar pictures, the daguerreotypes of his grandparents and parents, all in the old fashioned garments and hairdresses of long ago, the women in the white butterfly winged little caps, such as they used to wear on *Yontef*.

How low was the ceiling compared to that of his hotel room which he had quietly inhabited for several weeks!

"You did take a lot of trouble," he said, "It's like Pesach here. I appreciate that. I've got something for you, too!"

He bent over his valise on the floor, unstrapped it thoughtfully, took from it an object carefully wrapped in silk paper and handed it to her. She regarded the package expectantly. It contained a squarish, rather high souvenir box, set with shells and mother of pearl. Its little key hung from a cord of blue silk.

Into the middle of the cover had been set between the shells a little painting which represented in vivid colors the fountain in the square of the Spa, a pavilion surrounded by trees. Recha's smile was a little forced and she asked: "What do you expect me to do with that?"

"Well, put it on your bureau. Don't you like it? These things are fashionable nowadays."

In her heart she considered that this was nothing to her purpose; there was nothing she could do with it. She did not speak and drew up her upper lip a trifle. Nevertheless she unlocked and opened the top with the little key. An object lay there, wrapped in paper, and when she undid the paper she found two big, gleaming silver florins. At that she laughed aloud and turned to Raphael and kissed him repeatedly.

She busied herself with one thing and another. Perhaps he wouldn't take the revelation so hard as she had feared from day to day. She would make sure that he would never learn of the imprecation of Debele, whom she had driven out, which she could not forget and which had shown her the quality of her deed.

Next they sat at their table and comfortably dunked their coffee cake into their cups. She had served the cake on their handsome platter with its golden ornaments and its perforated edge. She asked him: "Well, what did you experience?"

"It's a good thing to get out into the world and meet other people. You learn what happens in *Kol Yisroel*. Almost daily Rabbi Salman, a great man among us, chatted with me. He treated us as though we were ourselves *Rabbonim*. A very pious man who explained to us that we did not quite realize wherein we failed, imaging ourselves to be so righteous. . . ."

"Well, you can overdo righteousness too," Recha said.

She was glad that he didn't ask how she had fared. While they had eaten their cake and coffee, the dusk had fallen. He got up and said: "I'll go downstairs a bit and greet our neighbors." In his shirt-sleeves and with his black velvet skullcap on his head he strolled into the street. Neighbors stood in their doorways, wearing their embroidered house shoes and spoke to him. For a long time he chatted with the cooper, Baechle, who had been his familiar friend from childhood on and with whom he was accustomed to discuss whatever happened.

After they had greeted each other, his friend said, not really meaning to be equivocal: "I'm sure Recha is happy to see you back home."

And also Michel Bloch strolled past and shook hands with Raphael without looking at him. Others, too, who happened to be strolling in this direction, stopped and bade him welcome. And suddenly it seemed to him as though they were all rather silent, far more so than was their wont, although he had not spoken with them in so long.

He went back upstairs for his supper. That sense of comfort came over him which we all feel when, after a long absence, we are once more under our own roof and can enjoy the consolation of the long accustomed. And Recha waited for him and they experienced a night that recalled to them their early days.

Raphael arose early in the morning and washed himself and put on his *tefillin*. After his prayers, they sat down with their tall coffee cups and ate the good white bread with the honey, fragrant of the pine forests. He had deliberately not asked concerning Debele, because he wanted to be tranquil during these hours of his return home, though nurturing an apprehension of the ugliness that might be in store for him. At last he uttered the question:

"And how is that *shlemihl*, Debele?"

And her answer was: "He's gone. A week ago he went to his kinsfolk in Kuppenheim, to his uncle, who is also his godfather. They wrote him. We can be glad to be rid of that pauper."

She gazed into her cup and stirred her coffee with her spoon, which was an empty gesture, since she never used sugar.

Oh yes, a number of days ago, without having mentioned it previously, Debele had suddenly presented himself to her with his square, brown-tinted, wooden box with a lock, which contained his few possessions, and had said:

"No good will come of this to you!" That's all he had said, not even goodbye. Then he was gone.

He had not told her where he was going. With a sombre expression and tense lips he had descended the stairs.

"The *chuzpe* of it—the, the . . ." The right word had not come to her.

And two days later the seamstress and midwife, Lizzie, whom she had met at the house of the baker Scholl, had told her in a tone meant to be reproachful and sympathetic toward Debele, where he had gone. It was Elias Gump who had loaned him the money for the trip. That's the way it had been.

Across the table she looked at the charm which was fastened by a special chain to the plated gold watch-chain which Raphael wore. It was a large, reddish, oblong, semi-precious stone. This charm had always seemed to make a stranger of him, ever since he had inherited it from his father. To her there was something excessive and full of vanity about it. Yet everything about Raphael pleased her, when she compared him to other men. Raphael arose. He looked at her full of distrust. He suspected that something had happened which he could not approve. Debele's kinsfolk in Kuppenheim had never before paid any attention to their poor cousin, although the *Chevra* had once written to inform them of his plight. Evidently those people had no realization of the duties owing to their *mishpoche,* such as are prescriptive in our old Law. In the *kehilla* the case had been discussed with marked disapproval. And so Raphael asked:

"How was it really? That's a fine beginning for you. I'm sure that that poor *bocher* didn't leave willingly. I hope you didn't forget that I promised to keep him in my house!"

But the woman, not considering that he did not yet know how things were, could not refrain from screaming in her accustomed manner:

"Now I've seen to it that we can rent out the room for real money; I've taken care of your business as no other woman would, and what I get is reproaches. No use having the house in lovely order! I get no thanks!"

"What happened? What did he do?"

"What he did? You ought to ask what he didn't do! He didn't pay, the good for nothing! And I had had my belly full of it!"

And thus there occurred a renewed moral collapse between these two human beings. Since they were deeply bound to each other and could not loosen those ties, despite the contradiction of their characters; it could not but be that they utterly lost their way to each other. In her mad impulsiveness and because, as we have observed, she could brook no contradiction, she now let herself go:

"Be glad he's out of our house. He cursed and threatened us, instead of being grateful that we kept him so long. And who will now pay the rent which he owes us? Get it from them to whom you've promised to keep him here!"

All that he had suffered through all the years came over Raphael at this moment. Silently he took up his hat and left the room; wearily he descended the stairs. She heard his tread on the wooden steps and beyond them on the paved street. And it seemed to her as though his tread was dreadfully tired; and suddenly something like compassion for him arose within her.

It was very early in the day. He went to Michel Bloch, who still had his *tefillin* on. Bloch smiled at him and nodded, but pointed at his arm on which the consecrated capsule was fastened. Raphael knew that he would have to wait.

Meanwhile Frau Bloch entered the room. She came from Hessen, from far away. Her name was Natalie and she had always remained something of a stranger here. No one addressed her in the old familiar forms; everybody used the new polite formalism with her. She was of a new type and wore no wig.

"Sit down," she said courteously, "and tell us about the great world in which you have been!"

She herself sat down and folded her hands in her lap and continued, without awaiting an answer:

"I'm sure you brought Recha something very nice."

At that he remembered exactly how he had come to buy that present for his wife. Both he and Avrohom Meyer had often discussed what they would bring their wives from the watering place. The older man had bought a handsome shawl of white silk with long fringes and he said that he could just see her before him, wrapped in that lovely shawl and accompanying him to *shul* on the approaching *Yaum*

Kippur. Raphael had not been able to choose so
quickly. He had decided to give Recha money, because he knew that that would give her the greatest
pleasure. And he had bought the souvenir box in
order to surprise her. He told the story to Frau Bloch,
keeping silence concerning the money but telling
her how on his last walk along the promenade he had
seen the box displayed in a window and had bought
it as an adornment for his wife's dresser. He described
it exactly. And Frau Bloch said:

"Oh, I've long wanted something like that for my
whatnot!"

She was glad not to have to discuss with Raphael the
matter which had been the substance of gossip for
weeks. And now her husband came up to them and
said: "Well, are you comfortably settled again?"

Raphael did not reply but, full of his errand and
his worry, asked brusquely:

"Do you know anything about Debele?"

"He's gone, and I can't say that I blame him."

And then he told the whole story, of how he had
accidently been at the court and there had met
Recha, pursuing her action to dispossess Debele. He
did not fail to emphasize the fact that the judge's
feelings had obviously been on the side of the poor
bocher, as was easily to be seen from both his words
and his expression, although in the end he had had
to decide according to the letter of the law. Michel
added that, frankly, he had been ashamed for their
whole *kehilla.* He carefully omitted the fact that he
had neglected to use his influence or to make a small
financial sacrifice, in order to help Debele.

For a space Raphael fell silent. Then he wondered
whether the poor fellow could not be invited back.
Bloch gave it as his opinion that that would be difficult; one didn't even rightly know whether he had
joined his kinsfolk in Kuppenheim. No news of any
kind had been received here. Raphael arose and
thanked them and shook hands with Frau Natalie
without a further word. He went out at the door and
through the long hall. Silently his lips moved, forming repeatedly the word *shlemasel*. He seemed deaf
to himself as he trod the street. It came over him with
a dull horror. What a shame that people could say
of him: he had broken his word and through his
wife transgressed the Holy Law by oppressing the
poor. For he could not repudiate her. It would be
talked about, this thing, and never forgotten. And
his family had always been proud of its *yichus*.

Nor was this all. What overcame him primarily was
pity for that abandoned and helpless friend. He had
a vision of him wandering the roads, sleeping in
rude inns with low people or even passing the night
in the open, cold and hungry. And he saw him at
the services in strange communities, standing wretchedly in the last row.

How had Recha been able to bring herself to do
this to him? He had always hoped that she would
change, not considering that the innermost character,
given us at birth, is not likely to undergo a transformation, wherever our path might lead us and
whether good or evil examples might accompany it.
Again and again she had been capable of actions
which were incomprehensible to him and alienated

her from him, deeply as he affirmed the binding ties
between them, the feeling that had once led him to
her, and deeply as he recognized the inescapable
obligation which our Holy Law imposes upon us.

. Slowly he proceeded toward his house. Having
reached it he remained standing under the arch of
the stone gateway. As though only half conscious he
returned the salutation of the passers-by, whether Jew
or Christian, whom he knew so well and who considered him as one of their own. None suspected, of
course, what went on within him: the hopelessness
ever to live again without a constant wounding of
his better self. And thus it had been from the beginning, because his wife could not resist an evil impulse stronger than all else in her life, even though
she clung to him not without affection. No, he
couldn't go up to join her. Perhaps she would realize
how deeply she had injured him, taking advantage of
his absence and of his confidence in her. He had never
before been as utterly disillusioned as by this action of
hers which seemed to show most clearly how little
she was able to master her own vulgarity and how,
indeed, she was bound to despise his yearning for
moral cleanliness—despise it, because she could not
grasp it.

He decided to take counsel with Frau Seligmann,
who loved him as though he were her own son and
to whom he had often confided his difficulties. She
always listened patiently to him and understood him.
She was more than eighty years old; she had been
his mother's best friend and had endured much in her
long life. Decades had passed since she had lost her

husband. Of the nine children she had borne him,
seven had died. One son had been lost sight of in
America. The single child left, a married daughter,
lived in a village at some distance and was not in
the best circumstances. Frau Seligmann lived a lonely
life. She had never left the little town. In any event,
he would have gone to see her after his journey.
It always calmed him just to sit beside her. She had
the magnanimity of the strong who, though they have
suffered, are serene. And so once more she heard
Raphael out, as he told her what he had suffered
at the hands of his wife. She, of course, had been
informed of the matter before. For a time she remained silent. There she sat, knitting a garment of
thick wool. A lock of her snow-white hair came out
across her forehead from her black wig. She looked
at him through her steel-rimmed spectacles.

"Of what use will it be, Raphael, to give you advice? You will have to overlook it, as you have over-
looked all that she has done before."

"It can't be done. The moment comes when one
can't go on. And this is the worst she's ever done.
How am I to face people?"

The old lady said: "Such cares as you have are not
the worst. Griefs that are in the very soul and which
cannot even be communicated—these can rob one
of all the joy in life. I tell you there are worse
things than those you have to bear."

"Care? Grief? This is like a sickness from which one
can't recover; that's what it's like."

"It's sinful, Raphael, to demand too much of God,
the Almighty. Aren't you a respected man? Have you

ever really wanted for anything? Haven't you just been able to indulge yourself in a pleasure trip, such as few in the *kehilla* can do? Many a man has had an ill-tempered wife and has yet been contented because he knows that we are all only human. And hasn't Recha some good qualities, too? Doesn't she keep your substance together?"

Raphael arose: "If she were only ill-tempered and contentious, I would bear it. But she has no feeling of honor or of *yichus* and cannot understand that there are things more important than money."

For a while he stood there in silence with drooping head. As though the solution of the problem had occurred to her, the old woman also stood up. She went over to him and in motherly fashion laid her old hand on his arm. She said:

"Come, sit down. You must have some refreshment. I'm sure you haven't eaten for a long time."

He smiled and patted the little old lady and said:

"I see you can't help me either. Yet I do thank you. How shall I cleanse myself of what she has now done by breaking my word for me and forgetting the *mitzve* of *Gemilus Chasodim*? What would our *ovaus avauseinu* say to this, not to speak of the living members of the *kehilla*? No, this cannot be mended. This I cannot survive."

Swiftly he went out. She called after him:

"Don't be *brauges* with me on this account; don't be angry, Raphele. Come soon again!"

No, she hadn't understood him either; she hadn't recognized what was at stake and what wounded him so deeply. But it seemed to him suddenly, as he found himself on the way home, as though he could no longer pursue that way; as though this spirit which, as it were, inhabited his house next to or in the semblance of his wife, could concern him no longer; that he was, in fact, homeless. Nevertheless he forced himself to go toward his house by a roundabout way. He walked along the wall of the town where cows stood in their stables and the path was strewn with hay and dung. Finally he passed through the vaulted tunnel between the two neighbors' houses which was always dark. He stood quite still there for a little in order to come to a decision. Yes, he would be tranquil and seek to overcome, once more to overcome the insuperable disharmony between his wife and himself, that indefinable force which made him powerless to shape his life and his future.

It was almost noon by now. At first Recha had waited for him impatiently. Thereafter dread had attacked her and the consciousness of her guilt had come upon her. But also, as often in her better moments, her affection for her husband had touched her. For, beyond all other circumstances, it existed. When he entered she acted as though she had forgotten everything. Suspecting that his long absence was connected with what hovered between them and her evil conscience warning her that he might have learned the true state of affairs from others, she said:

"I suppose you told other people much more than you told me? I've been waiting for you a long time."

And since in his heart he had concluded that it was vain to offer resistance, he was silent concerning what weighed upon him and gazed across the table

on which he had laid his outstretched arms. And so
this tragic problem lay between them like an illness
which could reach no crisis. Thus the first day after
his return home passed and thus, too, the succeeding
weeks.

Summer had come, with days of harvest and goodly
sun in which the Jews, too, rejoiced. For they, too,
had bits of land, partly assigned to them out of the
common lands of the town, which they either cultivated themselves or had cultivated by their neighbors,
as well as in the little gardens which the women
cared for.

Often and often Raphael sat alone and silent in
his rather carelessly cultivated garden by the river,
amid his berry bushes and ornamental shrubbery,
guarded by a decayed wooden fence. Now his fruits
were golden and ripe and dropped from the boughs.
Ah, how many years ago it was that he had helped
his mother set out the little trees. He was impelled
to think a great deal of the past. Although no member of the congregation had reproached him for
Debele's fate and some, indeed, said that it was a good
thing for the *kehilla* to be relieved of that burden,
and although, also, one man or another approached
him to cheer him up, as it were, because it was
understood that a deep conflict beset him and that
this conflict arose out of the matter of his former
tenant, yet he remained wholly silent in his depression and accessible to no consolation. Upon his in-
sistence the *Chevra* had written to Kuppenheim and
inquired of Debele's relations there whether their
cousin was with them. But no answer had been re-

ceived. And Michel Bloch had observed that, knowing
those people, he had expected nothing else.

And ever again, by virtue of that deep piety which
he had inherited from his fathers and their fathers,
Raphael was constantly reminded of that sin which
he and his wife had committed. Every morning he
read and spoke in the *Shacharis* prayer that the virtue
of *Gemilus Chesed* took its rank immediately after
the reverence due to father and mother in that hier-
archy of human actions which God has been pleased
to command us. And must not the others when in
their prayers they came to the passage that dealt with
it be reminded of him?

Recha, for her part, who felt clearly enough that
something very special occupied her husband, far
more than had been the case on the occasion of other
disputes during the long years, and who was not
unaware of the reason even though Raphael uttered
no word, tried hard, although he no longer offered
her any resistance even in the smallest details, to
approach him conciliatingly and even to make con-
cessions. In addition to the work which Jachet did in
the household, she herself performed many daily tasks.
On Friday she did the little shopping for over
Shabbos and haggled toughly over every farthing with
the fishwives and with the women who dealt in eggs
and onions who came from the villages and farmsteads with their woven baskets on their heads. She
accompanied her husband to *shul* on *Shabbos* and on
festivals, as all the other wives of the community did.

And now the *Yomim Nauroim* approached—the days
of self-examination and reverence and repentance.

All the members of the *kehilla* lived within that mood
which this period induces in the hearts of the faithful, because they feel nearer to the Eternal, blessed
be His name, than at other seasons, hoping for purga-
tion and renewal.

Raphael not only practiced all the religious customs, as he had been wont to do since his youth; he
actually took refuge in them despite the inner uncertainty smoldering in his heart, on account of that
which had happened. On the days of the *Selichoth*
prayers he arose before sunrise and with resonant,
lonely tread walked through the silent, sleeping street
to *shul*. Only here and there did a light glimmer in a
Jewish house. The fog was penetrating and he shivered. He prayed with the others; he saw them bent
over the old books beside the dripping candles, as he
himself was doing. He heard the familiar voices near
him and yet, in a sense, far away. In the first dim
light of day, when the peasants began to bring in
their morning loads, he returned home. There Recha
was waiting for him. In previous years he had had
to get up alone; his wife had not considered it necessary to arise with him on these consecrated days, as the
other women did. Now she got up with him and
helped Jachet to prepare the breakfast against his
return. And so on every one of these mornings there
was a cake between the pitchers of coffee and of
milk when he came home from *shul*. Raphael was
quite aware of the good will in this action and its
reason. But it was too late, as far as he was concerned.
It could no longer penetrate him. What he knew
and had now for so long experienced closed his heart.

On *Erev Rosh Hashono* before supper she offered him, as was the custom, a large golden and rosy apple, the fruit of his favorite tree in his garden, as well as a little pot of brown and fragrant honey. He cut a slice of the apple and dipped it into the honey and ate it, saying the appropriate *berocho* and then offered his wife a similar slice under the mild light of their silver candlesticks. At that moment she came close to him and stood before him and said:

"Can't we be friends, Raphael?"

All he could do was to utter her name and pass his hand gently over her head.

And thus they went to *shul* side by side on the two days and prayed among the others their special prayers and were deeply moved by the sounding of the *shofar*. On the second day of the festival they visited their friends in order to wish them a good year. When they left the house of Elias Gump, the latter said to his wife:

"I'm worried about Raphael; he's terribly careworn."

Several days later, as Raphael was leaving his house the letter carrier came and handed him a letter with these words: "It's from France; it must be mighty important."

The envelope did bear a French stamp. On it was the picture of the Emperor Napoleon with his pointed beard. Raphael did not open the letter. He slipped it into his coat pocket. He had a premonition that he must read its contents when he was unobserved and alone. He took a long walk beyond the boundaries of the little town. There he opened the letter which

was written on yellowish paper in an unknown hand
and signed with an unknown and almost illegible
name. The letter said that the writer of it had been
for weeks on the road with a certain David Levy.
The latter, before his death, in a poor inn in Zabern,
caused probably by consumption, by the want which
he had recently endured, had commissioned him, the
writer, to send this farewell to his kinsman, Raphael
Baer.

Now this letter was a trick and a deception, slyly
planned by Debele himself, in order to revenge himself on Raphael and Recha. For men do often find it
impossible to forget a wrong inflicted upon them and
harbor the impulse to revenge themselves at the right
time. Actually he had found shelter among his rela-
tives in Kuppenheim, which is situated on the other
bank of the Rhine not far from Zabern. They had
had need of a serving man on their farm and had
hired him. He was better off than he had been for
long.

As though to meditate upon the matter, Raphael sat
down on the edge of the road where the hazlenut
bushes with their brown fruit bordered the little road-
way which there joined the highway. The respected
citizen, Raphael Baer, crouched on the public road
like any insignificant *bocher*. But, truly, what was
there to meditate about? He shook his head and
murmured to himself: "It was fated to be so."

And although he asked himself what sense there
was in anything or in going farther, yet he found
himself walking for two long hours to the nearest
town. There the cattle market was in full activity.

The roaring and mooing of the cattle was audible from afar and the smell of the herds was in the air. A scene of this kind used always formerly to tranquillize him or to excite him agreeably, as something to which he had been accustomed from his youth. And when finally he strolled among the cattle which were fastened by ropes or chains to longish boards, and when he was saluted by acquaintances, peasants from the vicinity, traders from here and yon and by his own fellow townsmen, so that life in everyday plainness and naturalness surrounded him, he could have renewed his courage and been liberated from his cares. But he stood there and could not feel that anything concerned him anymore. To be sure, the other members of the *kehilla* were not here to strike bargains. It was a day between *Rosh Hashono* and *Yaum Kippur* on which it was better to practice expiation and to prepare oneself for the Day of Judgment. And so most of them just confined themselves to listening to what was going on, to the prices that cattle would fetch, to the state of the harvest in neighboring districts and to what were the hopes for the coming winter. Already the ground was covered with the withered brown leaves of the chestnut trees. But the sun of that late summer day made one a little weary.

In his aimless wandering about Raphael suddenly saw a group of men who were in the act of striking a bargain. One was a peasant in a dark-blue, long blouse, whom he knew well. It was Black Johann from the Bruder farm in Uhlingen. By a short rope he held a calf, a handsome brindled creature, which was the object of the trading. Near him stood little Menke

Weiler, from home, on his short legs, his hat on the back of his head and holding out his hand to the peasant. And behind Menke stood, with his back turned, as though the whole thing did not concern him, the latter's cousin, Josel, who resembled him astonishingly.

When the peasant caught sight of Raphael he called him to come nearer: "You've come at the right moment. You tell them whether this handsome beastie isn't worth seven Napoleons? He wants to give me only five!"

Now Raphael did approach. But before he could say a word and in spite of the fact that such estimates by a third party were usual and although Raphael had driven many common bargains with the man, Menke cried out abruptly, evidently fearing that Raphael would agree with Johann:

"What do you need him for? Let him mind his own business!"

This was not Menke's good day. For at that moment Josel, who seemed not to have paid any attention, swung around and said to his cousin:

"Bind the bargain, *gaulem,* you idiot. The creature is worth it!"

And so those two, the peasant and Menke, sealed the bargain with a resounding handclasp.

"But he's got to stand us a little treat at the 'Stag'; that's part of it," Johann added.

"Well, seeing that it's you, Johann," Menke agreed.

Raphael had gone on. For it was a sore blow to him that Menke had repudiated his judgment. Did the man already know? It must be so. Were they already

thrusting him aside? For he had failed to hear Menke
calling out to him that now when his business was
completed, they might drive home together.

Ah, he shouldn't have gone away upon receiving
the letter. He shouldn't have walked so far during
these penitential days. His father, of blessed memory,
had never performed the slightest work nor walked
any distance during this period. Neither, of course,
had his grandfather done so. Yet he hadn't really
willed this wandering. He had merely withdrawn
himself. He had had no definite goal.

He walked back at once and on foot. A plan had
occurred to him, a notion, as it were, toward redemption, the only possible thing to do. At home, they had,
as they did annually, prepared the *kappores* rooster
for *Erev Yaum Kippur*. This time, as always, it was
a small, young, little cock. He determined to purchase
this time a full grown rooster, as handsome a one as
possible, from the Spanish flock on the Erlen farm
in Uhlingen and, in addition, a handsome hen for
Recha.

To be sure, the peasants were astonished to see the
rich Raphael Baer, who generally bought only cattle,
turn up today in his own person to buy a couple of
fowl. At first they thought he was joking. In the end,
however, they gave him the bird which he chose,
although they had not intended to sell it, because
he refused to bargain and paid the very high price
they demanded. It was the handsomest cock which
walked proudly among the hens of the chicken run;
his plumage was steel blue; his tailfeathers, held
proudly aloft, were of a golden brown; his comb and

feet were scarlet. Next Raphael bought a big, snow-white Leghorn hen. For it, too, he paid the high price demanded. They wondered what had gotten into Raphael Baer that he should in his own person carry home a couple of fowl. On other occasions he did not even accompany the cattle he bought, but had them driven home by a manservant. He demanded a covered basket and put the fowl into it, promising to send it back. Holding it on his arm he left the farmstead. The peasants looked after him. All day long they discussed the profitable trade they had driven and the fact that Baer had himself walked off with the heavy basket. Also, they could not but observe his strange and silent behavior, such as they had not observed in him before.

On his way home, a quarter of an hour before reaching his town, he had to pass the *Kever Ovos,* the Jewish cemetery, which was situated on a flat hill. And although, as was customary at this period, Raphael had visited the graves of his fathers a few days before and had spoken the appropriate prayers, while here and there other members of the *kehilla* stood lost in memory and thus were deeply reunited with their fathers and mothers; nevertheless he was impelled to go in once more. He set down the basket in the grass. Then he entered by the sturdy, weathered wooden gate into the consecrated space, which was surrounded by a hedge of beech trees, still resonant with the voices of birds.

The scene was still a summery one. A group of broad, tall linden trees were still green with leaves and bent their branches low. Only a few wild flowers were left, but here and there the red heads of poppies still appeared among the evergreens and the grass. The headstones, unpretentiously hewn of weather-beaten sandstone, bore in the letters of the holy language, the names of all those who were now living in the little town. The same names were always repeated. And the sun shone brightly upon him as he stood in deep meditation and sought an inner redemption through communing with his forebears. He prayed and then fell into a long silence. And although it did him good to be among the dead here and feel that they were still alive, yet he did not feel liberated from his burden. He must put his hope in the sacrificial act.

Recha received him with rude excited words. She was suddenly ashamed to see her husband cross the public street with a poultry basket on his arm. Yet he managed to say calmly:

"These are the *kappores* birds. We need that kind this year in view of what has happened. The little ones aren't good enough."

"And two of them?" she asked. "Haven't we got enough?"

"Two," he replied. "I've got to swing yours also for you. A deep expiation is to be performed!"

She went on scolding about the extravagance. Didn't they have the little rooster and wasn't that enough? And she went on and on until night fell. And so the old peacelessness began again. Unmotivatedly she went on to scold and complain of all the things, irrespective of the immediate event, which she had recently restrained herself from mentioning.

Thus, for instance, she asked what had become of her own trip to Baden-Baden which he had promised her. He was evidently a man whose word was not to be trusted. And so she went on and on.

He did not answer her. He merely looked at her and then took the two fowl and placed them in a special compartment of the chicken house and fed them. For these birds were to be sacrificed in expiation of his own sin and of the sin of his wife for whom he was responsible according to immemorial pious usage.

The consciousness of his great sin, his disobedience to the Holy Law which had caused the death of a fellow Jew, as he was bound to believe, and which, though caused by his wife, had become more and more, as it were, his very own, increased the despair of that disharmony which had so long grown between them and for which there was now no help on earth. Both the sin and the discord worked in him like a living thing. In great dread he kept from all others what the letter had told him. But he was also torn by apprehension, lest the news reach the *kehilla* from some other quarter and so complete his moral destruction. Night brought him no sleep nor even repose of the body. How should he not attempt somehow to achieve redemption, since the death of poor Debele made it impossible for him to obtain forgiveness, which was granted to all the others on the Day of Judgment? For they could right whatever wrongs they had committed, as our Holy Law demands. Nor was that all. The dead man had cursed him in addition. How else than as the fulfillment of that curse could

he interpret the letter which he had caused to be
sent?

In the early dawn of *Erev Yaum Kippur*, when
Raphael came from *shul* after *Shacharis*, he fetched
the cock and the hen out of the chicken house and,
with one bird under each arm, went into the dim
kitchen where Recha was waiting. And while Recha
pressed the hen against her body, Raphael took the
rooster with his left hand by the feet and swung it
above his head again and again, after he had spoken
the prescribed words: "Let this be my expiation, *my*
expiation. . . ." He spoke with deep passion; indeed,
he cried it out aloud, as though it must surely be
heard.

Then Recha handed him the hen and he swung it
above his head for her and besought that her sacrifice
be acceptable. And she stood there with Jachet beside
her, awe-struck by this mysterious action—and all the
ancients of the centuries seemed to be in the room with
them.

When this prescribed and immemorial act had been
completed, Raphael, himself, once more took the two
birds, put them in the basket and, even before breakfast, took them to Salme, the *schauchet*, to be ritually
slaughtered. And Recha, though against her will, took
over the task which she usually assigned to Jachet.
She plucked the birds and took their entrails out.
Raphael watched her to be sure that no observance was
omitted. For the entrails, the heart, the liver, and the
numerous yolks of the unlaid eggs were thrown out of
the window into the yard for the gray cat who imme-

diately attacked the food with her eager skillful paws,
while a few fearless chickens came up and began to
pick. He, himself, thereupon, took the rooster to the
poor, neglected Mendele Weil, the most wretched
member of the *kehilla*, who lived in an attic in the
house of Shmul. He bade Recha take the hen to
Breindel, the widow of the former *shamus* Stern, who
had four children and who had been permitted to continue to live in a little house next door to the synagogue which belonged to the *kehilla*. But when
Raphael turned his back, she sent Jachet on the errand.

The day passed in that mood of pious preparation
which the Law demands. But toward noon they suddenly heard steps on the stairs and also voices and,
when the door opened, in came Avrohom Meyer and
Elias Gump. Cheerfully they approached Raphael
who was alone in the living room. After he had bidden
them to sit down he asked:

"How do I merit the *koved* to your visit on *Erev
Yaum Kippur?*"

It was Elias who spoke. "You will be a little surprised but indeed we come to do you *koved*. As you
know, our *Parnes* will resign in six months. And since
we understand that he would be too old to perform his
duties in any event, we determined to offer the
office to you. Your business leaves you enough time
and we all have confidence in you. Surely you will
not refuse."

It was Elias Gump, as a matter of fact, who had
proposed this move. Gump had the right feeling for
his friend's condition. Long discussions and even
opposition on the part of Michel Bloch had taken

place. But the majority had decided to prove to him even before the day of expiation, that he was as highly esteemed as ever. For, even had he not been as guiltless as he actually was, they would have judged him leniently. For it is not to be denied that those find forgiveness and extenuation among their fellows most easily who are distinguished among them by possessions and money. Yet these two who had come were sincerely Raphael's friends.

Raphael's reply was: "No, I cannot accept, honored as I feel. And I thank you, but I cannot tell you the reason."

Avrohom said: "Maybe we know something about the reason, but that doesn't matter and has nothing to do with it. Say yes, Raphael!"

In the meantime Recha had entered. She had been listening from the bedroom. She saluted the gentlemen and declared:

"If I may say anything, being his wife, I would say that he ought to accept."

But Raphael declared: "This is exclusively my business. I cannot accept because I cannot assume the responsibility and because I am not fit. Let us hear no more. I am grateful to you, Avrohom and Elias, and grateful to the others. Tell them so and tell them I will not forget this."

He shook hands with the two *balabatim* who also took their leave of Recha. She accompanied them to the door and said in a low voice:

"I'll try to persuade him."

Elias replied: "That will do little good, as I know him and the situation."

But when Recha returned to the room, she could not restrain herself from muttering the word *"shle-mihl."* Raphael simply turned his back on her. In utter silence they afterwards sat at their table to partake of the last meal before the fast. How much easier it would have been, if Recha had not been cursed with barrenness and if they had had children in whom to rejoice and whom to bless! But such is destiny, from the very beginning; joy and grief, guilt and redemption.

During the long day of expiation they both stood in the *shul* with their fellows. Raphael did not once leave the sacred precinct, nor did he once during all those hours look up to where his wife was watching him against the balustrade. He waited until, after the *Neila* service, darkness fell in front of the tall windows —bent deep over the stout, stained book, which the hands of his fathers had leafed through, on which their eyes had rested during years and during decades and which smelled of ancient paper and of the candles which had melted above it from morning to evening many times and on many days, such as this day. From dawn to the appearance of the first star he stood in the white shroud of expiation and did not sit down. He wanted to chastise himself, weary as he grew without food or drink. He wanted to seek forgiveness for what oppressed him and what no one observed beyond his outward bearing. And again and again he beat his breast passionately. The friends who were afraid for him hoped that this day would bring him peace from what oppressed him. But evening came and they chanted the last chant and the *shofar* was sounded for the last time, proclaiming final forgiveness to all. But Raphael had found no forgiveness and his soul had not been blessed.

Had he not just read once more in this old book the words of the prophet: "If thou seest one who is naked, clothe him. . . ." And what had he been guilty of? Not only had he not clothed Debele but he had suffered him to be driven forth, a wandering beggar, who had no place in the community. And had he not for long, even before the letter came, had a vision of him wandering about without food, without a roof over his head, perhaps freezing in the unsheltered night?

Yes, on this day it had been decided that there was no way out for Raphael. Nor was he comforted by the festive period of *Succaus,* when men seek hope again and serenity in their confidence in the renewal of nature and of the earth which brings fruits and nour-ishment for the winter. He stood with the others beside the great spring with its long iron pipes from which water streamed into the trough for cattle and men. It was situated near his house. But when the other Jews discussed the events of the day and teased each other and delighted in the festive tranquility of this day, so free of care, before they went to pray in the *shul,* he merely listened. It seemed to him that none of these things meant anything to him anymore, as though he were a stranger and had no longer any part in the in-terests of humanity. Yet all of them tried to show him that he belonged to them, as always before. Perhaps he could have liberated himself if it had been spring-time, if the winter had not been approaching; perhaps the sun of summer with its light and warmth could have penetrated his soul with healing. For we are indeed allied to the coursing of the constellations which God has created for us and perceive the influence of nearness and distance, of cloud and rain and wind and warmth and snow and frost, and of the rising of the sap in man and beast and plant, and the alternation of melancholy and serenity.

Like dragging steps from afar, Raphael heard one evening, shortly after *Succaus,* the rain fall on the flagstones of the street. And it went on raining endlessly, week after week. In order not to have to look out on the street, he now often sat alone in a back room from which nothing but the nearby roofs were visible. Continuously the water flowed over them; for days on end Raphael and Recha exchanged no word.

Winter came next, a winter without snow. But an iron frost hung disconsolately and gray among the houses, and the people of the little town were quite cut off from the world.

Once more it had been attempted to persuade him to become *Parnes* and it had been insisted that the very *yichus,* the honor of his family, demanded it of him.

"You owe it to your *ovaus avauseinu,* above all, to your father," the old *Parnes* Bernheim, whom they had commissioned to see him, had argued. But his reply had been: "Precisely on their account I dare not accept; just that would make the *avere* still greater!"

"What *avere?*" the aged man asked him. He wanted to calm him and pretended not to know. And, in fact, how could he have understood what the issue really

was? Raphael, who sat at the table, supported his forehead on his hand. At first he had been silent. Then
he had explained:

"The kind of sin that one can not get rid of ever."

And if a contemporary were to object that that for
which Raphael blamed himself was hardly so serious,
and that in any event there was no need for him to
feel so burdened on account of the circumstances
which we know, this may be true enough for the contemporary who asks the question. But we are bound
to reply that all this came to pass far longer than fifty
years ago when our fathers, at least in our part of the
country, still preserved the ancient faith and their
trust in God's might and consequently felt the obligation to obey the prescriptions of Him, blessed be His
Name, to the minutest detail and that they were cor-
respondingly careful not to transgress the most important laws. Nor should it be forgotten that we carry
the burden of our forefathers, of their lives, whether
they were good or evil, of their sins and beneficent
deeds—most heavily, indeed, of their sins; for their
blood flows in us; and we must not forget that Raphael's had come to him not only from his father, but
also from his mother.

The monotony of those wintry days in the small
town weighed heavily upon Raphael. He had never
felt that in the same measure. Always the same people,
always the same daily routine. He scarcely derived any
comfort even from the *Shabbos* when he had to appear among the others in *shul*. The alternation of its
festiveness and rest after the activity of the week did
him little good. For, on the one hand, he was in-

hibited from the demands of daily life so that the day
of rest meant little to him, and, on the other hand, he
found it difficult to endure the friendliness of his
fellows, because he felt guilty, whether they approved
of him or not. Like each one of us, he carried his own
law within him. Hitherto he had avoided visiting the
room under the roof, in which Debele had lived so
long. Late one November afternoon, after he had sat
a while at the window of his living room and looked
silently into the empty street and had just completed
his *Minchah* prayer, he suddenly arose, went up the
dark stairs and lingered for a moment in front of that
rude door. A remnant of gray light shone through an
attic window. The doorknob stuck. It had not been
used for long. It opened with great difficulty; when
finally it did open with a jolt, it frightened him. The
chill of the long uninhabited room hit him squarely
and the sense of its loneliness overcame him. There
was the empty bed, without pillows or coverlet; the
chair stood in the middle of the room quite as though
someone had just arisen from it. What did Raphael
want here? What did he seek? He took a few paces
forward. Since he had come from the warm living
room he shivered in this place, of which the ceiling
consisted of the bricks of the roof. And suddenly it
seemed to him that he was hearing a wracking small
cough and thereafter a voice very definitely. But he
did not grasp the words which that voice uttered. Yet
he knew that they were addressed to him; and from
whom could they come except from him who had
been driven forth, since no one else had dwelt in this

place? In sudden terror he fled and banged the door behind him so that the whole house shook.

Meanwhile Recha had remained given over to the sordid interests that seemed important to her: the chaffering over every farthing, the reluctance to part with even that which the necessity of every day demanded. And she had not observed that Raphael was wholly changed from what he once was and totally alienated from her; that, in fact, he led a new, strange existence, which separated him more and more, not only from her, but from everything which had once seemed of import even to him.

And so she was wholly unprepared when one evening, shortly before *Chanuka*, her maid Jachet, who was about to go to bed in her room, came screaming down the stairs, a flickering lamp in her hand, and cried out: "Raphel, Raphel," and wept aloud and could do nothing but repeat again and again: "Your husband —upstairs—your husband!" And Recha, who had been waiting for him because he had stepped out for a moment, and herself was about to enter their common bedroom, tore the lamp from Jachet's hand and mounted the stairway to the attic. There she found her husband, half sitting on a projection of the wall immediately beneath the beam of the roof, from which the spider webs hung down. And she also found a long rope of hemp which they had used to lead the cows from their stable. There he sat. His face was peaceful but rigid, and he was dead.

Now we know that little else is so great a *Chilul Hashem* as when a pious man among us can no longer

redeem himself through prayer and trust in the
Almighty, blessed be His Name, and himself ex-
tinguishes the breath of life that has been granted
him. But who of us shall decide why Raphael had not
been granted from the beginning more courage and
serenity and spiritual power, wherewith to withstand
the heaviness of his human lot?

Raphael had long been taken to the *Kever Ovos*.
For weeks the snow had gathered on his grave. At last
Recha recovered from a nervous breakdown. She had
herself been at death's door.

Therefore she had not even, as she should have
done, been able to sit *shivo* on a low stool for the
first week of mourning. The women of the *kehilla* had
nursed her and, indeed, a very stream of compassion
and dread had arisen during these long winter months
which had produced these tragic events and had
demonstrated once more how subject we are to the
great mysterious working of Him who is above us,
without understanding His aims and Whose ultimate
goodness we must trust. And they all came to console
her, each in his own fashion.

Michel Bloch, for instance, sat with her and told
her, one mustn't forget that, a great many years ago,
Raphael's uncle had taken his own life; if he was not
mistaken it had happened repeatedly on that side of
the family.

On another day Elias Gump sat opposite her at the
table for a long while. But he seemed unable to utter
a single word. He only once raised his hand from his
knee in a gesture which Recha understood very well.

Silently he left the mourner after having pressed her
hand.

The midwife Lizzie came and asked, if there were
anything she could do. Meaning to console Recha she
told her how, not very long ago, Raphael had complained to her concerning his childlessness. Perhaps
that had been the source of his despair. To discuss
that was, of course, her business.

In the end everybody agreed that he needn't have
done this deed! Yet how could they presume to judge,
seeing that we never know what goes on within the
soul of another or how a heart is shaken and suffers
under the evil and difficult things it is called upon to
endure.

And although Recha was so made as we have delineated her, yet now the *Yeizer Hora* was repressed,
if not indeed conquered, because it had been shown
her how one dare not challenge the infinite, incomprehensible power above, and because she learned the
meaning of that dark word: too late. She recognized
at last what she had lost.

How cruelly she suffered now because no children
had been given her, that she had no sons who during
the year of mourning could perform the sacred duty
of saying *Kaddish* for their father and thus bear witness for him to God and man and cause his name to
be remembered. Thus for a whole year she had the
chazan Jehuda say *Kaddish* and read from the Holy
Books every *Shabbos* in the rooms in which she had
lived with Raphael so long. And the people of the
community joined the *chazan* and commemorated the
dead. And she found no difficulty in paying the fees

demanded for this pious service. And in their bedroom, on the table beside his bed, there burned the
whole year long the memorial light: a little wick
steeped in oil in a glass which reminded her of him
during every hour of the day and the night. And on
the anniversary of his death she arranged, as is right
and proper, for a *minyan* to meet, and to continue to
do so on every anniversary of his death.

In the service of his memory her whole life was
transformed. She acted as though he were still with
her. On *Erev Shabbos,* when she blessed the candles,
the table was always set for two; and she did this for
many years, since she lived to a great age.

And during this long period she achieved a new
and other life, dedicated to the memory of her husband whom she now recognized in the purity of his
character. Repentance was in her and insight and
expiation. She sought to be what he would have
wanted her to be according to his character which only
now, as from afar, she saw clearly. And since he was
no longer there to contradict her, a thing she could
not bear, it was easy for her now to transform herself.

She visited his grave during the first winter, when
it was still a mound of barren brown earth and un-
cared for, as is customary during the first year. And
she continued to come in spring and in summer and in
autumn and recited the prayers and blessings.

And when the first year had passed, she caused a
matzeivo of plastic sandstone to be erected, handsome
and well designed as those of old. And a space next to
his grave was reserved for her, so that some day they
would rest together in peace. And it was clear that she

was intent upon making up for her errors, even though
Fanny Rothschild, who had an evil tongue, had tried
to spread the gossip, at first repeated by others, that
Recha did all this merely to call attention to herself.
But these slanders died down. Later it was understood
that anything is possible to the human heart, above
all, when it loves and finds the power to renounce.
And as year was added to year it was finally understood that Recha was deeply serious. For from now on
no poor man ever came to the *kehilla* to whom she did
not give sustenance. And if, on *Erev Shabbos,* a
stranger came to *shul,* he had to be her guest and none
other's. And it was understood that she would resent
having the guest taken from her and thus be robbed
of the *mitzva* which it was hers to perform. Nor did
any of these poor men leave her without being given
food until he could reach the next town. And so, in
the course of the years, that transformation in her became known among all who were wanderers in our
part of the country, whether merely pious old people
or else beggars or peddlers with their poor little wares,
and none left her door uncomforted. And because this
was noised abroad, there were sent her from cities far
away or from villages pious people with untrimmed
beards and *paiyes,* who dwelt in her house and prayed
for him who was dead so long. Thus she became the
typical widow of the little town, in black dress and a
cap with little ribbons and came to be, as it were, a
mother to all.

She had been shy of touching Raphael's clothes and
had let them hang in the wardrobe for long after his
passing. But one day of winter, when snow and rain

mingled in the streets, so that people stayed indoors,
a poor man had come to her door and begged for a
pair of shoes. She had seen that his coat was thin and
that his pale hands were trembling. She had gone to
the wardrobe and had taken one of Raphael's suits
and given it to the poor man. For time had gradually
wrought upon her, so that her loneliness no longer
prevented her from touching Raphael's possessions.
Her feelings had changed toward both him and toward
the visible remains and memorials of his life.

He, to whom she had given this gift, was almost
overcome and said:

"I can't accept that." Yet he took the garment and
held it up before him and felt the fabric and was as
happy as a beggar can be. He put his hand into a
pocket of the coat and found a paper, a letter, which
he gave to his benefactress. She read it and fell into
a chair. And she wept. For it was that forged letter
which Raphael had received so long ago from the supposed comrade of Debele. And it became clear to her
what her husband must have suffered and what had
at last seemed unbearable to him. And only now did
she gain a true insight into her husband's fate; for
she had long known, as everyone else in town, that
David Levy was actually with his family in Kuppenheim and served it and had both bed and bread.

And when the beggar had left her house, she went,
still silently weeping, to Elias Gump, who had long
been *Parnes* now, and told him the story and begged
him now, that her vision was clear, to write to the
Kuppenheims and beseech Debele to come back. He
was to live with her and to receive food and drink

from her as long as he would, even to the end of his days.

But this was not so simple. Debele had a good memory and the least among us, having been made in the image of the Lord, has his bit of pride. So it still stuck in him how he had been humiliated by Recha Baer. He was less resentful of her having driven him out than of the fact that she had often been *mevayesh* toward him, that is to say, had put him to shame in his defencelessness. In addition, he had no certain knowledge of what had happened in the meantime and how greatly Recha had changed. And so he replied, not accepting the offer at once, nor refusing. He said he would come only if Recha gave him the written assurance that it was her wish that he dwell with her without payment and that he be paid for his trip, for he was not coming for his own sake. In truth he was glad, because his kinsmen merely tolerated him and made him feel his dependence sorely. All his requests were granted and on a certain day he was back in the little town. And he, who had long given up hoping for anything, recovered his confidence and led a pious Jewish life.

At first, of course, it wasn't easy to return to that house with its peculiar odor and to be in constant contact with the woman of whom he had such disagreeable memories; and during the first weeks he sometimes caught himself sneaking through the hallway on his toes, so as not to be heard and scolded. But soon he recognized the fact that not only did she need him for the expiation of her sin and to ease her soul of what she had done to him through her greed, but that she had actually undergone a transformation and had become a different human being.

Thus he lived for many a year in that house by the fountain and belonged once more to the community and joined those who prayed on *Yahrzeit* days and on other occasions. And so it came about that they appointed him *shamus*. He kept the *shul* clean and formally handed the *chazan* the *Kiddush* cup and distributed the *mitzvaus* among those who had been called up to the *Tauro*; and on the *Selichaus* days went from house to house to summon the men to early prayers; and, of course, he was always present when *Kaddish* was said for Raphael.

As the years passed, Recha established a renewed and ever more familiar relationship with him who lived in apotheosis in her heart. She practiced all the commands of our teaching to the last minute observance. She omitted nothing. Yet, in the end, even this did not suffice her.

That souvenir case with its shells which he had once brought her from Badenweiler so many, many years ago, had now been standing for long on her bedside table. She guarded it like a sacred object. In it she kept the things that Raphael had had in daily use: his red velvet, gold embroidered *tefillin* bag and the *tefillin* themselves; his marriage ring and the flat watch and woven chain and the charm with its red stone which he had inherited from his father; also his purse of worn leather which his hands had touched daily and hourly. At first she had not dared to open it. When she had done so after many months she found in it sundry silver coins and an old, golden Napoleon.

She did not use the money; she let it stay there, keeping it for some future, unknown purpose.

The little key of the box she wore attached to a silk ribbon around her neck. Every morning she opened the box and took out the *tefillin* and unrolled the straps which had so often been about his forehead and his arm and which still faintly smelled of him. She touched the *tefillin* and let the straps glide through her fingers and put them back into the box. And this she did on every morning through the long years.

And often one saw her on the way to *Kever Ovos,* whether it was winter or summer or whether the leaves fluttered over the graves in the autumnal wind. On summer days she was seen almost at dawn hurrying through the street as always with a lock of hair, now gray, escaping from her cap. Then one man in his doorway would say to his neighbor:

"There is Rechele going to see Raphael." And even some said so who had never known him.

And from early morning until evening she remained there on that piece of earth which was separated only imperfectly from the neighboring field of wheat with its corn flowers and its poppies over which swept the pure wind of the season. She probably did not know what it was that moved her so and united her ever more deeply to her beloved when she sat by his grave which was now covered with an evergreen plant bearing delicate blue flowers, and when the nearby linden trees were loud with bees, mild humming voices of fruitfulness and immortality, and when the fledgling finches threw over the scene the pattern of their fluting. Thus she sat for many hours and sometimes

watched a golden brown bee working its way into a
favorite clump of blossoms; or else she gazed into the
deep blue of the sky in which a little white cloud
floated. And when thus a gentle weeping overcame
her, it was no longer a painful one but mildly sacrificial in its quality.

On such occasions one often observed Debele passing by the graveyard as if by chance and peering over
the hedges without disturbing Recha. And whenever
he perceived anyone, whether a peasant lad from the
fields or even a youngster from the *kehilla*, tempted
to taunt the woman who had now become strange and
eerie to them all, it would come to pass that he would
reprove such an one with harsh words and explain to
him the blasphemous thing he was doing. Truly, he
called it blaspheming God and fell into a great rage
until that other was silenced.

THE BROTHER

A Tale of the First Great War

I Samuel 18.1

It was our old comrade Wangen who, not long ago, told the three of us what is related here. He and ourselves were the only ones living in this city who had belonged at the end of the war to a certain regiment. And we have been meeting from time to time. It is, in addition, important to observe that it was not until now that Wangen felt able to speak of these things.

If you ask me, he began by saying, which was the worst day that I experienced during my almost forty months with the front line troops, I am bound to tell you that it was not those two days during which, in a little huddle of mud near Souchez, my comrades and I held a position against Senegalese Negroes with a single machine gun, while every five minutes, with a malevolent regularity, every five minutes during two

183

days and nights, a heavy shell made us its target, because we were definitely seen from the other side and the shells hit a little nearer or a little farther and finally I was half buried in the crater of one—no, in spite of everything, these were not the worst hours, when I consider the whole situation and in spite of the fact that the souvenir of those days is still in my left arm; nor were the worst those other hours when, at Korytnica, we were exposed to the fire of numerous Russian machine guns which faced us in a little wood and were ordered to proceed without any protection or means of resistance and heard our comrades here and there scream in the throes of death; neither this nor many other experiences were the most difficult when I compare to them the experience of a certain May day which was clear and sunny and which I will never forget.

The matter has to do with my brother, with Ernst. I've never told it before. We belonged to the same regiment in those days, an active infantry regiment with a good reputation. They called it the Green Regiment because it was the only one in the army with green shoulder straps. Now you may imagine that it was a good thing to experience battles and difficulties with one's brother in the same regiment. And, of course, there is a certain truth in that. It was a comfort to know that we were near each other, that we could see each other occasionally and thus check up on each other's wellbeing, to talk about home and about our two other brothers who were also in the field and exposed to danger. Even if one didn't belong to the same squad, each was still not far from the other. The circumstance was, upon the whole, a very favorable one and there were those who envied us. Many knew us brothers, because the regiment was pretty homogenous. It still represented our part of the country and we all still spoke the same dialect. You see, it was early in the war; it was in 1915.

This circumstance had its difficult aspects, too. I wouldn't like to go through that certain day once more. Actually it wasn't even a whole day; the thing lasted from afternoon until briefly before midnight, when it was cleared up. At that time I was the leader of a machine-gun squad—I, the simple Jewish private, Wangen.

We had been resting at some distance behind the front lines in a comfortable village. We were reserve material. Suddenly, one evening, the show started and the little clouds caused by shrapnel were so numerous on the horizon that they seemed to form a single row. We gazed westward into the sunset across the hills behind which the trenches were built. In itself it was a beautiful sight.

It was at the very moment when I was going to say farewell to my brother, whom I had been visiting in the quarters of his company in a nearby street. There the little houses stood in their gardens full of spring flowers. The alarm was being given. Ernst's company had to get ready at once and I ran as fast as I could across the fields with their small green shoots of wheat back to my own quarters, after we had bidden each other goodbye with affectionate intimacy. My company was still actually inactive; but we, too, had to be ready for the alarm. Perhaps the whole thing wouldn't

be so bad and even the seventh company, which was
my brother's, might return to its billet in the morning.

On this day, at all events, we were not ordered forward; we were restrained until some clarification
reached us as to what was really happening in the
front lines, what the enemy intended, in order to determine at what point our reinforcement would be most
useful. A curious, feverish condition came over us, the
feverishness and the tension which always set in when
one knew that something decisive was going on and
when one heard the dark thunder on the far horizon,
the meaning of which we knew well from many
battles. For by this time we were veterans. Nevertheless, we slept at last.

The new day had not wholly dawned and the streets
were still gray when I looked out through the ruined
window. At that moment the alarm was given us too;
we were to be prepared for an immediate start. Well,
that was a rapid process. In fifteen minutes at most
we were ready to march. The sombre thunder in the
West increased. It had probably eased while we were
sleeping. Now we heard immediately above us, or so
it seemed, the terrific yell of a shell from a heavy
piece of French artillery. The missile was meant for
our village and, indeed, in a moment we heard the
terrifying hit. The sound resembled that of gigantic
logs being hurled on top of each other. The splinters
fairly sang. Our village was so far behind the lines
that no hostile shell had hitherto reached it. Now
we knew that something very special lay ahead. One
of our comrades called out that the shell had been
aimed at the tall smokestack of a factory which stood

at the edge of the village beside the canal, on which the old freight lighters lay unused and rotting.

As we started on our march some of us tried to sing. In those early days we still sang occasionally. The voices had not yet fallen silent as later they did in the battles of Verdun and of the Somme. But now, too, there wasn't the proper spirit and soon we fell silent. For the tumult rose to gigantic proportions; we had not yet heard anything like it and we had the premonition of dreadful things to come. Nevertheless, we were not without confidence. We marched through the high, dewy grass of the meadows, past the bushes. The larks of the field rose singing through the air amid the thunder of the grenades, and this was a detail which clung very specially to my memory.

My comrade Vogt, who came from the Black Forest, remarked when he saw the willows with their yellow blossoms that he would rather stop now and carve himself a shepherd's pipe of a willow stalk and blow upon it and sit at home on a hill watching his goats than be a soldier here and kill Frenchmen with his machine gun. Actually he was not a trained gunner yet, but had to drag the cases of munitions. He was just twenty. Alas, two weeks later we had to bury him too. Shortly before we were relieved and before we set out for the Champagne, it was his fate to fall. He was the last one of our company whom we left behind us on the heights of Loretto. From that day on everything impressed itself in my memory with a precision unrivalled by anything else. It has stayed with me for life.

We were a small group, a squad of machine

gunners, that is to say, a dozen soldiers, accompanied
by the drivers and munition people. The leader of our
squad, Sergeant Baer, was all of a man. He proved
himself in danger, although behind the lines he sometimes rode us hard. Now he cried out to us:

"Pull yourselves together! It'll be gay today! You
fellows have almost forgotten that there's a war on!"

We had the notion that we were well hidden in the
wheat and the bushes. But when we came near the
site where our regiment was to assemble, forming part
of the right wing of our army, all hell broke loose. They
came, the howling voracious monsters of a primitive
world; and about us stood, nearer and farther, the
black trees which bore witness of the hits of the
grenades and the iron splinters with that shrill re-
pulsive tone which, you know, ploughed their way
through the air. We managed to reach the village
without anyone being hurt. On the village street
where, as we recognized at once, many more houses
had been damaged than a few days before, when we
had been here last, and in which new, deep shell
craters gaped, there met us, hurrying along in the protection of the houses, a messenger from the regiment.
One of our comrades who was from the same village
and knew him personally, called out to the messenger.
The latter cried back that the French were attacking,
that they had penetrated our first lines and that the
reserve companies who had been summoned during
the night were now being ordered to a counterattack.
These were the two companies of the second battalion,
to which the seventh company, that of my brother,
was attached.

Let me anticipate by saying that this counterattack succeeded—clearly, not without heavy losses. The combat went on for hours. Finally the whole position was retaken; we took a number of prisoners and two days later the report of the commanding general mentioned our regiment with praise.

We, ourselves, had a share in the attack, although we didn't enter the scene of actual shooting. It was toward noon when we had to move forward out of the cellar of a brewery, where we had been waiting. The conflict was at its height. There was still a question whether we would succeed; for the enemy had great superiority of artillery, although our own guns, as we soon saw, hit the trenches which had been ours the day before and which we were now supposed to take by storm. Just as we emerged from the village we saw a few hundred meters ahead of us a chain of marksmen of our infantry leaping forward between the craters and observed, too, how, now and then, one of them fell and arose no more. The shrill twittering of the French infantry and the great shell explosions surrounded us now like some dark manifestation of a catastrophe of nature. The machine guns rattled uninterruptedly and the hot sun stood high over the glittering landscape.

A little beyond the village, over toward the enemy, where the paved road divided, there stood a little chapel, just big enough to house the statue of the Madonna. There she was with the child, in a deep blue garment. I can see it to this day. A superstitious significance had attached itself to the little wayside chapel; seeing it, hitherto, always behind us, there had

been a feeling attached to it, as though it would protect us and had remained unharmed for that reason.
Whenever we hastened past, which was usually, for
very good reasons, by night, some of us had always
stopped or briefly kneeled before it and said a prayer.
It was as though Providence had preserved it. To be
sure, the wall exposed to the enemy looked like a
pockmarked face. The white plastering had crumbled
off under the accidental hits of the French infantry.

When I left the protecting houses of the village, I
had reflected: now we make a leap for the little chapel
and then lie down behind it to get our breath. A case
of munitions had to be dragged along of course, five
hundred machine gun bullets on a bandolier, no small
matter in this situation. . . . And it seemed at first as
though this plan would succeed; for I reached the
little chapel. But in this instant, suddenly, came the
howling of one of those monsters of the air, drawing
nearer by the second; I had just time, with an in-
stinctual movement, to throw myself down behind one
of the walls. Oddly enough, it was not the wall
turned away from the enemy, which was supposed to
offer a better protection; it was the wall turned to
the front, and that actually saved me. For the shell
struck not five meters from me into the hard road and
tore away, as I saw afterwards, that other wall and
swathed me in that storm of stones, dust, smoke,
sulphur and powder, with that peculiar reek which we
all, who were in the war, retain to this day. And the
statue of the Madonna had been hurled down from
her little platform and lay pitifully amid mortar and
dust. I had been saved once more.

But I had to go on. I passed by that blooming lilac bush, some of whose clusters of flowers I had plucked a few days before and had brought back to our billet. "He is quite mad," my comrades had said, "Next time he'll bring along the statue of the Madonna."

Alas, the lilac bush was in shreds. The shrapnel, of which the fragments still lay here, had stripped away the upper branches together with their blossoms which lay wretchedly in the dust. Of my comrades the last had just disappeared in the nearby connective trench which led to the position we were to occupy. Soon I joined him there and threw the case of munitions from my shoulders.

Already the wounded of the attacking companies had arrived. First aid was being given them. They were men of the third battalion and a very few of the second. Yes, of the second, too. And nearby sat three French prisoners in the sky blue uniforms which we saw for the first time.

We were not permitted to rest long. We had to move forward. Baer drew himself up: "Get up, march!" And behind each other, in single file, we stumbled and stormed through the trenches until we finally reached the place at which we were commanded to halt, namely, at the intersection of four trenches. The point of intersection was that of reserve trenches and several connective trenches which ran toward the front and must have been easily recognizable from the air. At this point we formed a reserve, ready to take its place. As I have said, this important place was known to the enemy, who seemed to have trained a battery precisely upon it. We recognized this

clearly from the succession of hits. They came from
the field artillery with its small malignant barking. As
is often providentially the case, none among us was
wounded, although our nerves found this hour hard
to bear. We looked at each other with those large, fixed
glances, which you have all seen; when the hissing
began again and we ducked down on our bellies.

And now from the trench that joined our own
emerged a new wave of our men, leaving all protection
behind them, and rushing straight amid the hostile
missiles. They were men of the second battalion and
of the sixth company, and even before they had
ventured out into the open field, one of them already
fell silently back into the trench and a little rivulet of
red ran from his forehead to his temples. We saw that,
although we did not stir. He lay flat on the bottom of
the trench; one of his comrades bent over him and took
the dead man's helmet from his head. Then swiftly
he arose and, his rifle under his arm, he leaped across
the edge of the trench.

The wild rattle of infantry fire came from the front.
And almost at once one of our messengers, bent far
forward, came rushing through the trench to summon
us. We followed him and observed that he was white
from the calcium of the ploughed up earth and that
the sweat poured down over his face. He led us into
the foremost position which they had just recovered
from the enemy and which was again completely in
control of our regiment. Soon we arrived and were
astonished. There was really, if one wanted to be truth-
ful, no trench left. In that early period we had not
yet experienced the effects of the cumulative firing of

the French artillery. From the time of this battle on it became known as drum fire. We had been accustomed to the trenches as accurately built, as though a ruler had been used. You all know how different it was later on, when we manned the craters of the shells, so that the hostile artillery, even though our position was recognized, had difficulty in aiming. But that was not so at this period. If a single target, say a portion of a trench, had been ascertained, then the situation was like that of a deer surrounded by a group of dogs. And we, the men of the infantry, had no escape open to us; we were delivered up to this raging without protection, without the possibility of a counter-blow. Our only reliance was on our comrades in charge of our artillery behind us. Nor had the very deep trenches of a later period yet come into use.

Such was the situation here. The trench that was to protect us was destroyed and level with the earth. And it was a wonder how any one remained alive. The hits had covered the ground so that no avoidance or covering seemed possible. It looked like a quarry, torn wide open between the greenery of the fields, dotted by innumerable flowers of the poppy, across which the attack had taken place the day before.

We were at once distributed among the various machine-gun crews. We relieved the men who had tended those pieces during the past two difficult days. To be sure, those whom we had relieved four days ago were no longer all there. We had five dead in our company and we did not yet know how many wounded. But three who were left from tending the gun position number five, and whose place we took, told us that their gun-layer, named Fromm—I could see him clearly with his little black pointed beard, which might have been that of a Frenchman, but actually he was a Jew, too—when he had been shot through both legs and had lain there for hours with his face growing more and more yellow, had murmured to himself: "Am I not going to be delivered, not going to be delivered?" He had said: "delivered" and not relieved. In his exhaustion he had not been able to guide his tongue any longer. He had been, I agreed with the men, a very kindly person.

And so we took up our position behind the guns, one by day and two by night. Next to us there were, in addition, infantry men who gazed from behind their cover across the poppied field into the threatening horizon. Slowly we began to rebuild the trench, to connect the holes and craters with each other. This meant a good deal of calling back and forth among us and of recounting a good deal of what had taken place. The first company had stood pat at the left wing of the regiment and had done so vigorously that, as our Sergeant Mehl told us, the counterattack against the enemy, who had occupied our position, could take place. And now we had succeeded. But what losses we had suffered! How many were missing? It seemed shameful, too, that nearly a whole company had been taken prisoner, although the men had not given themselves up until they had been totally surrounded and although we, too, had taken hundreds of enemy prisoners. A number of them still stood around with terror and dust and sweat upon their faces. Many lay upon the chalkstone, its whiteness stained red with their blood. And the tales went on and on so that the myth of this battle began to be formed.

No one seemed to know where the seventh company was and what it had experienced. I asked in vain. Unfamiliar troops had come to supply our losses, so that our regiment was split into alien parts. We tried to get our bearings. There were artillery observers, scouts of the armaments behind us who took advantage of a pause in the battle. The enemy in face of us had first to get accustomed to his new position. He seemed abashed, since his conquering mood had been turned into the reverse. But at our left, in the division that bordered our own, the noise of battle bubbled and hissed and thunder seemed to break out from the forest to the south of us.

We felt as though we were completely lifted out of the context of our lives. We had left behind us our old modes of being in this atmosphere of battle, which is a thing unique. We were other men.

And where was my brother? What had he experienced? For the moment I was still full of confidence. Nothing untoward had yet happened to either of us nor to two other brothers who had for long shared the menace of these battles. The mystic chain, the fated binding of our little group had not yet been broken at any point. Tragedy could arise at any moment.

The little Alsatian soldier, Striegel, when he heard me ask after my brother, said: "I'm sure he's all right. In his squad they really look after each other." Striegel assumed a paternal attitude toward us all. On his farm at home he had three children.

"How can they take care of each other when the grenades fly and the iron splinters hiss?"

And yet his words quieted me. I took up my position while my comrades, assigned to the same gun, sat on boards with which they had covered a crater. It was very hot; the sunlight quivered over the field. Next to us was a deep gallery of trench, the only one left. In it lay three company leaders; the leader of our own, of the second, and of the third. The latter had really no business to be here; his company was stationed at a considerable distance, but there was no protection over there. He did not leave this place all day long, but just cried out his commands. He had been quite a fine fellow in the garrison at home. Everyone had known him as an excellent athlete, horseman and skirt-chaser. But he loved life too well. The leader of our company, Asmus, was a different sort, even though I disliked him on account of a matter that doesn't fit into this story. He had that morning taken part in a hand-to-hand fight, carrying hand grenades; he had rushed from one machine-gun to another to make sure that everything was in order.

What was my brother doing now? Perhaps he was doing guard duty, obliged suddenly to duck down when a missile came or threatened through the air. Perhaps he suffered from thirst and from weariness. Where had they lain that night? Perhaps he had had no sleep while I had still been resting in our billet. He was young, younger than I, and had always in earlier years been a little frail. And now he had had to proceed into that storm of danger. How many eyes among

the enemy had had him as their aim? Had he suffered
from fear? He was brave by nature. Once in the
trench a comrade, Roll, had had to warn him: "You
get right in the dirt with your nose or I'll write your
mother!" He was a peasant-lad from the village next to
our own—and his chum. The anecdote had been repeated later. But perhaps now Ernst had not been able
to escape the nervous terrors from which we all suffered in hours like these. . . . Was he still alive? At
last that thought struck home. Perhaps he lay somewhere wounded, helpless, not yet found. These
thoughts must be subdued. The sun was shining; the
larks were still vibrating invisibly high in the air; it
was unthinkable that he was no longer in the light.

From beyond the woods of Bouvigny, behind the
hill of Loretto, came once again the well-aimed big
shells. The crashes beside us tore at our nerves, although our success had given us additional courage.
Many men ran forward through the trench, through
the holes, over the boards and timber that lay in all
directions.

Lieutenant Blattner of the seventh company turned
up. Now we would get information. When I saw him
it was like a message from home in this alien world.
Our father, who had long been dead, had known him.
He was the oldest soldier in the regiment and the
oldest officer of all. He had volunteered for service, a
big man with youthful eyes under his gray hair. He
saw me and stood still as I, my eyes turned to the
enemy, as was proper for me, stood at attention in
order to report.

"How are things going here?" he asked cheerfully.

"Very well, Lieutenant, but I know nothing about my brother."

"I wasn't with the Seventh myself; I was commanded for staff duty. All that I know is that the company suffered heavy losses."

"Would you have the kindness to inquire, when you have the chance to do so? I would be so grateful."

"Of course I will. I'll be back here in about an hour; then I'll be able to give you a report." He gave me his hand.

I stared unseeing. There had been heavy losses. What would that mean: heavy losses? If the company commander had already reported that to regimental headquarters, it must have been pretty bad. Dead and wounded to the number of fifty, an hundred, half of the company, that's what was called heavy losses. How could it have been different, seeing that the company had had to storm the enemy positions without any protection? And that had been followed by the hand-to-hand fighting in the trench itself with hand grenades and bayonets and rifle butts. That's the way it must have been. It had all happened before in the battles that March. But the same comrade who had threatened to write to our mother had saved his life by taking the butt of his gun to an enemy soldier whose bayonet was already at my brother's breast. This also became an ancedote.

"I do believe I saved his life," the young peasant had said afterwards. I had to think of that now. I knew, too, that that comrade would always watch over my brother, if it were possible. But could he always be

at his side? Was he, himself, still alive? The thunder
and the hissing from the forest behind the flat hill increased. There was one hit after another; the earth
seemed to tremble. The cries for first aid increased.
We sat and waited. Something special was going on
over there.

Next to us, near the rampart, there was a square
hole thinly covered. A shell had burst into it. Three
men had been in it, guarding a box of hand grenades.
These had not exploded; a fire had broken out. I
was ordered to go to see what had happened. But I
couldn't penetrate the short connecting trench. Everything was on fire and there was a smell of singed
flesh and the sound of moaning. At that moment the
hand grenades exploded and the pressure of the air
threw me back behind the rampart. I ran back. Suddenly it occurred to us that one of our little group had
been in that hollow; it was Muench, Vogt's best friend.
When I told Vogt his face grew white and he uttered
no word. But from that moment on he ceased to be a
good soldier. He would hide in holes when he was
supposed to stand guard; he would look at one be-
seechingly, like an animal going to its death.

Then suddenly someone's voice screamed across the
tumult: "They're coming; they're coming!"

Already we saw the figures in their light-blue uniforms. They were simply there; one had not noticed
their approach; bravely they made their way forward.
Our rifles rattled. We forgot to take cover; we stood
exposed, unless we were tied to a machine gun and
took aim, openly, uninterruptedly. The machine guns
rattled and barked. Everything was forgotten except

that combat in that hour. Life was forgotten and the future. We were strange to ourselves; each one was transformed. Our eyes burned and tingled with the heat; our faces were black with smoke and we breathed with difficulty in the stench.

Slowly the enemy line was broken; gaps punctuated it; finally there were only little groups left who ran miserably up and down, uncertain whether to proceed or withdraw. Black fountains of sand spurted up among them.

Then the men at our wings came out of the trenches and cut off their retreat and many prisoners were taken. Again we had won. And we were moved by the strange passion of that unheard of adventure.

And we had sustained no losses.

And at this moment when, with my comrades, I stood there with the incomprehensible emotion of power through a common deed, Lieutenant Blattner approached. He was coming back from the seventh company. I saw him from afar. Now he would be able to tell me that he had seen Ernst and that everything was well. He approached; he was there; I stood upright and gazed at him. He passed me by. In silence he passed me by. I wanted to cry out, but I could utter no sound.

What did that mean? It couldn't be; it mustn't be. My brother Ernst. My limbs were paralyzed; my soul stood still. He must be safe. It wasn't possible that anything had happened to him. His life had just begun; he had just awakened. He was too young to be conscripted and had joined as a volunteer. And hitherto he had done his share.

*

No, it just couldn't be. Blattner had simply not seen me. That's what must have happened. Even if he wanted to keep something from me, he would have had to say something after his promise. He was a friend; he knew all about us from home. How foolish were these notions of mine and this weakness. We had gone through a lot since morning; the tension of the day had been extreme. That's why I felt this way. We'd see each other again, when we were relieved. Tomorrow, as often before, for a few days behind the front we would again be squatting in the little garden of his billet and fry potatoes and eggs and be happy to be together and talk about home and about our mother and our brothers. I didn't know about our brothers either and yet I was not so anxious about them; they were far away in other regiments and the sacred number of us had at that time not yet been broken.

Our mother! It arose in me. What would I have to tell her and how?

Dusk fell. Toward the west lay that mysterious land, unreachable and uncertain, with those people who were, not only strangers to us, but in this hour hostile and malevolent and, as it were, identified with the raging of their artillery, so that the whole world that faced us seemed to threaten. That was our feeling.

The last brightness of the sky melted into the colors of evening. A silence rose as though no tumult of battle had ever been. Only here and there, farther or nearer, a shrapnel glowed whenever a plane ventured with soft roaring high above our lines. Now we had time to reflect. No news came from anywhere. Could not Ernst have sent a message? Couldn't he have gotten through some word? The certainty of doom came upon me. How was life to go on without him? He belonged to me, to us, like an organ of our body which we needed in order to live. I had to talk to someone. There stood Striegel, the short man with the big boots.

I said: "Something has happened to my brother; I'm sure. I've heard nothing from him and the seventh company . . . !"

"Don't worry! Look, we're alive too. Nothing has happened to him; he doesn't look that way; you can always tell."

I told him the incident with Blattner. It was his opinion, too, that the lieutenant had not seen me. But he was just using empty words to console me. Soon he was depressed too. I was certain of it.

"God damn it!" he said. "We're helpless. Fromm is dead. But you could see it in his eyes. You really could. And Jenne and Rohr and Mueller, all of them from our village. The death knells at home won't stop ringing. What shall we do? Maybe none of us will see home again."

Nightfall had made him emotional. Usually he was one of the bravest. He sat down on a munition case and with his right hand repeatedly struck his thigh. His little eyes were full of kindliness.

"You've got to look for him. If only we knew where the Seventh was stationed. They had a hard time. Maybe there's nobody left." Now it was out. "God damn it, you must ask Asmus."

It didn't occur to me that my brother might only

have been wounded. I could see nothing but extremes.
Dead! Dead! Somewhere on the field amid the poppies
he was lying with a little round hole in his heart. Or
he was torn to pieces by the splinters and was huddled
in the ploughed up earth with sand in his eyes and
mouth. . . . I couldn't rid myself of these images. Yet
I couldn't imagine it possible that death had torn
asunder our sacred circle. We had always been so
united; none could be without the others. Was all that
to be destroyed? And with it our youth; our games
with the other brothers beside the lake between the
sand castles we built and the secret paths we had between the endless reeds, and the long summers in the
orchards and our first attempts to fish with rods and
our sailboat all day long going from shore to shore
under the excess of the sunlight. In autumn we would
watch the cows grazing; we were so proud of that—
when the weed fires burned on the slopes and the
bluish plums hung in the trees. Then there was winter
with our long gliding over the smooth surface of the
ice; above all, there was our sitting about the common
table at home every day, year after year, and the hearing of our mother's kindly words toward all. All this
could no longer be real without our brother. Yet all
these scenes passed before my eyes as though I, myself,
were facing my last minute when, as the saying goes,
one rehearses the whole course of one's life. Despair
came over me and, though I knew that we were making these sacrifices for our homeland, we, the members
of the Wangen family, consisting of our fathers and
grandfathers, of the men of our blood who for cen-

turies had lived and grown up there—a part of the
land even as the peasants who had been our friends—
and that we were offering this sacrifice for those very
summers and autumns and for the fruits of the soil
and of the earth in which our fathers were resting, yet
the pain at my loss was too immediate and no equi-
librium of value could yet be established between what
had been given during the centuries and that which
had just been taken away. How was I to write to my
mother and how communicate what would have to be
told? Alone she was sitting in the house and listening
out into the unknown where her sons were embattled
and had not yet experienced the tearing away of a link
from that original chain of her children. And she had
been and was full of confidence and faith. How
would she bear it? These were the thoughts that overwhelmed me.

Suddenly night had fallen. Hither and thither
flashed the searchlights, distrustfully used by both
sides. The horizon seemed still to vibrate with the
heat of combat and death. The stench of burning was
in the air. Members of the medical corps rushed up
and down. Food was brought. But no one had any
certain news of the seventh company. Only one man
thought that it was stationed at our right behind new
troops who had been sent to reinforce us.

Once I perceived that the comrades were talking
about me. I turned around and saw Striegel in their
midst. And they all looked at me.

When our company commander stopped near us on
his rounds and I gave him my report, I pulled myself
together and asked him to give me an hour's leave of

absence in order to look for my brother. He gave me permission. He knew Ernst and had often seen us together. When my watch was over, I was to go. It was correct that the Seventh was now stationed at our right wing.

Well, my watch was the two hours left until midnight. Hope arose in me again. But never had a watch seemed so long before. I seemed feverish. I cooled my wrists against the metal of the gun. And just when the period was about to end, there was a last round of shooting. The machine guns began to bark and the fiery spheres of scarlet shells hissed above us. We covered the enemy with fire. An attack was at hand. Already our Sergeant Mehl gave the command for uninterrupted firing.

Everything else was forgotten. Madly my machine gun hammered and uninterruptedly the bullets flew. But the whole thing didn't take long. Swiftly as it had begun so also it declined. Perhaps they had enough over there. Those who were to relieve me were suddenly present.

I started out toward the right. I ran through all the ramifications of our position, now on top, now through trenches. Forward, forward, even though I stumbled feverishly over boards and holes and wire. High stood a bright and tranquil moon. Sleeping men lay on the earth. Men of the medical corps were everywhere.

I asked the men who stood guard. They were still members of our regiment, but never of the seventh company. Then I came across soldiers of another regiment, but still of our division. Hope sank again. What must have been the losses of the seventh company that it had been withdrawn so far behind the front? Perhaps there was no one left.

But I continued to inquire. I fell and hurt my right hand on the wire entanglements. But I remember so vividly how I asked a man whose pipe protruded diagonally from his mouth:

"Is there a company of the Green Regiment anywhere around here?"

"Yes, around the corner there one of that company stands guard."

Now I went slowly, very slowly; I almost crept and leaned against the wall of the trench. Sweat poured from my forehead, my throat was dry and my knees trembled. I could not face the dread certainty. Had I better go back? There stood a man and peered peacefully in the blue stillness of the night; his rifle was laid on the wall of the trench. He called out: "Who goes there?"

"Member of the Green Regiment," said I. "Who are you?"

"Seventh of the Green Regiment."

"Seventh of the Green Regiment! What group?"

"Group Holzer."

That was Ernst's group. That was my brother's squad. Courage now!

"Where is Wangen?"

"In there, asleep," the man said quietly and pointed to the rear. He's in there asleep—in there asleep. Man, what are you telling me? I put my arm around his shoulder. He was a new recruit and didn't know me.

"Where is he lying?"

"Right around the corner there."

I heard snoring and I saw a tent cloth hanging in front of a square hole in the wall. I lifted it. Someone cursed. It was our comrade Roll.

"Where is Ernst?"

"Where the hell do you come from? Over there!"

Yes, there he was lying, a tall soldier, with white dust on his boots and his little cap pulled down over his eyes. He was sleeping quietly.

I took his hand and he awoke. And saw me: "You!"

For a long time we said nothing. We only felt our common blood.

He never knew what this day had meant to me on his account.

Thereafter they all recounted adventures of battle. Needless to say that Roll was the chief hero in them all. . . .

So this was for me the most difficult day of the entire war. For up to that point we had still been spared. Fate had not yet insisted upon its necessary share to equalize and justify the fact that my two other brothers or, rather, the first of them, fell in battle, whom the other had to follow, so that the sacred circle was broken. But of such things one can scarcely speak.

Wangen fell silent. In the end his voice had quivered a little and become hoarse. For, as has been said, it isn't so long ago that he told us his story; and we others, who had listened to him, felt very clearly how more and more, as his tale progressed, the breath of a great and fateful doom came over us again. And when we considered what was happening to us, the Jews of Germany, today and what had been experienced by our comrades in the days of the Great War, we perceived with deep emotion the heavy tread of history over our heads. . . .

THE SIN

What I want to tell you today is a story concerning my grandfather, of blessed memory, who was an old and very pious Jew. The story, it seems to me, has a meaning beyond the mere anecdote.

When I speak of his age that is because I only knew him as an aged, venerable and proud personality. His life was contemporary with the dawn of the nineteenth century. He was born shortly after the ending of the twenty years of war, when tranquility settled down on Europe for the following decades, indeed, for half a century, during which the Jews began to be peacefully integrated into the life of their environment and shared its speech and fate. It always moved me to realize that through him I was allied with that age which seemed to us boys in some sense an heroic one and which laid the foundations, not only for a dream, but also for a reality, in spite of everything that is happening today.

Thus his birth and my father's, of blessed memory,

who died far too soon, and my own span an entire
century; and it was one of the most moving experiences of my youth, indeed, of my whole life—which,
after all, survived the First World War and its battles
—to see my grandfather, then more than eighty years
old, arrive from his native village in order to accompany his young son, my father, to his last resting
place. For we had already long moved to the city. His
great form was still upright; his long white beard left
the shaved chin bare. We children surrounded him and
nestled against him and he uttered soft laments in
loshaun hakaudesh, as it were, to himself. Then he
laid his old hands in blessing on our young heads and
pronounced the appropriate prayers again in the holy
tongue.

But it isn't this that I wanted to relate today. Some
day I may—this and much else, which would take me
too far at the moment. Already you will perceive what
manner of man it was concerning whom the following
anecdote was truthfully related.

He was so devout that in his community not only
the Jews but also our kindly peasant neighbors gave
him a name of such extreme significance that I would
rather not record it in this place. There was no hint of
irony in this appelation; there was the expression of
high esteem, for they were all aware that it was a
true faith and a true fear of God which guided the
conduct of his life.

One day, watching the *schauchet* of the community,
Salme, slaughter a six-months-old male calf, he seemed
to observe a detail which made him doubtful of the religious validity of the action. I can't tell you exactly

what it was; perhaps the details were never communicated to me. It may be that long custom had
made Salme disregard the necessity of every detailed
prescription; perhaps he forgot to utter some necessary
prayer or benediction. These matters are not important in regard to the anecdote. Grandfather carried
his observation tacitly in his mind until at length his
conscience began to trouble him. Could he be responsible to the congregation, not to speak of God's
all-seeing eye, to subject the *kehilla* permanently to
the danger of an infraction of the religious law which
would render the meat it ate actually *treif?*

At all events, he wrote to the regional rabbi, who
lived in a neighboring village, and with all proper
respect communicated his doubts to him. The *Rav* in
question was much younger than himself, perhaps in
reality not as pious; yet to him the rabbi was a consecrated personality and his judgment the norm in all
such matters. Thus he wrote concerning what troubled
him, for his own sake and that of others and waited
for an answer.

This answer, when it came, was entirely different
from anything he had expected. After he had read the
letter he was, in a sense, more tranquil; on the other
hand, a new element of depression seemed to arise
from it. For the *Rav* asserted not only that whatever
the *schauchet* did was quite as it should be but, beyond
this, that Salme was the best *schauchet* in the whole
region and that the community, like himself, should be
very happy to have so able an official. It is needless to
say that my grandfather nourished no doubt concerning the rabbi's veracity.

Now, as I have said, my grandfather was satisfied. His new trouble arose from the great wrong that he had inflicted on Salme. By making a false accusation he had become guilty of a serious sin. Hence, when on the next *Shabbos* after *Mussaf* he left the synagogue, he stopped the *schauchet*, who always walked as though somewhat bent down by the burden of his worries, and begged the man to call on him on the following forenoon.

When, at the time appointed and suspecting nothing, the man appeared, grandfather asked him courteously to be seated and caused a bottle of the red wine of his own vineyard, which is as refreshing today as it was then, to be brought and placed on the table. He then sat down in front of the little man and offered him a pinch of snuff from his silver box and said:

"Listen, Salme, I have committed a wrong against you and I desire to beg you for forgiveness. That is why I asked you to come. Do forgive me!"

He gave the man a detailed account of what had happened and then stretched out his hand which the other took in some embarrassment; for my grandfather, of blessed memory, was known, as I have intimated, as a proud person who was on terms of intimacy with almost no one, except his two brothers. Salme then replied that the matter was of small importance. Things like that could happen and the result had been very favorable to himself since, under the circumstances, he had received the special commendation of the rabbi.

But grandfather was not satisfied: "Nevertheless,"

he said, "I did commit a sin and I am bound to make atonement for it. I beg of you that from now on you send one of your boys to me every Sunday morning for three months and I will give the boy a thaler each time. Doubtless you will be able to make good use of it."

I should add that in those days our family belonged to the wealthier group in the village. For many decades, indeed for more than a century, our fathers had driven their trade industriously and had lived frugally and had also profited from their fields and meadows and orchards and cattle. Even the father of my grandfather had been a man who, for those days, needed not to worry about material things. Heaven knows, all this has changed, you may be sure. Time has not spared us either, which is why I can tell this tale.

The little *schauchet,* with his slightly inflamed eyes and his thin, pointed little beard, had six children, which was a good many for the small trade in goats and chickens which he drove to eke out his income. Nevertheless he replied that this thing which my grandfather had determined upon was not at all necessary. In brief, he was polite. But he left the house very much pleased with the first thaler in his hand.

Needless to say, the promise was kept. Every Sunday morning during twelve weeks one of the sons of the *schauchet* came and received the gleaming silver coin. The money had a great deal more value then than now; in addition it was a symbolical coin and in this case was really worth something quite beyond its purchasing power.

And it was one of the *schauchet's* sons, who was a comrade of mine in the war, who told me the anecdote years later.

And I am glad to set it down here because I am afraid that no one among us in this age would act as my grandfather did and as many of his generation would have acted under such circumstances. This kind of people today are arrogant and cannot bear to right wrongs they have committed unless they are forced to do so, because the fear of God is no longer in them. They let their cigars hang diagonally from the corners of their mouths and utter empty words concerning justice to those who are dependent upon them. Hence my little anecdote concerns *shechita* and a sin, but also *zedoko,* namely a charitableness which is also justice.

THE FISH

Whenever Jaune, that is to say, Jonah, a name long associated with the story of a fish, went to the bank at Emmern to deposit as little as fifty francs to earn him an interest of three percent, which was high in those days, he put on his black and solemn, though quite shabby, morning coat and also put on his formal hat, green though it had grown through many years of use. For on each occasion of this kind it still seemed to him important and almost festive to consider that he had succeeded in putting money aside again. The little town, where the only bank in the region was situated, lay on the other side of the Swiss frontier, not far from Werblingen. The other Jewish people also deposited savings there. They were not forced into many expenditures and nearly all the liquid cash which they took in could be deposited in the bank. They lived on the produce of their own gardens, fields and stables. As for extravagances—well, on *Shabbos* afternoon before going to *Mincha* services,

the men would sit in the wainscoted parlor of the
inn and, amid the flies which crept along the table,
play a game of cards which is indigenous to that
region. But Jaune, unlike the others, grudged himself
even this. However careful he was, he might lose
something; in addition, he would have to pay for at
least a coffee with kirsch or for a quarter of a bottle
of Veltliner wine. He was well along in years by this
time, in his later sixties. Moreover, he was quite the
largest man in the village and had had many decades,
together with his wife Gidel, to accumulate capital
through an habitual behavior which one need not
call by the polite word thrift but could fairly call
avarice. Those two grudged themselves everything,
and everybody in the village knew it. To be sure,
they were all saving by nature, but what those two
were capable of, that was going too far. People asked
themselves what, in the end, those two lived on. Because there, in our village, where people lived so
close to each other for so many years, there were no
secrets, whether one wanted to pry or not. And so
everybody knew that Jaune and his wife, as the
mohel Rothschild once remarked, grudged themselves
the very air they breathed. That made it clear enough.
If they did have to buy something like wine for
kiddush for *Erev Shabbos* or meat and fish for the
holidays, it went without saying that they bought the
very cheapest stuff obtainable; indeed, they were satisfied with the very refuse that everyone else rejected.
For instance, no one else in the village bought the
stomach of a cow from the butcher Wolf; it was not
considered *bekoved*. But for them the butcher would

himself have had to eat this part of the animal, concerning the tastiness of which when well prepared
opinions might differ—or he would have had to sell it
to people who could eat *treif,* if on the slaughtering
days Jaune had not regularly turned up to buy the
stomach for a few farthings for Gidel and himself.

There he would come along on the village street,
holding his purchase in his hand in front of him,
slightly bent forward and regarding his cheap booty
with an air of satisfaction. Everybody was bound to
see it and to feel a touch of contempt. In the same
way, when he would haggle for half an hour with
a fishwife over two whitefishes for Friday night, trying to beat the woman down by a farthing or two,
the others, listening at their windows, or standing
beside him, would laugh with a touch of malice. For
this species of fish seemed to everybody else too cheap
to be used at the meal which ushered in the Princess
Shabbos. All these purchases Juane had to make himself. For his wife Gidel had been badly paralyzed
for a long time. All she could do was to move about,
to drag herself about, as it were, in their house. Leaving it was out of the question for her. No one remembered the last time that she had taken a walk;
but all over her part of the village her voice was
familiar. That's the way those two were. In brief,
as has been said, they stank of stinginess.

The best way to characterize Jaune is to record an
answer which he once gave to the community's
chazan, Stein, when the latter explained on a certain
occasion that, according to our Holy Law, concrete
animal sacrifices need no longer be brought, but that

it sufficed to fulfill the highest duty through prayer. Jaune's comment was: "Well, by God, we do get off cheap!"

Thus, necessarily, their store of cash increased, which made them only the more an object of laughter. People were pretty sure that they were worth not less than fifty thousand francs, though this may have been an exaggeration common in such cases. And the older they grew and the wealthier they grew, so their avarice increased too; perhaps it was because they had no love in their hearts and so the greed for money took its place.

Across the street from them, where the village began on the public road, there dwelt in an equally dignified house, the old Seligmanns. Frau Seligmann, Breindel, was Jaune's sister and so her husband Aron was his brother-in-law. These people were utterly different; they were generous and lived a good life. Nevertheless, Aron was Jaune's friend beyond the friendliness of their kinship. Yet between these two, as is common among coevals who have been accustomed from their youth on to a measure of competition, there existed a definite rivalry in certain matters.

All through the summer, up to autumn, the women fishmongers would come from beyond the mountain around the lake. It is a long trip they had to take; for hours and hours they pushed their baby carriages plaited of willow withes in front of them in which, wrapped carefuly in great, fresh leaves, they brought their fish. There were perch, striped like tigers, smooth, moss-colored tench, whitefish with their reddish fins, grayish-green pike; there were lake trout of delicate texture without the many bones which the others had and, once in a long while, there was a big brook trout, which was bought only by the very prosperous and by them only for the High Holidays.

On a certain Friday which happened to be *Erev Shevuaus,* on a sunny morning, when all the apple trees were in bloom, there stopped on the road which came down from the mountains between the first houses of the village, a certain Frau Hofer, who was a fishmonger from one of the nearby villages. Everybody knew her. She had had a three-hours' trip with her little perambulator and there she stood slightly sweating in the June sun, with her face red under her white handkerchief.

"Fish, fresh fish!" she cried in her high voice, prolonging the syllable as much as she could.

After a little while Aron Seligmann came forth from his broad house on the left side of the road as one comes from the hills. He stepped out on his stone steps under the little, green, tin roof and cried out to the fishmonger:

"Wait a minute, Frau Hofer; my wife is coming right out!"

"That's all right, Herr Seligmann!"

But Aron didn't go back into the house, although he himself never made such purchases; he considered that his wife's business. He went up to the woman's little cart.

"What kind of stuff have you got?" he asked.

"All kinds. But for you and for the holidays I've got a wonderful brook trout. It's a long time since we've caught such a fine one; it weighs four pounds."

"You don't say so! Let's see it!"

From between the broad cool leaves the woman lifted an exceptionally handsome fish and proudly held it up. The trout gleamed and its little red spots shone in the sun.

"A handsome fish; you're right! What's the price?" he asked.

"Three mark, because it's you."

At that moment a man's voice was heard from the first story of the house across the street. Although Jaune had not been able to hear exactly what was being said, yet he had a notion of what was happening; he had also seen the handsome fish and he now called out:

"What's going on? Have you got something very good, Frau Hofer?"

But before the woman could answer, Aron Seligmann informed his brother-in-law:

"It's nothing for you; it's much too expensive!"

"Well, I wouldn't ask you for the money to pay for it," Jaune answered.

"Well, I'm sure that Gidel will have her say in the matter, so far as I know," Aron said laughing and a little tactlessly, when you consider that he was a friend.

Jaune called down:

"You tell me the price of the fish, Frau Hofer!"

"Three mark," the woman repeated.

"Consider it sold!" he cried out at once. He hadn't really considered; he had called out those words, suddenly impelled by a sort of pride.

He shouldn't have done that, considering his char-

acter. He had done it out of vanity and to slap at
his brother-in-law who thought he was something
better just because he spent money more easily. On
the very stairs a confused regret came over him, and
when he was on the street, he couldn't help trying
to bargain: "You can't let me have it for less?"

"Look, you said it was a bargain!"

And so he was stuck with the expensive fish and
his sister Breindel, when she finally came downstairs
and her husband told her with a good deal of amuse-
ment what had happened, had to be satisfied with a
two pound pike. Jaune stood there and scrabbled
in his purse, which was a dried piece of swine's
bladder, and for good or ill brought out the thaler
and handed it to the woman with reluctant fingers.
Then he took the fish and, holding it in front of him
with both hands, he carried it upstairs. And it wasn't
long before one heard the screeching voice of Gidel,
his half-paralyzed wife, and one couldn't mistake the
words *meshugge* and *shlemasel*.

What were they to do with a four pound fish,
above all, with a trout that cost three mark? This was
a piece of extravagance never to be expiated. Something had to be done. They took counsel with each
other. The upshot was that, after a while and after
they had carefully looked out of the window to ascertain that no one was watching, Jaune left the house
with a little basket on his arm and hurried toward
the upper village. In the little basket reposed the
fish among a stingy little mass of grass and wrapped
in a slightly soiled cloth. Jaune was going to try to re-
sell the fish among the prosperous people in that

part of the village. He didn't conceal from himself the fact that this would be difficult. He found that he was not mistaken. For, on the one hand, the fish-mongers had visited every house and, on the other hand, even the well-to-do weren't going to buy so expensive a fish, although it was *Shevuaus*. In addition, he felt that he was making himself ridiculous. But there was Gidel to be thought of, and there was his own unconquerable avarice which made him grudge both enjoyment and expenditure. Three mark for a fish which would soon be eaten and exist no longer! It was unthinkable! He had to get rid of it. But when he tried to sell the fish to the wife of the *Parnes* Bernheim, a fat, cheerful woman, she laughed in his face even before he could really explain his errand and said:

"Since when have you become a fishmonger, Jaune?"

What was he to say? What reason was he to give? Well, it did occur to him to say:

"Gidel thinks it's too much for us two people and we know that you're expecting company over *Yontef*. I'll let you have the fish for three mark; I paid three and a half for it."

"God forbid, that's too much for us; anyhow, I'm well supplied."

And Jaune was forced to believe her, because the whole house smelled of fish with a green sauce.

So he trotted along with his fish. He called on three or four other families, but it did him no good and it was humiliating, too; and finally he had to go home without success. First he had considered whether

he shouldn't deceive Gidel and tell her the fish was
sold. But then his lie would come to her ears almost
any day, and how was he, in addition, to hide the
fish which, even at this moment, began to smell the
way a fish had no business to smell.

And so, when he came home toward noon, he had
to confess to Gidel that his attempt had failed. Whereupon away out in the street one heard the voice of
this supposedly feeble woman. Eat the fish? Were
they to eat it? How would it taste to them? It were
better to eat poison than to be guilty of such extravagance. Maybe he might still get rid of it. There
wasn't much time left; soon *Yontef* would set in and
it would be time to go to *shul*. And so he decided
to try to preserve the fish to the beginning of the
next week and then to try his luck when people had
eaten up everything that they had bought for the
holiday and when their cupboards were bare. There
was no question of course of trying to sell anything
on the morrow, which was not only *Yontef* but
Shabbos to boot. He carried the fish down into the
cellar, where onions and potatoes were stored and
where there were two empty wine kegs. To protect
the fish from the cat he weighed down the little
basket with two heavy stones.

That evening when Jaune came home from services,
his friends not only wished him Good *Yontef*, but
several asked him:

"Well, Jaune, did you sell the trout?"

They asked him again and again and finally he
said:

"Don't bother me about that fish!" Or he said: "What business is it of yours?"

And finally there was a rumor all over the place that Jaune had joined the fishmongers and ran around with a fish in a basket. For, of course, Aron, his brother-in-law, had not been able to hold his tongue. And for weeks the whole village laughed, because everybody knew about this couple and their nature.

The fish lay in the cellar and, undoubtedly, the cellar was cooler than any other place in the house. But after all it was summer and the days were bright and warm. And the fish lay for one day and then for a second day, because it was *Yontef,* and one could neither buy nor sell. Monday, however, bright and early, Jaune went into the cellar and picked up the basket and looked at the fish and smelled it too and forced himself not to be too aware of the odor. Again he hastened to the other part of the village and to Frau Bernheim who still, as he knew, had house guests and who might be happy to acquire this delicacy. Jaune thought that this was a sound idea on his part and confidently stepped into the house which was reached by a little bridge across the brook. Frau Bernheim met him as she came out of the kitchen and was drying her hands on her blue apron. He said nothing but took out the fish in order to prevent her saying that she didn't want to see it, because she was well supplied. Well, no words were needed. Before he could say anything, the woman quickly held her nose with her hand, even as it is delineated on old, old pictures, where people are shown following a corpse. The fish smelled. But it didn't smell the way

fish should smell. It smelled the way a fish smells
which has been dead out of the water for four days.

And so Jaune had to realize that there was nothing to be done. He had enough! On his long legs
he went home through the village by the garden
paths and, walking along the nettles beside the
wooden withered trellises, it suddenly occurred to
him that he had never yet confessed to Gidel how
he had come to buy the fish, how he had committed
this extravagance which he couldn't blame her for
considering a piece of madness. And the reason was
because, as soon as he had shown her the fish, she
had started to scream and scold concerning his senseless action and thereupon they had been "mad" with
each other and had not spoken. When he now entered
at the kitchen door and found her sitting on a low
stool peeling potatoes, he threw the dead fish on the
table and began screaming on his part:

"I'm through with the damned fish! Let the cat eat
it! I didn't want to buy it. But that brother-in-law
of yours was bargaining for it and he had the im-
pudence to say that the fish was too good for us. And
so I bought it to spite him!"

At last the confession was out.

The woman asked: "Did Breindel see it all?"

"Certainly, she saw and heard everything."

That calmed Gidel: "If you did it to spite them,
that's worth three mark to me. And the cat can have
her fun."

And so they took the once handsome fish, which
was a sacrifice to their avarice and to their feeling
of kinship, and threw it behind the house on the

dunghill for the cat who rejoiced in it, and they were both satisfied. . . .

This is the story of the fish. But don't laugh too self-righteously about those two. Who hasn't made a purchase from such motives? You and you and, yes, probably I, too—only out of the motive of boasting before others who are really our superiors and whose superiority we are unwilling to admit. Of course, the object in question, the sacrifice, need not be a dead fish. Sometimes it is an object of far different character. . . .

TWO MOTHERS

To my sister Lotte, in Israel

Always Frau Fradel—Aunt Fradel, as everyone called her, whether they were related to her or not—was there. Of course, she was not obliged to be what she was, namely, the most beneficent woman of the little town, if this is the right word for her. Perhaps it is too general in its meaning to describe her character. Whenever anyone needed her, she was there; and there was no need for her to give herself any importance, as everyone said, because she and her husband were among the most prosperous members of the Jewish community; and they were respected, as few others were.

The point was not that she gave money or things that could be bought with money, that she fed the hungry and clothed the naked wherever there was need. Others did that too in obedience to our holy precepts, even if not in the same generous measure. But wherever there was need of counsel or of active

227

helpfulness, she was inevitably there. It is of her that people thought, when they were at the end of their rope.

What was it exactly that she did? Well, there are many things needed that cannot be bought with money or have material value.

There was old Salme, who could hardly walk any more and who lived alone and who was taken care of only briefly every day by the dumb girl Balbine. Who was it that, on *Erev Shabbos* shortly before service, brought him wine for the *kiddush* in a little bottle and two home-baked poppy-seed rolls, summer and winter? It was Fradel. Who was it that, skillfully and with a special knife, removed the pip from the tongue of the chickens, so that they could take their nourishment again like healthy animals? It was Fradel to whom both the Jewish women and the peasant women went full of confidence, with their sick, obstinate hens under their arms. And after *havdolo,* to whom did Black Ella go—her dark hair had turned white long ago—who was full of sorrow because her children, two daughters and their husbands, neglected her in their avarice, a woman full of troubles, and brought a few farthings, sometimes twenty, sometimes only ten, which she had saved during the week, for safekeeping? And to whom did she say almost each time: "I trust you more than anyone else, Fradel. Save the money for me until they take me out to the resting place of the fathers, and buy me a *matzeivo* with it, because my daughters won't do it. God will bless you for it."

And when there was an epidemic in town, whom

did the doctors send to help the awkward people?
It might have been diphtheria among the children,
and there were as yet no specific injections to give, and
powdered sulphur had to be blown down the throats
of the little ones, not too much and not too little.
They sent for Aunt Fradel. She knew how to do
this and sundry other things and imposed these
duties upon herself according to our eternal law.

Can't you see her hastening early in summer along
the paths between the meadows, concerned and light
of foot, because she had heard that Menke Gump's
Jewish field-hand had driven the scythe into his leg?
She had said on that occasion: "It takes real clever-
ness to do anything so stupid." But she felt that
her presence was needed, just because he was a
stranger and had no one of his own in the town.
Or, on some winter day of bitter cold, when the
gray, massive clouds oppressed the little town, can't
you see her, bareheaded and with only her black
woolen shawl about her shoulders, dash around the
corner to the alley behind with a heap of faggots in her
apron? It had suddenly occurred to her that perhaps
old Salme didn't have enough wood to heat his room.

Her own household, meanwhile, was always in
order and spic-and-span. You should have seen the
pewter jugs on their shelf in the vestibule scrubbed
and shining all year long as on the day before *Pesach*,
or, above all, the brass lamp with the four arms
which hung from the ceiling.

Her own marriage to her husband Simon was a
happy one. How could it not have been? And they
had one son who had long been helpful to the father

in his cattle trade—one son and no other children, whom his mother in private moments regarded as a reward for her life as she sought to lead it.

The most important source of care to her had been for long the duty imposed on her by the situation of Hannchen Lipschitz, the old woman who occupied two attic rooms behind the synagogue. Lipschitz? You are right, that is a name which does not occur in our part of the country. No one knew where the old woman had come from. But there she was, all alone, a sort of counterpart to little old Salme. Well, her origin is not important. What everyone knew was that originally Hannchen had spoken a language which seemed to us in those days like that of our brethren who dwelt in the East of Europe and who were very pious, more so than our people deemed themselves to be. And so everyone respected her. But this was not the only reason. She was also respected from the circumstance that she had a son. No one in town had ever met him. But it had been proved that he lived and, of all places, in America. And everybody knew where he lived and the foreign name of the place had a strange and mysterious effect upon our people. The town where he lived was called Keokuk and it was situated in a state named Iowa. Keokuk and Iowa—odd, that there should be such words. And someone had once said that they were pronounced quite differently from the way they were written. But how, he didn't know either.

And all this was proved, which is the chief matter,

by the circumstance that every month there came a
letter with foreign postmarks and stamps; and this
was no ordinary letter, for it was registered and contained not only written news but each time a five dol-
lar bill. Five dollars! Everybody remarked on that to
everybody else. It is comprehensible how deeply that
impressed our people. From so far away, from America, somebody got money, enough money to live on it
for a whole month, as, indeed, Hannchen did. This
explains the respect in which Hannchen was held, as
may well be understood even today.

To her, herself, what was of greater importance
was the enclosed letter which gave her news of her
son who had now for so many years dwelt beyond
the seas.

In all likelihood he prospered. Nay, it was certain.
How else could he regularly every month send the
money, which must have been in excess of what he
needed for himself. It was said that he had been
gone more than twenty years. But he hadn't ever
married, although he had been in his early twenties
when he had emigrated. Often and often his mother
reflected on this.

This, too, everybody knew, that his name was
Heinrich; but what calling he followed remained a
mystery.

His mother knew it. But she told no one. For the
fact was that her son had *had* to emigrate, for some
reason or other, and had finally over there been ap-
prenticed to a cobbler and later had become a journeyman, but had not been able to be a merchant any

more. Hannchen was ashamed of this, although she loved him as a mother will love the child of her own flesh and blood.

The old lady, who always wore a black lace cap with a lilac velvet bow, had never read one of these letters herself. So, in a sense, what was the purpose of writing the letters? To be frank, she could neither read nor write; she had never been able to do so, aside from the circumstance that her old eyes could not have been used for this purpose anymore.

Now who was the helper in this need? Aunt Fradel, of course. For years and years, ever since the letters had come, it was she who had undertaken to read them to the lonely mother. This was a task after her own heart. Whenever one of the letters arrived, the mother sent a message to Frau Fradel, usually by one of the children who played in front of her house; and Fradel hastened to her to read her the news and also to take the money and have it exchanged by her husband, who occasionally visited one of the nearby cities of Switzerland.

To be sure, there wasn't much on the four sides of the small, ruled sheets of cheap paper. He was all right, the son wrote, and he was working. Such was always the content of the opening phrases. During the early years he had sent no money. Then one day he wrote that he was all right and that he had now established himself; he had a shoe shop of his own and would soon be able to send more dollars. But the money never did increase, so that Aunt Fradel drew her own conclusions. And it should be emphasized she never told anyone of the details

of these letters, so that, as it were, they remained quite
private to the mother. She, for her part, was now
again very proud of her son who was a merchant in
America.

Finally Fradel proposed that Harry, as the son now
called himself, be advised to address the letters directly to her. This would simplify matters. She would
then know at once when one had arrived. This would
be well because, as we have forgotten to say, she,
too, had undertaken to answer these letters. She did
not do so in her own person. Ostensibly it was his
mother who spoke to him and who gave him good
advice, sent him counsel from the little home town,
which wasn't even on the railway, out into far away
America. Aunt Fradel contributed only her handwriting.

Thus the years passed and Fradel was happy over
the part she was playing in this matter and always
thought of her own son who was at home and a well
behaved chap, and she was grateful in her heart.

There came a period with no letters—one month,
two months. Aunt Fradel did her best to console
Mother Lipschitz: America is far away, there's a
whole ocean to traverse; one ship or even two might
have foundered. She did her very best. Finally a
letter did come. It was addressed in an unfamiliar
handwriting and it was written in German by a
countryman, that Hannchen's son had died of tubercu-
losis, from which he had suffered long; moreover, that
he had left nothing but his worthless working clothes,
because, he had, like the writer of the letter, worked
in a shoe factory and had often talked about his

mother. Concerning a business or such important matters or any inheritance, there was nothing in the
letter. Perhaps one should observe that it was under-
standable, and even to be approved of, that the son
had at a certain time wanted to awaken at least the
dream in his mother that he had become a respectable
merchant once again.

Now, of course, Aunt Fradel, as we know her,
was in a dreadful situation. For some days she went
about much oppressed and wondering just what to
do. How could she wound that poor mother by com-
municating the tragic news, especially since the old
lady had recently become more and more fragile?
Finally, difficult as it was, she determined to lie. But
she had faith that God would forgive her for the
sake of the good that might thus be done.

She went over to Hannchen Lipschitz and read
her from the letter, which she carefully took out of
its envelope, whatever could console her. She invented
reasons for the delay and communicated things which
the son had actually written in former letters. The
old mother was relieved and satisfied. . . .

But another month passed and again a letter was
due; the mother had already reminded her. At that
Aunt Fradel sat down and wrote a letter from America and read it to the careworn old lady. She did the
same thing the next month. To ease her own task
she sat down one day and wrote a letter to the dead
son and answered that letter in the character of the
dead son. And she continued to do this for a long
period. . . . But now you will ask how about the
money that was expected? Well, our good Frau Fradel

had a way of raising that too. What was the purpose of her husband's being a member of the *Chevra Kaddisha,* the charitable organization of the community? She explained the situation to him and he, in turn, narrated the matter to the charitable members of the *Chevra.* Thus every month a sum was set aside which could satisfy the modest requirements of the old lady. Frau Fradel told her that, once and for all, she had a way of exchanging the dollars into native currency at once.

Thus some time passed again. One day war came, that first war against the French. And the son of Aunt Fradel, who had satisfied his military service among the red-collared cavalry, had to go, too. Well, there now set in a great deal of correspondence to and from the scene of war. We know from our own wars how that is.

And now Aunt Fradel, a mother herself, had a great burden of care. We needn't emphasize that; we know how mothers are. But she did not on that account in any wise forget that self-imposed duty of a correspondence with America. Every month she went with one of those feigned letters and mounted the creaking wooden stairs to Hannchen Lipschitz in that house behind the synagogue.

And indeed, she, who was herself now getting on in years, visited the old woman more often than was need, because, as everyone knew, her end was not far off. All that kept her alive was her looking forward to her son's letters; nay, she hoped to see him once again. Because Aunt Fradel, when Hannchen had uttered the wish to see her son again before she died, had read to her a reply in which the son promised to visit whenever his business affairs would permit him to do so.

It was on the very day of that hard winter, when it was clear that Hannchen Lipschitz was on her death bed, that Aunt Fradel and her husband Simon received the news from the front that during a battle that lasted several days, beside a river, Lisaine by name, that flows past the fortress of Belfort, their son, as the message read, had fallen for King and for Fatherland. It was, as we have said, the very day on which only hours separated from her death that old lady whom the other mother had so compassionately cared for for so long. The dying woman was very weak in body and quite conscious of that content of her poor life, her son, whom she believed to be alive. And she spoke of him and begged for a letter from him, as though that could still save her. And they came and described her condition to Mother Fradel, who was almost out of her mind with grief. And she arose—although, as the Law requires, she had already been sitting on the low stool of grief with her husband—and, with eyes that could hardly see for their tears, she went down and in her black dress joined that dying woman, sat down beside her bed and read her a cheerful letter from that son who had now long been dead: that he was well and that he would soon journey home to see her. And thus she brought her, until she fell into the sleep of death, the consolation of all those years for the last time.

As for Aunt Fradel . . .

THE DARKEST HOUR

He was suddenly awakened and, under his doublet, felt for his coat of mail which he never doffed by night abroad, ever since he had been attacked in Alsace by some of the rebellious peasants and would have been killed, had he not at once been recognized as a Jew and not as the knight for whom he had been taken. He half-lifted himself from the sack of straw which was his bed. A repeated ringing had awakened him. It was still dark. The sudden, shrill, bell-like sounds were like sparks flying out of night and silence. This sense of brightness had aroused him; at first he did not know whether there had been a ringing in his ears or a glittering before his eyes. Also he felt a great weight, as it were, upon him; it had remained with him from the day before. And suddenly he knew what that ringing sound was: in the nearby smithy they had on their anvil the iron that was being hammered into shoes for his horse.

He recollected the details of yesterday. Late he had come to this village. During the afternoon he had crossed the Rhine on a ferry just above Strassburg, where Jews had always been well looked upon, and on account of the importance of his goal had been minded to stay on horseback all night. Suddenly he had observed that his roan mount was limping and had found that it had lost the shoe from its left forefoot. He had not noticed it before, though it must have happened hours ago. Thus he had been forced to look up the local smith, although the smithy had already been closed and its fires had died. The smith had examined the horse's hooves and had seen that other shoes were loose and about to fall off. He had rather noisily refused to take the job upon himself, now, after nightfall, and had insisted on putting it off until morning, even though Yossel had offered him a reward far beyond the customary price if he would undertake the work at once. At all events he had promised to work at dawn.

So Yossel had been forced to pass the night here and to lose a second night since the evil news had reached him.

The inn had been nearby; it had room for only a few guests. They had not recognized him as a Jew, partly because the tallow candle shed only a dim light; above all, because he was not forced to wear the yellow badge beyond his native town of Rosheim and that section of Alsace under the governor of Hagenau; moreover, though his speech with its Alsatian tinge was not native here, yet on the edge of the

Black Forest they spoke not very differently from himself. Finally, he was accustomed to use a lordly bearing and he always had money enough to pay for whatever he wanted; and money would pay for almost anything.

For only a few minutes did he continue to lie there on the wooden bench covered by the straw sack. He leaped up, almost fully dressed as he had laid down. He stepped over to the little window with its thick, leaded, almost opaque panes; yet he could perceive that the early dawn was rising over the meadows and over the trees. Only this little room was still quite dark. Through the ringing of the hammers he now heard the manifold chirping and fluting of the birds, which announced the hour. From afar came the cry of a cuckoo bird.

It was a day in the month of *Sivan* of the year 5289, which is, according to the chronology of our exile, May of the year 1529. It was during the reign of the mighty but unhappy Emperor Charles V. The sun of spring had been warm and everywhere the land was green and virginal. Although Yossel was weighed down by the circumstance which had forced him to this hasty journey, hope arose in him as he watched the awakening of nature. He was alone in this little cubicle which was really only a lean-to of boards. A wooden bowl filled with water stood there. He washed himself as best he could. He took his phylacteries out of a bag fastened to his belt which, completing his dressing, he had fastened around his hips. He placed them on his

forehead and about his left arm and performed his
devotions with a slight forward and backward sway-
ing of his body.

The moment he had completed his prayers the
innkeeper appeared; he saw at once that he had
given shelter to a Jew and cried out:

"Accursed Jew and Christ killer! You sneaked in
here without telling me! That'll bring me bad luck!"

Yosselmann, not inexperienced in such matters—
alas, how often had he had this experience!—but
quite ready and able to meet them, took his long
sword from the corner where he had placed it the
evening before and calmly, without looking up,
girded himself with it.

"A Jew with a sword; a Jew with a knight's sword
and a slashed doublet!" The innkeeper was astonished.

"Yes, and more than that," Yossel replied. Out of
a leather bag he took a parchment and smoothed it
out and asked:

"Can you read?"

"No, I have no use for this new-fangled stuff!"

"This is a letter of safe conduct made out by his
Imperial and Royal Majesty for me as the commander
and ruler of all Jews in German lands."

The innkeeper laughed. Commander of the Jews!
There was no such person; there couldn't be! How
could you rule something that didn't exist? He knew
individual Jews, wretched, obsequious creatures who
would come wandering along and who, above all here,
where they were not permitted to settle, were properly despised and hated because they had killed the

Saviour and so had no rights at all. They had come
begging to do a little business; never had he permitted
one under his roof. You could rule over a people,
but these curious single individuals could be the
objects only of disdain and jeering and force. He
laughed again. But Yosselmann held up before him
the imperial seal, vividly stamped in red and recognizable; it hung from silken cords. Slightly abashed,
the innkeeper retreated by a pace or two.

In a hard voice Yossel asked: "What is my reckoning?"

"Two farthings Rhenish, two farthings!" said the
innkeeper, glad enough to get out of an obscure
situation. Ruler of the Jews! Was that possible?

Yosselmann threw the money on the rude table
between them and went forth very erect. The other
stood and gazed after him.

"He doesn't even wear the Jews' hat," he murmured to himself. That was supposed to be a Jew?
He had to go over it again and again in his mind.
Look at this one! He held himself erect and walked
in a stately fashion and had the eyes of a lord;
he wore a sword and had a slashed garment, a doublet
with sleeves, with openings at the top so that the
brilliant cloth of his undergarment showed. True
enough, he wore a beard like the others. But it
wasn't quite like the others; it was even blonde and
a little red only at the edges. Shaking his head he
descended the dark stairs and, in puzzled fashion,
rubbed his nose with the back of his hand.

Before the door of the house he saw the smith
beside a horse. There was an odor of burned hoof

about. The horse was a genuine Flemish roan, with brighter tail and mane, such as was never seen hereabouts, heavily built and with a broad rear. The tail had been tied short with a ribbon, after the manner of the knightly horses; and at this moment the horse neighed, as though to greet its master. The smith was accompanied by his journeyman who wore a leather apron and held out to the horse two handfuls of oats which he had taken from the nosebag attached to the saddle.

"Is everything ready?" Yossel asked.

"Oh yes, quite! He's a beauty!" And the man patted the horse with his rough hand. When Yossel had paid the smith, he swung himself into the broad saddle and rode off. . . .

Immediately behind the village he passed through the narrow valley of a brook, a hollow in reality, with sandy hills on both sides. But it soon spread out in fields of the early grass which was dotted by innumerable dandelions. For this was the cheerful season of the yellow flowers of the plains, and everywhere on the edges of the road cowslips nodded in the wind.

A lightness of heart would have come over him as he rode slightly upward, had he not been so deeply depressed by that which had forced him to undertake this journey. He was almost tempted to talk to himself concerning that which exercised his thoughts. But his lips did not stir.

A heavy duty had been assigned to him once more on account of his brethren. Three days ago a Jewish messenger had come with evil news from a village, of which he had never heard the name, although Jews dwelt there, as he now learned. It was situated beyond the Black Forest, where a river issued forth from the mountains, and was subject to the Count of Württemberg. The message had been in the German language couched in Hebrew letters. The mysterious character of the holy alphabet intensified the greatness of the danger.

The messenger had come on foot, covered with sweat and dust. At first he had scarcely been able to utter a word from his dry lips. But at last he had told how one had given him this writing in his village, who had similarly brought it from the nearest town and had bidden him to make the greatest haste, for it had been given to that previous messenger by still a third one who had brought it from the mountains beyond. The writing said the following, that a Christian child, a man child, had been found dead in that place and that the others had arrested all the Jews of the town with the intention of burning them at the stake. Haste to bring help was needed, because sundry Jews had already been tortured in order to wring a confession from them, and poor crippled Solomon, without confessing anything, had suddenly died while the thumbscrews were being applied to him.

"And only you can help us, Rabbi, only you who have seen the Emperor face to face, you who have been able to help so often." Thus the messenger had ended his message.

They had given him refreshments and then had let him tell his tale. Rumor permitted him to add to

what was written. It was bad enough. More than
thirty people were in prison, torn forth from their
homes a week ago. They faced the worst, if help did
not come. For always one had to face the very worst,
as they had known for centuries, unprotected and
defenseless as they were in the midst of the crowd
of the others.

At first Yossel had wanted to leave that very evening. But his wife had persuaded him to spend the
night at home and to set forth at dawn. And he had
been happy to be persuaded. Only two days ago he
had come back from a journey into the Lowlands
which he had undertaken once more for business
purposes and had wedged in between other journeys
which he had taken for the sake of the community
of Israel. He had been glad to stay for his wife was
beautiful and still young, almost twenty years younger
than he, who was now around fifty, and she loved
him and she was always new to him whenever he
returned from his journeys which took weeks and
sometimes months. Sometimes, when he had been
able to do good to his brethren, it was she who seemed
to him his great reward when, after a long absence,
he was with her again. He saw her before him at this
moment and a great tenderness arose within him.

But from this image confidence came to him too.
He would put things to rights, even though he had
lingered those few more hours. He had always been
lucky in these matters, whenever he had attempted
something for all of them, for the Jews of the German
lands, ever since he had become aware of the circumstance that it was for him to help them in their

narrow lives and in their fearfulness concerning their
fate. Ah, he could see them before him, how they
dwelt among those who kept hatefully aloof from
them even though they had spoken the same speech
since time immemorial; how they sat in those villages
and small towns west, south and east since they
had been scattered by the bloody rage and the horrible
murder that had taken place in the narrow towns
at the time of the Black Death almost two hundred
years ago. Two hundred years had passed. And yet
it was in their hearts and in their blood, the awareness
of an eternal shadow. . . . But things would be better; he felt that more and more and reflected about
it. Again and again he sought to penetrate into
the future and into days to come beyond the veil
of the uncertain. For new things were happening
in the world. People were daring to criticize the
Church itself. And even though the poor peasants,
who were the neighbors of the Jews everywhere, had
been defeated in their uprising only a few years
ago and had been slain by the thousands for their
blasphemous revolt against the lords and knights and
priests and monasteries, yet much had changed. A
lighter air was to be perceived in all quarters; words
were spoken against oppression and the sin of greed
which had not been possible a while ago. And a Christian had actually translated *Chumish* into the German
language in order that all might read it and perceive
from their Holy Book what the Jews actually were.
And had not the Emperor, long may he live, summoned him before him? Never before had such a
thing been heard of. He had conversed with him

as with others at his court and had not made him
feel that he was a Jew, nor been contemptuous of him
on account of his Jewishness, as all other Jews before
him had had to suffer. Sundry times it had seemed
to him as though the proud imperial man had wanted
to convey to him that in his own loneliness and
mournfulness, young as he was, he had felt a kinship with him and with his brethren. And all this
passed through Yossel's mind in such moments as
these.

Upright he rode along. A pride rose in his breast
and a sudden confidence too in the thought of that
which had forced him to this journey. How they
always received him, his brethren, oppressed as they
were by their lowliness and small daily troubles,
but also fulfilled with the unshakeable belief in their
holy calling and confident of Messianic fulfillment
at the end of days. This he always experienced again
when he came to help them. They would kneel
down before him; they would kiss his hand if he
permitted it. So deeply did they trust him whose
reputation had now for years gone through these
lands. He was deeply aware of his own calling and
election. In his heart of hearts he confessed this to
himself and had done so ever since one of their rulers,
the governor of Lower Alsace, had first called him
the governor of the Jewish community and had
shown him an appropriate respect. And what it meant
to him to be received by his brothers as the helper,
the helper in need!

The valley became narrower. The fir forest with its
bright green crowns came nearer and nearer. Beside

him a clear refreshing brook flowed downhill. Straight ahead, in the height of the cloudless sky, soared suddenly an eagle, noble and secure upon its wide-spread pinions.

According to his calculation it must now have been near noon and he should have been able to come forth from the hills and reach the plateau on the farther side of which lay the village to which his tragic task drew him. As yet he knew no details. He had no confidence in the exact account which had been conveyed to him. He knew from experience the exaggerations of terror. And perhaps it would be, as it had been often before, that he would have to face and fight down evil looks and derisive words and to combat hatred and greed and bloodthirstiness. Perhaps money would help, as it had often done before. But it occurred to him that in his haste he had perhaps not sufficiently supplied himself with money. And to appeal to the brethren in the neighboring communities would take too much time, not to speak of the circumstance that certain of them might even refuse. For several times in recent years it had happened that monies loaned and used for those in need, or for others who had pledged themselves for them, had not been returned. And he had had to undergo reproaches from those who thought only of themselves, as though he had profited from these transactions. He thought of this with bitterness.

Yes, it was always the threat of murder and arson— or else money. This time he would have to deal with villagers; perhaps they would take less money

than the merchants and the guilds in the cities, who
always haggled. For, indeed, the peasants and others
who were themselves oppressed were more easily
dealt with, because they felt a commonality of fate.
Had they not, at the time of their great tragic rebellion, when they destroyed and burned and plun-
dered the castles of the nobility in his home region,
had they not spared the Jews, when he himself nego-
tiated with them? This matter should be manageable
since the occasion was of less moment. And yet,
when the great terror and the delusions concerning
their faith came over these people, it was always
difficult—more difficult, perhaps, than dealing with
the burghers, because these did remember the law
and the agreements made with the Emperor concerning the Jewish servants of his Chamber and consequently inaugurated various legal procedures before
anyone was condemned or executed. In this way time
was usually gained which meant a great deal. Would
he be in time on this occasion?

Suddenly it came over him. Perhaps his journey was
in vain; perhaps the worst had happened and there
was no rescue to be achieved! He must hasten. He
spurred his horse so that it began to trot. If only he
had not ridden forth alone; his wife had tried to
persuade him to take a manservant along; had he
done so he would have felt the oppressive loneliness
less. Thus he was overcome by a tumult of feelings,
until at last his faith and confidence that all would
be well prevailed once more. In his own experience
it had not yet occurred that a sentence had been
executed without some sort of legal proceeding; in-

deed, it happened ever more rarely, compared to former times, that the angry delusions of the mob led straight to murder. His mood grew brighter when he recollected the days of his own youth when his father, of blessed memory, as the latter had often told him, had had to flee from his native village beyond the Rhine after two of his brothers had been burned at the stake. The terror of those memories had still vibrated in his father's voice and had left in him a dread which often pursued him into the very dreams of childhood.

No, he would probably succeed. He was sure of it. And how they would all thank him, the fathers and the mothers for their children's sake and the white-haired old people whose memories went back to a more evil time and who knew what it meant that things were easier now that someone, that is, the Emperor himself, listened to them through him. They would *bensh* him, and his.

Serenely he thought of his family and had a vision of his son who, like his grandfather, was named Gerson, a free man, a leader of the others, as he was himself, riding through the German lands and pursuing his affairs untroubled. He had already considered that he would try to get him very special privileges, to beseech these from the Emperor himself, who had so kindly an attitude to himself. He remembered how his brethren hung upon his lips, so to speak, when he told them of his visits to the Emperor, when he described how graciously Charles had listened to him and had replied to him. Like a fairy tale it had seemed to them, one never heard before,

and they were glad that one of their own had been
raised so high and been respected among the others
who surrounded the Imperial Court. Soon he would
ride to the far city of Augsburg, to the Great As-
sembly, to which all the estates of the Empire were
invited to deliberate concerning the thing that was
all-important to them, namely, the unity of Christendom. There he, too, would express his petition, nay,
his demand, to the Emperor and the lords of the
cities for a protective regulation and for right conditions for all the Jews in the German lands.

From time to time he now saw farmsteads, and peasants standing at the edge of their fields. Ploughing and
sowing were over. It was now the time of growth
under the wide heaven and of warmth and moonlight
and rain, as God chose to send these. How familiar
all this was to him, since he was accustomed to spend
so many of his days riding through the country.
Soon he and his brethren must be permitted to own
land too. That was one of the things he wanted
to gain from the Emperor, the privilege of owning
forest and field beyond the houses and to cultivate
the earth and reap wheat and fruit and grapes. He
would see to it, too, that his people traded scrupu-
lously, as the Holy Law commands; indeed, he would
insist on certain agreements and invite to the con-
firming of these emissaries from all the important
kehillaus.

Dreams, dreams. Now and then he heard the
sharpening of the scythes; the earliest crop of grass,
food for the sparse cattle, was being mowed. Here
and there a man swung his scythe. The high white

clouds in the infinite blue touched him with the majesty of God's creation. How could evil come to pass under that sky, especially the kind of evil which had impelled him to this journey? By noon he reached the ford of a river, near which the wheel of a water-mill turned slowly, and from afar he saw a town with walls and towers and churches. He would try to bypass it, in order to have no trouble with identi-fication and with tolls and with a possible delay.

Here by the river were others. A knight in full armor with his squire were also fording the river; the water swirled about their mounts. Yosselmann tried to keep aloof as the only other rider on the scene. With heavy tread a miller journeyman, with a sack of flour over his shoulder, greeted him. It was of him that Yosselmann asked directions and when, a moment later, the master miller, an older man with flour stained eyelashes and, indeed, white all over, joined his servant and took part in this con-versation, Yosselmann soon knew that he was on the right road. He learned, too, that the rumor of a new blasphemy committed by Jews was already spread abroad in the country. For he had now reached the territory of the Count of Württemberg. Thus he crossed the river without delay and kept his horse at a trot.

Slowly the dusk descended. On the edge of a wood he dismounted briefly. Sitting by the road he ate a bit of smoked beef and bread, which he had in his saddle bag, and pronounced the evening prayer. He intended to ride through the night in order to arrive where they waited for him in the morning. He

knew how they would yearn for his approach, because they believed that he could help them. He
pictured the very scene; it seemed to him as though
he were already among them, bound to them, a very
part of them.

There was no moon. But there was a faint brightness over the landscape because innumerable stars
were in the heaven and glimmered there. Now and
then a bird flitted softly from tree to tree and now
and then the lonely man heard the small thud of
waking animals on the almost indistinguishable path.

The sense of loneliness came over him. He was
the only human being far and wide, the only one,
moreover, who knew what might befall, who was
riding into uncertainty, into a kind of infinity. It
was not exactly fear that befell him. He was aware
of danger, as all created things must be. It was not
even a threat to himself which suddenly, like something thick and objective, robbed him of his breath,
so that he clung tensely to his faithful horse. He
felt within his breast his people and the threat to
them and the uncertainty and mystery of the surrounding night. He was indeed alone. He alone had
to bear what afflicted all; nor did they know, not
one, what he desired for them.

He felt the moisture of gathering dew. At first
he had thought that it was sweat upon his forehead.
He must arrive at the right time and soon enough.
But even if he did, what guarantee of success did
he have? Now doubts beset him which he sought
to allay by counter-arguments. Hitherto God had always helped him, as though He had chosen him,

whenever he had had full confidence that he could help his people. It would be so once again.

A haze appeared in the sky and a wind caused the leaves to rattle over Yosselmann and brought it home to him that he was weary. His eyes were heavy. If he could only sleep. . . .

The horse stumbled on a stone and almost fell. This awakened him; he pressed his flat, hatlike cap over his forehead and spoke a prayer. Also he now felt the coolness of the coming day. Between the trees and fields, which emerged ever more clearly from the light haze of morning, the sun rose at his right. It warmed him and warmed him within too, so that he recovered his confidence. In a few hours he would have reached his goal. And all would be well. He recalled to himself again and again that what he most feared had not happened for long. And he smiled to himself when once more he thought of the joy of those who were expecting him.

He took a deep breath. His chest expanded and he took the reins firmly into his hands, although he left the bit loose. The pressure of his knees gave his horse the signal to trot. He sat his mount well; no one would have suspected him of being a Jew. To be sure, the country Jews had always been more courageous and held themselves more erect than those in the cities and had sometimes smiled in pity when they observed the lives of their brothers in their dark alleys into which they were pent by the distrust of the others. It was better in the country where they lived among the peasants who knew them and were well known by them. Thus it would probably be in the village to which he was riding. People there would have friends among the Christians to whom one could talk, who might themselves negotiate with the more malevolent ones and seek to save those who were threatened, if only to avert from the village the eternal reputation of its wicked madness. He had never before heard the name of the village. It must be small and the peasants poor. To be sure, that so many of his brothers lived there with their families seemed to prove that there was enough business to nourish them.

He had come to the end of the forest and the sky was now wholly bright. It was the morning of a beautiful spring day. A bell rang from the distance. Was this the place? Suddenly again his heart was oppressed. The decisive moment was at hand. But when he had ridden for yet another while he saw a convent with tall walls lying amid the meadows and gardens. And as he approached by the road close to the convent he heard in that garden the singing of women's voices, a high devout singing. From his horse he could look over the walls and in the garden of the convent he saw the nuns, two by two, in their yellowish-white robes and hoods. They were Dominican nuns and he now heard too the deep tones of an organ. It was a peaceful picture amid the flowers and blossoms; on the edges of the walks and between the flower beds grew the festive tiger lilies such as one often saw delineated on pictures of their Madonna. Were these nuns, too, not full of confidence in God? Did these not, too, sing to Him? Was it possible that their people would do what was so to be feared and which he had come this long way to prevent? Was not this a picture of peace and love? Inconceivable that this journey of his should be in vain; such wrath of God was not to be thought of. Had he incurred it? It now seemed to him that everything was directed against him alone.

Yet how did he dare to doubt? He had conquered worse than this. Perhaps everything was already well and he would but arrive to share the joy and relief of his brethren. Or else, some negotiating was still necessary, or a reference to the power of the Emperor, on which he knew that he could lean. Yes, the humble folk still revered his majesty; it was the princes and the big cities who cared very little and compounded the imperial demands for cash. It was the common people who needed someone to revere, in whom to believe and whom to obey. He would show his safe conduct which implied the Emperor's protection and negotiate with the leaders. Perhaps he would need to confer with only a single priest who could be influenced by a gift for his church and his tithes. He felt quite sure of success.

A gravel pit suddenly interrupted the meadows along the way. The stones of the gravel were radiant in the brilliance of the sunlight, so that one could not bear to look at them. Here and there stood amid the gravel the tall candles, as it were, of purple thistles.

After brief reflection Yossel guided his horse between the high bushes and weeds and halted. He wanted to say the morning prayer. But hardly had he taken the *tefillin* from his saddle-bag, and the horse started grazing nearby, when he he saw a figure emerging from the hazel bushes and immediately turning to run away. Yossel at once recognized him as a Jew and called to him: "Bar Yisroel?" "Shema Yisroel!" cried the other identifying him as a fellow Jew.

It was a man with touseled hair, and sand all over him, and feverish eyes, and torn garments. With wide fearful eyes he looked at Yossel.

"Who are you?" the latter asked.

But the other did not answer the question. He cried out: "Terrible, terrible!" and then: "Help us! You are a Jew and rich."

"Where do you come from?" Yossel asked.

"I ran away from them. But they are on my trail. They want to catch me . . . like the others."

"You must be from Baisingen, where misfortune threatens. It must be near here."

"Misery such as no one has known. And there is no help!"

"You mean that nothing fatal has happened and help can be brought?"

"I ran away two days ago. All our people were still alive then, but they were gathering wood for the pyres and each of our enemies contributed wood." He laughed convulsively and went on: "But who are you? One of our people who bears himself like a knight? I saw you from afar and hoped that *Shem yisborach* sent you to save us."

"My name is Yosselmann."

Upon hearing this the other fell to his knees.

Sobbing he laid his head upon the pointed shoes of Yossel and embraced his ankles. "You! It is you! We will be saved!"

Yossel drew back a little: "Don't! Don't! It is all in God's hands!"

And the other raising himself up turned to the East and cried in a loud voice: *"Boruch ha-Shem. . . ."* And then he added: "Quickly! Hasten, hasten! Then you'll get there at dusk or even before. My wife and child are in their hands. They separated them from the men and I escaped to seek help. . . . And now that you have come perhaps there will be help."

Yossel did not try to begin his prayers. He put his *tefillin* away and mounted.

"Stay with me and show me the way. What is your name."

"Yecklin ben Shmuel," the other replied.

"Tell me what is to be told, Yecklin!"

He let the horse walk slowly, for the road was an upward one. With his left hand Yecklin clung to the stirrup so that with this support he was able to keep up with the horse. In spite of his exhaustion, he told his tale.

A peasant woman, Red Kate, his own neighbor, had suddenly one morning run screaming and accusing through the village. The Jews had stolen and hidden her child in order to use its blood. It was just a month old. This woman had ordinarily not been evil; she had good relations with Jews and had even been the *Shabbos goie* at a Jewish house across the street. At first they had laughed at her and some had said that she must be *meshuggah*. But at noon, when her hus-

band had come home from working in the fields, he
had himself gone looking for the child and had found
it in the yard of that very Mennlin, whom the woman
had served and with whom she had been friendly. The
child had been found dead among tall weeds. At once
a general tumult had arisen. All the other men had
come in from the fields, armed with scythes or with
pitchforks or with flails, which they had fetched from
the barns. And sundry had immediately cried out that
all the houses of the Jews should be set on fire and
they themselves burned with their children in order to
avenge this crime. But others had objected that thus
their own houses might go up in flames, and so they
had refrained. But how dreadful the matter was could
be seen from the circumstance that when he had
escaped they had already begun to gather wood and
to plant stakes in the earth. . . .

Breathlessly he fell silent. It was clear to Yossel how
necessary haste was. Yecklin had had to interrupt himself again and again and had scarcely been able to
get his words out.

"Show me the way, Yecklin, the exact direction, and
then follow me slowly. I'll hasten all I can."

Yecklin called after him a fervent blessing and remained behind.

In spite of the story he had heard, Yossel could not
believe the worst. And even in Yecklin's words there
was a gleam of hope. It was unimaginable that such a
thing could happen, that it could already have happened. He spurred his horse to the utmost speed. The
day grew hot and the landscape glimmered; his eyes
hurt and he could peer out only under lowered lids.

How beautiful the country was! As often before in
difficult situations, he sought to summon all his moral
powers. This thing, too, had to be conquered. Then he
would go upon a decisive mission to the Emperor, so
that threats like this could not recur. It must be done.
The very fact that such a thing as this could happen
would demonstrate to the Emperor the necessity of
such an intervention as had not yet been used. Nor
was his plan without an element of reciprocity. It
would commend itself not only to the Emperor but to
all the estates of the realm. Laws should be issued for
the Jews, which they were to obey in all their occupations and which would raise them from their lowliness.
Turning this plan over in his mind he almost forgot
the immediate object of his errand. He was riding
swiftly to save people; this was a race with death. And
suddenly he was forced to imagine what it would be
like if he received such an account from his own home
and were to be told that his own wife and children
were in such danger. At that moment he felt as though
the ground were being withdrawn from under him and
his heart contracted. But as we are all reluctant to
believe in evil, insofar as it might touch us, so now,
too, he dared not doubt the success of his mission.
Indeed, the magnitude of his responsibility gave him
additional courage.

He had long left the mountains behind him, where
the paths between the black fir trees were damp and
earthy and had cooled him. His heavy horse was sweating; foam dripped from its mouth and he himself felt
the heat intensely. He pushed his hat back and wiped
his face and eyes. The road now led straight to a

little town. It was a much traveled road. Wagons met
him now and again and the drovers made way for him
respectfully, as for a knight. The little town, the name
of which he had long known, lay on the slopes of a
moderate elevation. From afar he could peer into the
steep lanes. He could not avoid traversing this town,
even though he were to be delayed by tolls and an
examination. He knew that the village where tragedy
threatened was only a couple of hours' ride distant
from here. Ah, perhaps the situation had been clarified
and his brethren were free!

Chains rattled as the bridge of the city gate was
lowered. As Yossel's horse tramped resonantly over the
planks, forth from his sentinel box came the warder
of the bridge, big-boned and broad in many-colored
trunks and with a long mustache. He planted himself in front of the horseman. Yossel, without dis-
mounting and in silence, showed forth the imperial
safe conduct. He knew how it affected people. Although the warder evidently could not read, yet he was
impressed by the horseman's bearing and let him pass
without toll or other hindrance. And he had seen the
great Imperial seal. Yosselmann rode swiftly up the
street. His horse's hoofs were resonant on the cobble-
stones. Here and there a window opened and the
curious gaze of a woman followed him. Everywhere
the smell of tanning, which he was accustomed to from
home, assailed him. There were hardly any men to be
seen. Were they at their day's work or had they been
summoned to participate in the evil deeds of that devil-
ridden village? Such things always had their lure. He
dared not ask if anyone knew of that matter here. The

uncertainty seemed more bearable to him than any confirmation, since soon he would see for himself.

On a small square there was a stone well. Children were at their play. A barefoot little girl in a clean frock laughed at him and then called the attention of her playmates to him. They surrounded him and cried out to him: "Sir Knight, Sir Knight." But instead of this easing his soul, the sight of these children and their natural behavior oppressed him the more in contrast to what was ahead of him. Their images dwelt in his mind long after he had left the little town by its upper gate. He saw his wife and his children before him, and the son who was long past becoming *Bar-Mitzvo* and was promising to become a veritable *talmid chochem,* and his little daughter who was only ten and blonde and very dear to his heart. And suddenly it seemed to him as though he were riding for their sake and must hasten not to come too late; as though he were riding homeward because from thence he had been told of that which was happening in the village of Baisingen. . . . A strange transformation went on in his imagination. He saw his own family tied to the wooden stakes, surrounded by that mad and evil crowd; he saw the torches kindled; he saw them defenceless among the others who cried out and prayed for help that did not come. It was like a heavy nightmare, which he could not rid himself of. At last the vision narrowed itself to that of his little daughter. Alone she stood with the flames shooting up on her, weeping softly, her tears still streaming down into her hair which hung disheveled over her face. . . . He couldn't get rid of the image. It was for her that he was riding, for his own child and for the others who were everything to him, for whose sake he lived, and for himself too, although he was bringing help to people that he did not know. He rode upon this way for all Israel, not only for those who were immediately menaced. A fever came upon him. He dug his spurs into his horse and galloped on.

He emerged from a narrow forest and came out upon a slope between fruitful fields. At this point he perceived a strange odor which had nothing to do with the fresh country smells up to this point. At the same time he saw a thin vapor above the valley, a static windless smoke which did not stir. The odor of plants and blossoms had disappeared. Yonder—that must be the place with its low houses and huts. Now horror befell him. Was he too late? He urged on his horse. There was a farmstead, but he saw no human being; and after that came the first houses of the village. Not a soul. The road which was filled with dung and refuse was empty. A dead cat lay there with singed fur and open eyes. His frightened horse rose on its hind legs, so that for a space Yosselmann had to concentrate his attention on the immediate situation.

And suddenly he became aware of a dreadful odor which did not recede and which he was never to forget during the rest of his long life. It was the odor of burned flesh. He recognized that at once; these were the charred and murdered bodies of his brethren. Too late! Too late! But perhaps there were a few survivors to be saved. It could not be, it must not be that they had all been murdered. But why was no one to be seen of the people of the village which extended far. The church with its shapeless brown tower of wooden tiles—he had seen it from afar—lay at the other end of the rows of houses. On the fields, too, he could catch sight of no one. Had they all fled after their blasphemous crime?

Out of the narrow window of a low house which stood diagonally to the street, with its wall of crumbling plaster between the dark brown beams, there suddenly protruded the head of a gray-bearded old man. It vanished again almost instantly, before he could address a question to it. From another nearby house he now heard the sound of many voices in prayer, after the manner of a litany. But no one was out in the open. He was about to dismount when the street took a sudden turn. Shortly thereafter it spread out to a wide square in front of the church. There it was—there! Two great linden trees stood there with their enormous crowns of foliage. But on the nether rim the leaves were singed and yellow; tongues of flame had touched them; beneath them there had been a conflagration.

At first he saw only masses of charred matter from which arose a thin column of smoke, as though a smoldering were still going on. Black stakes still stood and smoldered too, and from them hung dark forms, contorted bodies which had been men. . . . Too late, too late! Those were his brothers.

So this could happen to animated beings, like himself. Was this conceivable? Tall and quiet his horse stood above all this, but it trembled; and he himself seemed to have blended with his mount, as though they were a single creature. Dazed by the scene, he had forgotten to dismount. But when he stood on the ground a faintness came over him and, to prevent himself from falling, he had to lean against his faithful steed. And ever again he was assailed by that odor which aroused both horror and revulsion. There was no escape from it. And it seemed to him as though it were his own flesh that had been burned to ashes here. So lowly a creature is man that his fellows, who are also supposed to have been made in God's image, could treat him like an animal. And it came over him like a bitter illumination, that his life would never again be as it had been before.

Why had he come too late? It was his guilt. He had delayed and thereby committed a sin. He should have gone forth on the instant when the news reached him. But he had lingered a whole night with his beloved wife, for the sake of his own heart, while death threatened his brethren here; that was it . . . that . . .

He looked about him. No living creature was to be seen. They had all hidden themselves, these madmen, these murderers. The emptiness round about and the silence were like the face of the evil conscience of the criminals; they dared not look upon a stranger; they dared not look at each other; they had crept into hiding.

In his confusion Yossel wandered up and down. What was he to do? Never had he seemed so helpless to himself. At last he heard footsteps and turned around. A young man, a peasant, barefoot and in tattered linen breeches stood before him. One of his sleeves seemed empty. Evidently, his left arm must have been broken and was supported by a rope which was fastened to his shoulder. His face, too, with his red-lidded eyes was full of bloody welts, as though he had been beaten.

"Whom arc you looking for, Master?" he asked.

"I'm looking for the Jews, for all those who lived here. But I see, it is too late."

"I tried to save them; I fought with those crazy creatures until, as you see, they fell upon me too. They came near to burning me. My girl was among them; we loved each other in secret. Her name was Shoenle. And now, look what has become of her and, oh, she screamed so pitifully. . . ."

He walked up to a little heap of charred matter and took a handful of it and held it before his eyes and gazed at it and wept.

"Let us bury them, Master Jew!"

Yosselmann could bring up no word out of the drouth of his throat. Suddenly he saw them, all of them, all through the ages, who had been burned thus at stakes, he saw them in a single horror-stricken vision and he thought that a fever had befallen him.

And as he was about to agree with that young peasant and accept his help, the Jewish messenger, Yecklin, whom he had left behind, came rushing on the scene. You cannot say that Yecklin came running. It was a plunging forward, a mad rage in every limb, and he roared as though bereft of his senses and rushed from charred remnant to charred remnant, seeking for the identity of all he had loved. And he threw himself down and beat his forehead against stone and dust and cried again and again: "This you have done to me, to me . . . !," and tore his garment from collar to edge. And then suddenly he began to laugh, to laugh uninterruptedly.

Yossel found his self-control again. He went over to his poor brother to console him.

"Let us pray, Yecklin," and he turned his face to the East.

"Yiskaur Elauhim es nishmas. . . ."

This was the prayer for the martyrs. But the other no longer understood; he laughed and went on laughing.

Meanwhile, partly out of curiosity, partly impelled by their feeling of guilt and their evil conscience, a number of people came out of the houses. At first they were women, but then men joined them, so that soon there was a little crowd which surrounded the two Jews. And suddenly they, too, began to pray; they seemed like children who, conscious of evil, wanted to make some amends. And now, when the knacker of the village, a great, ragged fellow, joined the group and laughed and asked whether one hadn't better dig a ditch or trench beyond the village in order to bury what was here, a great, beardless peasant with short blonde hair brought his fist down on the knacker's nose, so that the latter retired bleeding and scolding.

But Yosselmann now sent one of the peasants to the neighboring village where Jews, in great dread over the fate of their brethren and their own, had waited in prayer and fasting. They had known what had happened. And so they came and buried the martyrs in a common grave and used all our holy ceremonies.

And this was the last time for centuries that Jews in the German lands were martyred on account of their faith and on account of the superstition of the others.

But from this hour on Yosselmann knew that it would in a sense always be too late and always be in vain to fare forth and to save his brethren. And when he reflected upon the original reason for his belatedness, it also became clear to him that none dared nourish any joy the while he knew that anywhere his brethren were in danger.

None ever saw him laugh again. And when, after sundry days, though he made all haste in his recurrent dread for his very own, he came home, it was found that the hair on his temples was quite gray. And when, with a rigid face, melancholy and mournful as never before, he stood in front of his wife, she wept and took him in her arms because she had an immediate presentiment of what had happened and that this time his journey had been in vain. . . .

It was, furthermore, authentically reported, that the dead child of Baisingen had been accidentally smothered in bed by Red Kate, its mother, and that in terror of her husband's reproaches, the woman had accused the Jews. In her later years she told the tale to her confessor who, at a still later date, was able to divulge what she told him because he had gone over to the new Protestant faith which arose at that time.